For Adam

THE GUARDIAN OF DETRITUS

A Motor City Mystery

Assembled in Detroit
by Chuck Snearly

aventine press

Published by Aventine Press
55 East Emerson St.
Chula Vista CA 91911
www.aventinepress.com

ISBN: 978-1-59330-881-0

Printed in the United States of America

It is never too late to be what you might have been.

—George Eliot

We hope for better things; it will arise from the ashes.
(Speramus meliora; resurget cinerbu)

—Motto given to Detroit by Father Gabriel Richard
after the city burned down in 1805

The City of Trees

—Early nickname for Detroit

All hail Detritus! What was, what is, what will be…whatever.

—The Guardian of Detritus

Prologue

Murphy in the Bushes

Running was not Murphy's strong suit.

He did much better when he left the road, scrambled down a hill, and began creeping through the bushes in the dark, gliding silently through the shadows. Still, by the time he got to the motel, he was dirty, wet, and gasping for air. Worst of all, his targets were already inside.

"Choi!"

Murphy cringed when his vulgar assessment of the situation drifted across the parking lot in front of him, bounced off the white cinderblock building on the other side, and returned to where he stood crouching behind a bush. His reaction to this breach of professionalism was immediate and regrettable.

"Ikuh!"

With the echo of his second ill-advised expletive still ringing in his ears, he squatted down to figure out what to do next.

His plan had worked well up until now. He had followed the target couple at a discreet distance as they drove away from the city. When they turned off a rural two-lane highway into the parking lot of a dimly lit motel, he kept driving, not pulling over until he was a hundred yards down the road.

That was when the plan began to unravel.

He parked on the road so he wouldn't be spotted, knowing he would be most likely to get a good, clean shot while they were still outside and confident that he could make it back to the motel before they made it to their room. But it had been many years filled with cigarettes and beers since he had humped it through the back country in 'Nam, and his Ranger training hadn't included how to avoid getting old and fat. Even with his cross-

country shortcut, by the time he got there, they were already in their room.

He could see directly into the motel office across from him, where a clerk sat alone behind the counter watching television. From the front of the office, a sidewalk traveled the length of the building, past double windows and doors that opened directly onto the parking lot. He could see their car parked halfway down the row. They could be in any of the rooms, behind any of the curtains rimmed in light.

They definitely wouldn't be coming out to the car to get any luggage.

Murphy briefly considered uttering another one of the curses the Cambodian monk had taught him, but instead he set down the gear he was carrying and started working on Plan B. He had to figure out a way to get them into the open.

He thought about going to the office and asking to see the couple who had just checked in. But he knew from painful experience that clerks in cheap roadside motels guarded the privacy of their clients like pit bulls in a party store. Persuading them to change their minds was always expensive or dangerous. Besides, it would create a witness who could identify him. In his business that wasn't a deal-breaker, but it also wasn't a good idea—it left a loose end that could come back to haunt you.

He briefly considered setting off a car alarm to get everyone to look out their windows, but that would be messy and risky, and increase the chances of being seen.

Another alternative began forming in his mind. He peered over the bushes to read the name on the pale-blue neon sign at the front of the motel and discovered he was standing in the bushes of the Time Out Inn. He pulled out his iPhone and Googled that name to get a phone number. If he called the office and asked to be connected to the couple who had just arrived, he would be able to hear the phone ringing and figure out which room they were in. A quick knock on the door and his work would be done.

But the flaws in this plan were apparent to Murphy almost as soon as he thought of it. Someone might trace the call to his cell phone. A phone in another room might ring at random. Most importantly, he preferred to do his job from a distance to avoid the chance of a physical confrontation. His Ranger training still served him well in a fight, but why risk it?

The least desirable option was quickly becoming the only one left to him. He would hike back to his car, park it at the end of the lot, and wait for the happy couple to emerge from their room. They certainly wouldn't be staying all night, and if he rummaged through the leftover fast food bags scattered throughout his car, he might even be able to find something to eat. There also was a half-full bottle of Jack Daniel's under the seat to help take the chill out of the night air.

The more he thought about it, the more desirable this option became.

He grabbed his gear and began to move out, but after a few steps, he was stopped in his tracks by his first lucky break of the evening. At the far end of the parking lot, in the last room in the row, a woman threw open the curtains and stood staring out at the line of pine trees in the distance.

It was her.

Murphy ducked down and began moving quickly and quietly toward her behind the cover of the bushes. If she kept the curtains open for just a minute, he would have a perfect spot to shoot from, behind a bush directly across from their room. He was gliding through the underbrush in total silence and seemingly without effort, happy that this skill hadn't deserted him and confident he could finish the mission.

Then the light in the room went out.

He stifled the urge to curse again by reminding himself that he was equipped to do the job in dark. As long as they didn't pull the curtains closed, he was still in business.

When he reached the spot directly opposite their window and looked out through the night vision, Murphy saw that the man had joined the woman at the window. He watched as they embraced and kissed in an eerie world of green-shaded twilight. Suddenly they turned away from the window, and he cursed himself silently for not acting faster. Then he realized his good luck hadn't deserted him; in their haste to continue, they had left the curtains open behind them.

He had all the time in the world.

For a few moments he indulged himself, looking on as they undressed and stood beside the bed. Even in a sickly shade of green, she was a real looker, with a pretty face and a firm, well-rounded body. A lot of times his job sucked, but sometimes it was pretty cool.

When they embraced again, Murphy started shooting.

Chapter One

Larry in Accounting

Will waited for the call that would change his life in an office with no door.

Nothing to hold out the sights, sounds, and smells of his co-workers.

Nothing to get in his way if he wanted to leave.

Nothing to prevent senior executives from sticking their heads in and annoying him.

"Harkanen, you're coming to the meeting this morning, right? It starts in ten minutes."

Will looked up to see Larry in Accounting standing in the open doorway, looking like he'd just stepped in dog shit. Larry was the Chief Financial Officer at Technart Innovation Corporation, which made him the CFO at TIC in corporate speak. He made no secret of his deep disdain for Will and his colleagues in Public Relations, being famous for walking by a group of them having lunch together in the cafeteria and declaring, "This must be the overhead table."

"I thought the meeting was at eleven o'clock, Larry."

"That's the pre-meeting for Orlando. This is a smaller group meeting to get everyone aligned for the pre-meeting."

"You're having a pre-pre-meeting?"

"Orlando is important to me. I'm not leaving anything to chance."

"I can't make it; I'm expecting an important phone call."

"I sent out a notice on Meetus, didn't you get it?"

"I don't use TIC web apps, they're too complicated. If you want me to come to a meeting, you have to do it the old-fashioned way: send me an e-mail or call my cell phone."

"What's the matter, Harkanen, afraid to try something new? Let me bottom-line it for you: I need everyone at this meeting with their budget numbers, including PR. You're the Director of Media Relations; that's why they gave you this extravagant office. I'll see you in ten minutes with the PR budget numbers, or I'll see your boss when the meeting's over."

Larry disappeared from the doorway, and Will sat staring after him, trying to decide what to do next. He thought of a speechwriting cliché he had used on more than one occasion: the Chinese word for crisis consists of two symbols—danger and opportunity. He knew that wasn't really accurate, but right now he was desperate enough to hope there was a glimmer of truth in this romanticized lie.

In *Monty Python's Life of Brian* terms, he was chewing on life's gristle.

A month ago his soon-to-be ex-wife had informed him that their marriage was merely comfortable, and that was no longer acceptable. He was told it was time for them to seek fulfillment and happiness—separately. It didn't take long for him to suspect she had gotten a head start on her search long before she delivered her devastating performance review:

"You play everything safe, Will, you're never spontaneous, you never take chances. You're so predictable, and so boring, and we are so over."

On the advice of his attorney, he had let slip the dogs of war, or in this case a tired old hound named Murphy. Will smiled at the metaphor, then tried to figure out what movie had brought it to mind. Marlon Brando in *Julius Caesar*? Sadly, no—it was General Chang in *Star Trek VI*.

Murphy was hot on the trail last night and had promised to report back this morning.

Will hoped the call came soon; TIC had strict rules about keeping your phone turned off during meetings. He thought about it for a moment but couldn't decide which was worse:

missing the call or attending the meeting. One held the potential to radically change his life; the other was certain to be more of the same meaningless bullshit that continued to fill his days.

He wasn't sure what scared him more.

It had taken him years to get to where he was—a lifetime, if you counted the false starts before TIC started sucking the life out of him. But still, he was not living the dream.

As a young man he was determined to change the world with his music. That ended in a way that was spectacularly bad, even by the high standards set by rock band cautionary tales. After that he had worked hard as a reporter to save the city he loved. He was branded a liar and thrown in jail for his efforts—a Detroit thank-you.

Will knew from painful experience that things could end quickly and badly if you weren't careful. And yet being careful was exactly what had led him to his boring job in this boring company.

His thoughts drifted again to *Life of Brian*: perhaps it was time to give a whistle.

The angry accountant had just presented him with a perfect opportunity to boldly go ahead of schedule. He had ten minutes to get a head start on the banging new lifestyle he told himself he wanted so badly.

Was "banging" a word a man his age could use without embarrassing himself? Didn't it mean something dirty? He couldn't remember and he didn't care. He was going to use it.

Banging.

Of course, he could always take the call later or listen to a message left on his voicemail. But a banging new life shouldn't begin with a timid compromise: giving in to a bullying bureaucrat. On the other hand, even if the plan worked and he avoided paying out a massive divorce settlement to his cheating wife, he was still going to need a job and a steady income.

He looked at his watch; seven minutes to decide.

Time for some more movie magic.

It was his favorite game, a mental trick he had taught himself years ago: visualizing a movie that paralleled his current reality. It helped him put things in perspective or, in some cases, ignore an ugly truth. But at the moment it wasn't working; at the moment the only thing that came to mind was Eric Idle singing and whistling enthusiastically while suffering an excruciatingly painful death.

Five minutes.

He tried to visualize Lauren Bacall asking him the question she asked Humphrey Bogart in *To Have and Have Not*: "You know how to whistle, don't you?" It didn't help. The only new image that flashed through his mind was a brief montage of car chases and shootouts. He gave up and looked at his watch again.

Three minutes.

He was trying not to look at his watch when a new image started playing in his head. It was some kind of Frank Capra film shown in reverse, where everything started out sunny and bright, then turned dark and desperate: *It's a Horrible Life*.

He needed to rewrite his script, and soon.

Maybe just not right now.

Will was reaching into a drawer to get the budget file for the meeting when his phone rang. The ringtone was the song "Back in '72" by Bob Seger, chosen to commemorate the last time he was happy with his path and purpose in life. He answered the phone and heard three words that filled him with hope and horror.

"I got them."

Chapter Two

Sucker Punch

Paddy wanted to blast off from the city on a wall of sound but his car wouldn't cooperate. It ignored his polite requests to "play music"—a slap in the face to a music freak and audio geek. He thought about his options for a moment, then tried speaking the song titles he wanted to hear in a clear and commanding voice:

"Gimme Danger."

"Search and Destroy."

"Death Trip."

Nothing happened.

This was serious.

He needed the music of the Godfather of Punk to take him away on the drive home, especially after what he'd been through in the last few weeks. Unfortunately he was heading onto the Chrysler Freeway, where he would be surrounded by maniacs racing back to the suburbs as darkness descended on Detroit. At that point any attempt to operate his iPod by hand would be suicide.

It was eyes on the road, hands on the wheel—or else.

Paddy tried to remember back to the thirty seconds he had spent skimming the section about the voice activation system in the owner's manual of his new car. With his musical background and technical knowledge, he had assumed getting it to talk to him would be easy—one more item to add to the growing list of things he had been wrong about lately.

Buying a new car when he was broke. Thinking he could make it talk to him without bothering to read about how it worked. Trying to cash in on some sordid business from the past that he should have left alone.

Maybe if he spoke the name of the Album or Artist.

"Raw Power."

"Iggy and the Stooges."

The silence that followed was breached by Paddy's angry shout.

"Go screw yourself!"

To his amazement, the car responded.

"Calling Sue Ursell."

Paddy cursed and ordered it to stop until he heard the familiar voice of his administrative assistant coming through the car's speaker system from his iPhone.

"Wagner and Associates, how can I help you?"

"Sue, it's Paddy. My dumbass car called you by accident. Why are you still at work?"

"I'm leaving in a few minutes. I had to look up some numbers the accountants need to finish our taxes."

"The government can wait one more day to pick the bones of our carcass clean. I'm not paying you overtime, that's for damn sure. Go home."

"Yes, sir. By the way, you left those files you were going to take home on your desk. If you want to come back and pick them up, I'll leave the lights on."

Paddy thought about it for a moment as he headed onto the freeway.

"It turns out those won't be as useful as I thought they would be. I'm just getting onto the freeway. Do me a favor, put them in my top drawer, and lock it."

"Will do. Have a nice evening."

"Whatever."

After trying several voice commands that did nothing, Paddy found a button on the steering wheel that hung up the phone.

In the silence that followed, he heard a faint thumping sound behind him. As it grew closer and louder, he realized it was some moron playing cranked-up rap music with a booming bass line.

His car began trembling as Greektown Casino and Ford Field flew by on his left. He started cursing, then remembered the voice activation system and stopped. This time his obscenities didn't generate a random phone call; he assumed they were drowned out by the noise that was filling the car.

He wished he could be cooler about it. Even at his advanced age, he still imagined himself as the young upstart who pissed off old farts with his loud, obnoxious music. He was, after all, Padrig Wagner, aka Paddy Wagon, the bad-boy rebel from the golden age of Detroit rock. But there was no getting around it—he considered the rumbling vibrations he could feel in his chest from fifty feet away to be an invasion of his personal space.

He glanced up at his rearview mirror and spotted the source of his irritation: a shiny black Dodge Magnum with smoked-glass windows. With the help of a strong instinct for self-preservation, he fought off the urge to flip off his fellow music lover. It was never a good idea to give the finger to a stranger in Detroit. Instead he pulled over into the far right lane to let the Magnum pass.

To his surprise it pulled into the right lane behind him and closed the gap between them. Steady, repetitive thumping filled the car, shaking his body and pounding his brain. It was impossible to think, so his instincts took over. He swerved back into the middle lane and stepped on the gas. The driver of the Magnum did the same.

He was being followed.

He swerved into the far left lane and pushed the gas pedal to the floor. He looked in the rearview mirror again to try to figure out who was after him, but he couldn't see the driver's face in the growing darkness. What he could see was that the Magnum had followed him into the fast lane and was closing the gap between them once again.

He was being chased.

This was no ordinary case of road rage or rush-hour roulette. Whoever was in the boom box behind him meant to do him harm. He was certain of that, just as he was certain that he had brought it on himself.

Paddy told himself to stay calm and scanned the road ahead of him. He saw a sign for the Ford Freeway and an opening in the traffic to his right. It was time for a Detroit Slide—a high-speed exit from the left lane without the use of a turn signal. He waited until he was almost to the exit, then cut across two lanes onto the ramp heading west.

The Magnum did the same, narrowly missing cars in both lanes.

The ramp made a slow arc to the left, passing the ghostly white ruins of the Fisher Body Plant on the right. The abandoned building, where Cadillacs had once been made, was a Rorschach test of broken windows and graffitied obscenities. Paddy sped past the old plant and a billboard urging drivers to donate their cars to Mother Waddles to help feed the hungry.

The traffic on the Ford Freeway was surprisingly light for rush hour. Paddy found he could maintain a high speed by weaving from lane to lane around cars. But so could the Magnum, which continued following closely behind him. He moved back into the fast lane and saw the exit to the Lodge Freeway on the left. He took it at the last second and found himself sliding to the right, all four tires squealing like pigs being slaughtered.

The Magnum followed, still ticking away like the world's loudest time bomb.

He was headed south on the Lodge, back toward his office downtown in the Renaissance Center. At this time of day, traffic headed in this direction was almost nonexistent, so Paddy floored it. Motor City Casino zipped past him on the right, and MGM Casino was coming up on his left. He wondered why the cops hadn't pulled him over yet, then remembered that Detroit cops rarely bothered anyone on the freeways unless there was an accident or a crime.

Going fast in a car was not a crime in the Motor City—or, at least, it was so far down the list of crimes as to not draw attention to itself.

Then he thought, why not get their attention himself?

"Call the cops."

"I don't understand."

At least the car was talking to him, despite the noise. The relentless "boom, boom, boom" was getting closer and louder again, making it hard to think. He had to speak more slowly and clearly, lose the slang.

"Call the police."

"I don't understand."

He felt a sudden jolt as the Magnum nudged him from behind. This guy was nuts; he was going to get them both killed. *No,* Paddy thought, *he is just going to get me killed—that's his job.*

He decided it didn't make sense to call the police; whatever was going to happen would be over in a minute or two, long before they could do anything about it. Cobo Hall was looming straight ahead. He braced himself for the sweeping left turn into the tunnel that went underneath it and spilled out onto Jefferson Avenue.

Once again his tires screamed in protest as he asked too much of them. The car drifted to the right, and Paddy made a split-second decision: instead of heading straight down Jefferson to his office, he would turn left onto Woodward Avenue as soon as he emerged from the tunnel. He moved the car back into the left lane without slowing down and got ready for the hard turn he hoped would lose the Magnum.

He looked ahead for the landmark that would show him where to turn: a traffic island that held a twenty-four-foot-long arm that hung from a four-legged pyramid frame. The statue's formal name was the *Joe Louis Memorial*, but everyone in Detroit called it *The Fist.*

Paddy wasn't used to coming out of the Cobo Hall tunnel going this fast; there wasn't much time to think. The traffic lights at Woodward were green, which meant he would be cutting across traffic going in the opposite direction on the far side of the median—a chance he was willing to take at this point. But there was more: some kind of construction on the corner he was hurtling toward; poles with bright lights that cut through the twilight, piles of dirt, yellow sawhorse barricades.

The split-second distraction of this unexpected scene was costly. This time Paddy's instincts failed him.

He yanked the wheel to the left to make the turn, but it was too much, too soon. A small crowd of people scattered as the car crashed through a barricade, slammed up a dirt pile, and launched itself into the air.

The last thing Paddy saw was an enormous fist heading toward his windshield.

Chapter Three

Motion Pictures

Old Main had started out as a Detroit high school more than a century ago; now it served as offices, classrooms, and revered icon for Wayne State University.

Not a bad second act.

The stately old building's first floor had a stone exterior that looked like the foundation of a castle; above that yellow bricks cut with arched windows were topped by a slanting, silver-blue roof. A number of pointed spires reached upward from the roof, and a massive clock tower stood at the front of the building.

As he approached it in the vanishing twilight, Will thought Old Main looked like a slightly more sensible version of the castle in *Harry Potter and the Sorcerer's Stone*. Perhaps he, too, was a special person whose exceptional talents had been overlooked his entire life.

Unfortunately the magic spell of the building's charm was broken when he sat down in his lawyer's office to hear the private detective's report, which began with a simple question.

"Do you wanna see naked pictures of your wife doing it with another guy?"

Before he answered, Will paused to ask himself a question: was this the worst moment of his life? The monumental failures and traumatic embarrassments of his past had set the bar high. But the only thing that prevented him from declaring this moment the all-time champion was the possibility of worse moments to come.

"I paid you to get them, so l suppose I ought to."

The detective handed Will a large manila envelope streaked with dark-red smudges.

"Be careful, I got a little barbeque sauce on the envelope."

Will pulled out the photos and shuffled through them. They were grainy black-and-white photos taken with a night-vision camera, but there was no doubt about who was in them and what they were doing.

For a moment Will thought he was going to throw up.

"You all right?"

His lawyer walked around the desk where they were seated and put a hand on Will's shoulder. Will stared at him blankly for a moment, then nodded and handed him the photos and the envelope. His lawyer walked back around the desk and put the photos in a drawer before he spoke.

"Mr. Murphy is quite insensitive, not to mention fat and sloppy…"

"Hey, I'm sitting here."

"But he is very good at what he does. I know these pictures must make you uncomfortable, but they are going to save you a lot of time and money. I just need your okay and we'll proceed as we discussed. Do you want me to go over the details of the plan again? If not, do I have your permission to proceed?"

Will knew the details of the plan all too well: he had agreed to have Murphy follow his wife and her boyfriend around and take photos that would prove adultery. It was a trump card to be played during the divorce settlement talks that would cut his losses considerably. But now that he had them and was confronted with the ugly but undeniable truth, he wasn't as sure about taking action as before.

Earlier in the day Will had passed on the chance to begin his new life following his bliss, whatever the hell that was. But that had been a minor test of his resolve, easily dismissed as meaningless. This was the real deal, a decision that was potentially life-changing.

He decided to stall for time.

"How did you get these, Murphy? They look like they are inside a hotel room."

"It was a motel out in the sticks. I was trying to get shots of them going inside, but I didn't get there fast enough. Then we got lucky; they opened the curtains in their room. They turned the lights off, but I had my night-vision equipment with me just in case. When they started humping, they didn't even get under the covers. Who knows, maybe they got turned on by doing it with the curtains open. She was really getting into it, there's one picture near the end where she—"

"That's enough, Murphy. I'm sure this is difficult enough for Mr. Harkanen, he doesn't need you adding commentary."

"He asked, I told him."

"Will, we talked about this at length. You agreed to do it. You know what we have to do."

"Let me ask you a question first, Baxter. What famous movie does this remind you of?"

"What?"

"The three of us, sitting in this office. We look like three of the main characters in a classic film noir, made in the early forties. You know it."

"I know *you*, Will. You're procrastinating. I need to let them know we have these photographs right away. We'll need time to reach a settlement before our court date."

Murphy looked a lot like Sidney Greenstreet, who played the Fat Man in the movie, only a lot more rumpled and stained. Baxter Fineman had the same short stature, finely tailored suits, and refined mannerisms as Peter Lorre. His office in Old Main resembled the worn, poorly lit office of Sam Spade, who was about the same size and build as Will. But the similarities ended there: Will knew he was no Humphrey Bogart.

"*The Maltese Falcon*. That's the movie I was thinking of. We kind of look like the guys in *The Maltese Falcon*."

"None of the main characters in *The Maltese Falcon* were black."

"I know, but you sort of look like a black Peter Lorre."

"You're stalling, and you're insulting me. That's great. Let me ask you a question, Will—why did you hire me?"

"You're the only lawyer I know—or at least the only lawyer I know that I trust."

"I told you when I took this job that I wasn't a divorce lawyer. I'm a law professor, not a practicing attorney."

"You saved my ass when the Detroit Police were after me."

"That was twenty years ago. And that case involved libel law, which I taught *and* practiced. I don't teach divorce law."

"What can I say? You're my friend and I trust you. I assume you're still passionate about fighting injustice. Everything else is details and excuses."

"How long have we known each other, Will?"

"Thirty years, at least. I took your *Law of the Press* class. It was the beginning of a beautiful friendship…"

"Yes, yes, *Casablanca*, I get it."

Baxter Fineman stood up and began pacing back and forth behind his desk, presumably to address the jury in Will's mind. He held up his hand and raised a finger for every point he made.

"You've known me for decades. You trust me. I've gotten you out of serious trouble in the past; more than once, I might add. You hired me despite my strong protests, you agreed to my plan, the plan is working—and *now* you don't want to follow my advice."

It was hard to argue with all those fingers, so Will kept stalling.

"I haven't said 'no.'"

"You haven't said 'yes' either. And if you don't, Jane is going to stomp on your heart *and* pick your wallet clean at the same time."

Will thought about his options, then thought about the photographs—here's looking at you, kid, indeed. He was certain they would work, but he also was certain they would hurt and humiliate his wife. A lot of people, including his attorney, would argue that she deserved it. But Will couldn't ignore their shared history, the two great children they had raised, the good times they had together.

"I'm sorry, Baxter. I'm more Rick Blaine than Sam Spade."

"What the hell does that mean?"

"At the end of *The Maltese Falcon*, Bogart turns the woman he loves over to the cops to pay for the crime she committed. But in *Casablanca* he lets the woman he loves leave with another man because it's the right thing to do."

"Which means?"

"I'm not going to do it."

His lawyer said nothing at first but just sat there, shaking his head. Finally he spoke.

"I was afraid this would happen. You're making a huge mistake, you know that. You're letting your emotions influence your decision. You're a nice guy, you don't want to hurt anyone, you don't want to make waves—I get all that. You still have feelings for her, but she doesn't deserve them."

"I'm sorry if I'm screwing up your plan. I thought we'd get a few pictures of them holding hands, maybe kissing in a restaurant."

"I know they are unpleasant, but these will be much more useful to us than a picture of them holding hands."

"I'm not going to destroy the mother of my children just to save a few bucks in a divorce settlement."

"All right, then. I won't waste any more of my time trying to talk you into doing something you don't want to, Will. I ought to know better than that by now. So tell me, what *do* you want me to do?"

"Burn the photos, delete all the images, and settle. Whatever she wants is fine, just end it. I'm tired of this whole mess, I just want to put it behind me."

Once again his lawyer just sat there shaking his head, but now the detective spoke up.

"That's good karma, man. Keep it up and you will overcome your dukkha and be reborn onto a higher plane."

"Mr. Murphy, my client has already chosen a foolish and self-destructive path. Please don't use your dubious second-hand religious beliefs to encourage him to go any further."

"I know what I'm talking about. I learned about Buddhism from a Theravedin master in Cambodia."

"You hid out with a group of forest monks for three months, and one of them taught you how to swear in Khmer. That expertise may prove helpful to Mr. Harkanen after he loses everything to his wife in the divorce, but until then I would ask that you engage in shikantaza."

The detective nodded but said nothing, which caused Will to ask a question of his attorney.

"What the hell is shikantaza?"

"It's a word that describes a popular Buddhist practice. It means 'sitting quietly.' I recommend it for Murphy, but not for you. Even without the photos I can still try to stretch this thing out and get something out of it for you. I can ask that the court date be postponed and—"

"I'm flying to Orlando tonight, I'm going to be at a meeting there for four days. Get the deal done while I'm gone, Baxter, I want to put this behind me as soon as possible. I'm sure Jane will be reasonable. This is all on her, after all."

"Unfortunately I don't share your high opinion of your wife's sense of ethics. This could cost you a lot of money."

"My job sucks but it pays well. I'll get by. Call me when you have a deal."

"It's your funeral. I'll make the arrangements."

Chapter Four

Corporate Retreat

On the first day of the meeting, Will did everything he could to avoid people like Larry. It might have been the fresh scars of his impending divorce. Or the fact that it was getting increasingly difficult to pretend to be enthusiastic about the work they were doing.

Maybe he just didn't like phony assholes.

In any case, he didn't want to "network" or "bond." He didn't want to exchange pleasantries with people who weren't pleasant or share ideas with people who had none. After dinner he went right to his room so that he could spend the evening alone, surfing the web on his laptop.

His plan had worked remarkably well until late that night. He was about to turn his laptop off and go to go to bed but instead decided to do one last thing—check the online edition of the *Detroit News* to see what was happening back home. Two articles caught his attention, and he read them back-to-back. If he had read them separately, at different times and different places, they would have done nothing. But he read them both together, and together they changed everything.

The first article was a review of a book by an Australian nurse who worked with dying people. In it she summarized the five things they regretted most:

The five regrets of the dying: "Number one: I wish I hadn't worked so hard. Number two: I wish I had stayed in touch with my friends. Number three: I wish I had let myself be happier. Number four: I wish I'd had the courage to express my true self. And number five: I wish I'd lived a life true to my dreams, instead of what others expected of me."

He was still wrapping his mind around number five when he read about the traffic accident that killed Padrig Wagner.

Padrig and Will were childhood friends. They had been very close as young boys and had started a rock band together when they were teenagers. But they had a falling-out years ago and hadn't spoken since then. Despite their differences and the years that had passed, when Will read about Padrig's death, a wave of sadness washed over him; he was sorry for Padrig, for their lost friendship, for all the years that had gone by he could never get back.

He suddenly felt himself in serious need of a drink.

He took a tiny bottle of scotch out of the minibar and drank it down in three gulps. But that small gesture felt more pathetic than cathartic, and not at all appropriate to the occasion. Paddy Wagon was gone; a quick drink in an empty room was a woefully inadequate way to mark his passing.

Sleep was no longer a priority.

Fifteen minutes later Will found himself sitting in one of the hotel's many bars at midnight, sipping on a single-malt scotch and talking to the perfectly arranged young woman serving him. After a few drinks he began unpacking his troubles and sharing them with her in the timeless manner of drunks and bartenders everywhere.

"My wife is leaving me after twenty-five years. I thought we were doing okay. Then one day she tells me I'm dull and boring and stifling her."

"Uh-huh."

"She said there wasn't anybody else, but I was sure there was—and there was. I've seen pictures of them. Nasty pictures."

"Hmmm."

"But you know what? I'm okay with it. I consider it a wake-up call. I've been sleepwalking through life. I've been muddling toward mediocrity my entire life. Just trying to get through it, not trying to make the most of it. That's going to change. I've got to muddle higher."

"You want another?"

"Why not?"

Will and the bartender had just reached an important mutual understanding about the shortness of life and the need to do the things that really matter when he heard a voice behind him.

"Hey, it's the wordsmith—just the guy I need."

He turned around on his barstool and there was Larry. On this particular evening Larry seemed to have had a change of heart about public relations people. He sat down on the stool next to Will and put his arm around him.

"You're really good with words, right?"

"I guess so, that's what they pay me for."

"I need some good words. My presentation is tomorrow in one of the breakouts after the first full-group plenary session. You know what? I'm going to tell you a secret, don't tell anybody. I hate public speaking, it makes me nervous. I've been touring the bars in this dump all night trying to calm down, and now problem solved because I ran into my old friend Will."

"How much have you had to drink, Larry?"

"Plenary."

It took a few minutes for Larry to stop laughing at his joke.

"I thought you were all set. Isn't that what we had all those meetings for?"

"I have a PowerPoint with notes that I read from, but I need more."

Will started to tell the drunken accountant to go back to his room, sleep off the drinks, and rehearse his presentation in the morning before the session started—but Larry interrupted him.

"You guys in public relations, that's all you do is talk, right? They say that talk is cheap, but in your case it isn't. I know, I see the numbers—I'm a numbers guy. You call us bean counters, but at least we're adding value. All you guys are adding is bullshit. Expensive bullshit."

It was at this point that Will decided to be a little more— what was that word they loved so much around here—proactive.

For starters, he could imagine a universe in which he would have succeeded in seducing the woman behind the bar if Larry hadn't interrupted him. The fact that Larry couldn't stop himself from piling on insults even as he asked for help was another factor in the decision. But, as bad as they were, under normal circumstances he would have ignored these routine transgressions.

It was the news of Padrig's death that put him over the top. The memories it awakened were a painful reminder of the vast gulf between his youthful dreams and his current reality. He realized, with great sadness, that it was far too late to ever bridge that gulf, and he did not intend to try. At this point all he could do was gather the courage to pursue whatever dreams were left for him. He wasn't sure if he could do it or even what those dreams were, but the hope that it would happen soon was all that kept him going these days.

In the meantime an immature prank would serve as a fitting tribute to his lost friend.

"How can I help you, Larry?"

"I want to be the next CEO."

"Can't help you there, they don't ask for my advice about senior management promotions."

"I know that, you dumbass. I want you to help me give a great presentation tomorrow. What's-her-name, the marketing guru, is a slick talker. The moron in charge of sales operations is a world-class bullshitter. That's why they have the inside track to the CEO job. Everybody thinks I'm a boring bean counter with no personality. I need to add some pizzazz to my presentation."

"You want pizzazz? Tell me what your presentation is about."

"I went through it at the pre-meeting yesterday morning."

"I know, but I wasn't paying attention. Tell me again."

Larry spent the next five minutes describing his presentation. Cash flow, return on investment, debt-to-asset ratios—it was as dull and unengaging as Larry himself. But listening to him ramble on gave Will enough time to come up with a plan.

"You need to tell some jokes."

"Jokes?"

"Jokes, Larry. I'll give you an example. You see that dish of mixed nuts at the end of the bar? Did you know that if you take a can of mixed nuts and shake them up, the biggest nuts go the top? The same thing happens in corporations."

"I know what a joke is. I can't make fun of senior management."

"That's just an example. It's the type of joke that works best in a speech, jokes that are related to the message you are talking about. That was a joke about becoming a CEO, which is what we were talking about. You get it? That's what you need in your presentation."

"I told you, I don't want to say that our senior management is a bunch of nuts."

"Forget the nut joke, Larry. Pay attention to what I'm saying. You need to tell jokes that are related to what you are talking about—jokes that help you make your point. One at the beginning to loosen them up, and one at the end to bring it home and emphasize your message."

"I can't tell jokes."

"Yes, you can, you just told one. That plenary gag was a riot. I almost spit out my drink when you told it."

"That's the only joke I know. I heard someone tell it here last year."

"Don't worry, I'll give you two great new jokes you can tell. Grab one of those napkins and write this down."

Will knew that the only advice most people have ever heard about giving a speech is that you should tell a joke at the beginning. He was counting on the fact that Larry had probably heard this advice at some point too. It would make what he was about to suggest to Larry seem well-intended and reasonable.

He was not a strong advocate of forcing humor into a speech—over the years he had seen too many speakers squirming in awkward silence after attempting to be funny and failing. If the speaker wasn't good at handling humor, it was best not to include a joke in the remarks.

Larry was as bad at handling humor as anyone Will had ever known.

"So the first joke plays off the fact that we are at Disney World and also the fact that one of our competitors in the automotive components business is in trouble. You've heard the rumors about Innolution Industries?"

"Those aren't rumors; they're losing contracts right and left and we're picking them up. We're eating their lunch."

"Okay, so at the start of the remarks, you say that when your daughter heard we were coming to Disney World, she asked you to buy her a Mickey Mouse outfit."

"I don't have a daughter."

"Okay, your son."

"My son is thirty years old."

"You're missing the point here, Larry—it's a joke. Pretend you have a daughter who is ten years old."

"Everyone will know that isn't true."

"It doesn't have to be true."

"But they'll know."

"Okay, let's make it your niece. Nobody will know if you have a ten-year-old niece or not."

"Well, I guess."

"Here's the joke, Larry, write it down: when your ten-year-old niece heard we were coming to Disney World, she asked you to buy her a Mickey Mouse outfit. So you told her that Innolution Industries wasn't for sale."

"As far as I know, they're not for sale. We would never buy them, anyway; they have way too much debt on their balance sheet."

"I keep telling you, it's a joke. It doesn't have to be true, it just has to be funny. They're going to laugh at it, especially if you tell it. It will surprise the hell out of them."

Will believed this statement to be completely true—in fact, he was counting on it. No matter how badly he delivered it, seeing Larry attempt to tell a joke would strike his colleagues as extremely funny. And their laughter, in turn, would give Larry the confidence to finish his remarks with a second joke.

That's when Will would have his revenge.

"Okay, here's the second joke. Get another napkin and write this one down."

The second joke was dark and disgusting. Will wasn't sure Larry would go for it, even as drunk as he was right now. There was even less of a chance he would tell it to a mixed audience of company executives when he sobered up in the morning. Most likely he would realize how inappropriate it was, even for a small-group session outside of the main meeting, and curse Will for stringing him along. But whatever happened, it would be worth the effort.

Will would try his best and hope for the worst.

"There's this guy who loves B.B. King. He's a guitar player and B.B. is his idol."

"Someone told me you used to play guitar in a rock band, is that true?"

"Yes, I did."

"Is B.B. King your idol?"

"He's one of them, but that's not important right now. Let me finish the joke. His wife doesn't know what to get him for his birthday, so as a special gift she decides to surprise him by secretly getting a tattoo of the initials B.B."

"Is this based on facts?"

"No, but it's funnier than hell, and it's related to your message."

After he explained the joke, Will was pleasantly surprised by how enthusiastic Larry was about telling it. Apparently he was certain it would make him appear to be "one of the guys" and greatly increase his chances of becoming CEO.

Will was even more surprised the next morning when, sitting with his throbbing head in his hands at the back of a room filled with half-asleep executives, he heard Larry actually launch into the joke at the end of his presentation.

"So the wife gets a letter B tattooed on each of her butt cheeks, and when the husband comes home for his birthday party, she drops her pants and moons him, and he says—"

At that point the sound system went dead, and a visibly upset woman from Human Resources ran to the stage and began hissing into Larry's ear. He managed to squeak out a "thank you" to the audience and followed her out of the room.

A half-hour later a man and woman came to the room where Will was attending his next breakout session and took him away.

Chapter Five

The Bottom Line

At some point during the interrogation, the small conference room Will was taken to stopped being the Happiest Place on Earth.

The two Human Resources representatives—John and Marilyn—were taking turns asking what Will assumed were rhetorical questions. In any case, he wasn't answering them.

"Do you know that what you did was a serious violation of company policy?"

"Do you know how offensive it was?"

"Do you know that it could cost you your job?"

"What do you have to say for yourself?"

They stopped talking and looked at him expectantly. Eventually it dawned on him that this was his cue to speak.

"I didn't do anything."

This caused the HR people to begin another round of rapid-fire rhetorical questions.

"You didn't do anything?"

"You didn't suggest that 'Larry in Accounting'—as you refer to Mr. Washburn—add some jokes to his remarks?"

"You didn't tell him to use your joke about B.B. King?"

"You didn't think that joke would be highly inappropriate for a global leadership meeting?"

"You don't think that joke is degrading to women?"

They stopped talking and looked at him with expressions of disgust and disbelief. Apparently that was the signal for him to speak again.

"I told you, I ran into Larry in the bar, and he asked me to help him with his presentation. I gave him a few suggestions, had a drink, and went to bed."

"You don't deny that you told him to tell the joke?"

Will knew this wasn't a rhetorical question. He also knew that the path he must follow from this point on would lead him slowly but inexorably away from the truth. The conference room felt close and warm, and the overhead lights glared in his eyes. His head throbbed and his throat was dry—telling them he had *a* drink was a serious departure from the facts.

No sense stopping at one.

"I told him the joke, but I was joking. I didn't think he would actually use it."

"That's not what Mr. Washburn says. He says you told him it was a great joke, and the audience would love it."

"I was kidding. I work in public relations. It's the twenty-first century. I know that joke is offensive, I assumed anyone as intelligent as Larry—smart enough to be a senior executive in this company—would know it is offensive. I have way too much respect for what we are trying to accomplish here to do anything that would distract from this meeting."

The path he was on was going downhill fast, and he had already left the truth far behind.

The truth was he thought Larry was an idiot. He thought the senior executives of his company were smiling sharks swimming in extremely shallow waters. He thought a corporate offsite meeting that gathered executives from around the world in a resort hotel for four days was the tenth circle of Hell.

Now the two of them were exchanging glances and nodding at each other, and then the man spoke.

"So you're sticking to your claim that you were only kidding when you told him to use the joke?"

"Yes. It's the truth."

"That's not what Mr. Washburn says. He says you urged him to use the joke at the end of his presentation because it summarized and reinforced his main message. You do remember what that message was, don't you?"

Will knew the HR man was trying to lure him into a trap, but he couldn't resist responding to the question. It was too good of a line not to repeat.

"Keep your eye on the bottom line."

"Keep your eye on the bottom line—do you think that's funny?"

Another obvious trap, this time set by the woman. The trick here was to keep from laughing out loud or even smiling. Will's face remained grimly frozen as he responded.

"Not in this context, no."

"In what context would you find this funny, Mr. Harkanen?"

"I don't know. Maybe a frat house mixer or a bachelor party."

With growing alarm Will realized that the boldness he had been hoping for was making a sudden appearance at the worst possible time. He wasn't sure where his smartass remarks were coming from—maybe it was the hangover, or perhaps he wasn't quite sober yet. Whatever it was, they were about to let him off the hook if he could just keep his mouth shut.

More glances and nods, and the man spoke again.

"Mr. Washburn is lucky; he's too high up in the organization for us to fire. I really shouldn't share this with you, but he's lost whatever chance he had to be CEO. Of course, he'll get to keep his job. You, on the other hand, are not too high up in the organization to fire."

"I take it I won't get the CEO job either."

"You really are a funny guy, aren't you? Do you know how close you are to being fired?"

"If I'm close to being fired, I guess that means I'm not fired. So what are you going to do to me?"

The man cupped his hand and whispered into the woman's ear, then it was her turn to speak.

"We're going to offer you the same deal we did to Mr. Washburn. If you apologize to the entire management team at the start of the plenary session this afternoon, you can keep your job."

"That's it?"

"That's it."

Despite the disdain and indifference he had displayed to his HR inquisitors, Will was greatly relieved to hear he would keep his job. Being duped and dumped had rekindled a deep desire to be and do something different with his life. Last night the regrets of the dying and the news of Padrig's passing had fanned those flames once again. But this morning his head hurt, and whatever he had been longing for was fading into forgetfulness. As bad as things were in his life, he desperately wanted them to stay the same.

After his meeting with HR, he ate lunch by himself in the main dining room: the news about what he had done had traveled fast, and no one wanted to network or bond with him anymore. That was fine with Will. He skipped the next two breakout sessions and went back to his room to kill time until the afternoon plenary session began.

He got out his laptop and surfed the web, looking for information about the band he and Padrig had been in years ago. It took a while but he finally found an article about them at a web site labeled www.detroitmademusic.com. Halfway through the story he began thinking he had made a big mistake. Or, more accurately, that he was about to make a big mistake.

Then he got the call, and he knew it for sure.

"Will, it's Baxter. I've got some bad news."

"You called just in time, I'm having too good of a time here. I could use some bad news to come down from the euphoria."

"I'm not kidding, Will. We destroyed the photos and deleted all the images like you asked. Then I met with Jane's lawyer."

"And…"

"They want it all, Will. They're claiming mental cruelty, that it's all your fault."

"I was lot of things, but I was never cruel."

"We'll have to prove that. It's going to get ugly. I wish we still had those photos."

"I'm glad we don't, I might be tempted. Just settle the thing, Baxter."

"What?"

"Give them what they want, end it now."

"Are you crazy?"

"No, but I'm going to be."

When the call was finished, Will was ready to go. By the time he left for the afternoon plenary session, it was too late to turn back.

He had finished the article about his old band, then read the story about regrets again. After that he went back to the *Detroit News* online to see about the funeral arrangements. The obituary in the *News* referred him to a funeral home web site, where he learned that Padrig's funeral would be held in two days. He used an online travel service to book a flight back to Detroit, packed his bags, and called for a bellhop to carry them down to the lobby. Then he walked to the main ballroom, where five hundred of his fellow employees were waiting for him to apologize.

The ballroom was strangely subdued, the usual nervous buzz of loud talk and laughter that preceded a big meeting noticeably absent. Ordinarily it took the functionary who handled the logistics of the meeting several minutes to quiet the crowd and introduce the first speaker. This time the crowd listened in silence as he explained that before they got to what was on the scheduled agenda, Larry and Will had something they would like to share with the group.

Larry appeared to be in shock. His apology was brief and sincere. He told everyone he was sorry for what he had said. He was especially sorry if he had offended any of the women in the room. What he had said was sexist, degrading, and unacceptable. By the time he stepped down from the stage, he appeared to be nearly in tears. He glared at Will through bloodshot eyes as they passed each other in the aisle.

Will made his way slowly up the steps and across the stage to the lectern. He had imagined that he would be feeling exhilaration and triumph at this moment, but he wasn't. Instead he felt tired and sad, for himself and for the people he was about to address.

Youthful folly was best left to the young.

Will adjusted the microphone, looked out over the sea of business-casual blazers and open-neck shirts, and made his statement.

"Who's Bob?"

Chapter Six

Funeral for a Friend

By the time Will arrived at the funeral home for Padrig's visitation, the parking lot was full. He circled twice, cursed, and drove away to park on the street.

"Give the people what they want," he said.

He walked back toward the funeral home with growing unease. He had gone through hell to get to this place, but now that he had arrived, he wasn't sure he wanted to be here. This was a fresh hell with ancient roots—his friendship with Padrig had ended abruptly and traumatically more than thirty years ago. Making things even worse was the fact that Padrig's widow, Jacqueline, figured prominently in that disaster.

Still, at one time he and Padrig had been friends, band mates, and musical collaborators. He felt a deep sense of loss for his friend, for himself, for what had been, and for what might have been. Besides, what happened was decades ago, and he hadn't spoken to any of them since then.

It was time to forgive and forget.

Inside the funeral home a black sign with white stick-on letters directed Wagner guests to the Garden of Remembrance. Will walked down a hall and through French doors into a long, narrow room filled with chairs and couches. Small groups of people were gathered in clusters, speaking in low tones and looking uncomfortable. At the far end of the room, a wax figure that looked like Padrig was resting in a shiny, black coffin, surrounded by a wall of flowers.

Jacqueline stood in front of the coffin, talking to an elderly couple and smiling. Her blonde hair was piled up instead of hanging down, and a black dress and high heels had replaced blue jeans and sandals, but she was still as beautiful as he remembered.

Will wrote his name in the guest book. It felt like he was filling out an application to become a mourner, and listing a motel as his home address made it even more awkward. When he finished, he made his way toward the grieving widow. As he got closer, she looked up and saw him. Her eyes narrowed and the smile disappeared. She said something to the old couple, then crossed the room quickly to meet Will.

"What are you doing here?" she said.

"I came to pay my respects."

"Why?"

"Padrig was my friend."

"Some friend."

"We had our differences. It ended badly. But we were friends."

"Padrig was never your friend."

"I know some bad stuff happened, but that was thirty years ago. It's time to let it go."

"*Some* bad stuff? He kicked you out of your band and stole the woman you said you loved."

"I did love you."

"Now he's dead and here you are, I assume to gloat or try to make me feel guilty. You're not welcome here, Will."

"I have no illusions about what kind of person Padrig was, but I'm certainly not here to gloat. And I didn't come here to make you feel guilty. When I read about the accident, it really affected me. Even after everything we went through, I was sad about Padrig. I wanted to come here and pay my respects to him, and my sympathy to you. But it was more than that. It was like some sort of wake-up call or something. It made me think about what I was doing with my life, or wasn't doing. I wanted to reconnect with the band, reconnect with something I had when I was younger that somehow got lost over the years. I had to come here."

"You want to start up the band again? You want to be rich and famous?"

"I don't want that. I want the feeling I had back then. The world was full of possibilities and potential, and I was eager and excited. Like it was Christmas Eve and I was lying in bed waiting for morning to come. I want that back."

Jacqueline stood just looking at him for a moment. She seemed to be considering something very carefully; perhaps what to say or how to say it. When she spoke again, her voice was softer, the edge of anger gone.

"So Padrig dies and all of a sudden you're feeling old and nostalgic. When was the last time you talked to him—1978? You don't know anything about him, then or now. You don't even know half of what he did to you, and you don't know anything about his so-called accident. You're having a late-life crisis, Will, but it's got nothing to do with Padrig or me. Go have it somewhere else."

"So-called accident? What do you mean?"

"You're the college graduate. What do you think 'so-called' means?"

"He crashed his car into the Joe Louis statue in the center of the city in front of dozens of witnesses. Are you saying it wasn't an accident?"

"I heard you were a reporter. I suppose that means you believe everything you read in the paper."

"So what are you saying?"

"I'm not saying anything. Not to you, anyway."

"What about what he did to me, you want to tell me about that? He kicked me out of my band and stole my girlfriend—and that's only half of it? You want to tell me what the other half was?"

"Not really."

"Then why did you bring it up? Are you trying to make me feel worse after all these years? Because I doubt very much that you can."

Jacqueline glanced around the room and Will followed her gaze. People were beginning to notice the quietly heated discussion the widow was having with the vaguely familiar stranger. She hesitated for a moment, looked into his eyes, then spoke.

"We can't talk here," Jacqueline said. "Go down in the basement, there's a coffin showroom at the far end. Wait for me there."

"A coffin showroom?"

"Just do it."

She turned abruptly and walked away toward the body of her husband. Will stood for a moment and tried to process what had just happened. His first instinct was to leave—he didn't need this crap. He had imagined a tearful, heartfelt reunion, not a confrontation. But he *had* been a reporter at one time, and a good one. He loved digging in, uncovering the truth, and connecting all the pieces of a good story. This had all the makings of a good story—and it involved him.

He turned around and headed back toward the French doors and out of the Garden.

Chapter Seven

A Clean, Well-Lighted, Creepy Place

The coffin showroom turned out to be surprisingly bright and cheerful. It creeped the hell out of Will.

The large, rectangular room was filled with coffins on stands surrounded by samples of different exterior materials, liner fabrics, handles, and other fixtures. When Jacqueline didn't show up immediately, Will found himself browsing among the different models and styles, wondering what he would pick out for himself. At this point he was unaware of how quickly he would need one.

As he read the display boards, he quickly discovered that a majority of the floor models in the room were actually caskets—square boxes with hinged lids. A coffin was the more traditional tapered box with a removable lid.

"That's the kind vampires prefer," Will said.

Movies had taught him a lot of things.

As he circulated among the various displays, deliberating about colors and textures, it gradually dawned on him that this was the ultimate exercise in foolish vanity. After a lifetime of sweat and toil on this Earth, why care about what the box they bury you in looks like? Would anyone reevaluate their opinion of him based on what he chose to go out in? Would they think he was more fashionable? Classier? Sportier? A vampire?

And if they did, what difference would it make to him? Even if a cool coffin could change his legacy, he wouldn't be around to enjoy it. All of this begged the bigger question: why care about what anybody thinks about you in the first place?

Will felt a shiver go through his body. He wasn't certain what caused it: the thought of the nothingness of death, or the idea of being trapped in a padded box. Whichever it was, metaphysical angst or physical apprehension, he was certain of one thing: this place was getting on his nerves.

He picked up a catalog and found himself playing the "can you believe how much these things cost?" game. This was less frightening than the picking-out-a-coffin game but couldn't hold his interest for long—frankly, he didn't give a damn. He checked his watch and began to wonder what the deal was with Jacqueline. Was she playing yet another cruel joke on him, or had she simply forgotten that he was down here?

He was working up the courage to leave when she suddenly appeared, closing the door behind her. She walked straight to the back of the room and disappeared behind a mahogany casket. Will followed her around the corner.

"I don't have a lot of time, people will be looking for me," she said.

"Okay."

"You need to know the truth about Padrig, about what he did to you."

"I told you, I'm at peace with what happened. I came here to pay my respects and try to get a fresh start on my life."

"You don't know anything about what happened. Why do you think he kicked you out of the band?"

"Creative differences. We wanted to go in different directions."

"Bullshit. He was scared. The Exits had just signed with a major label and were about to take off. You had done most of the good work on the first album, and you were really coming into your own on the second album. Padrig was afraid he was losing control of the band."

"Creative differences, control of the band, whatever. That was a long time ago."

"That's not all—he was jealous of you, of us. He wanted me."

"So you fell in love with him. I lost my girl to another guy. It happens."

"It's not that simple. He didn't win me over…we made a deal."

"A deal?"

"He told me he was going to kick you out of the band. Everybody thought the Exits were going to be the next big thing. He promised me if I was his girlfriend, I could come along for the ride. I'm not proud of what I did."

"I guess not."

A sharp slap stung Will's cheek.

"Don't you dare judge me. I was young and stupid, and I wanted to be a part of the excitement. It's your fault too, you know. I thought you would fight for me. I thought you would fight to stay in the band."

"You hedged your bets."

"You should talk, you invented hedging your bets. You never were fully committed to the band. You were still in school, getting your degree. And when things got tough, you turned tail and ran."

"The band never made it—they fell apart. Why did you stay with him?"

"Why does anybody stay with anybody? Why did you stay with your wife? What's her name?"

"Jane. We're getting divorced. She left me for someone else."

"I'm sorry to hear that. Kind of a pattern with you, isn't it?"

"Why did you stay with Padrig?"

"We had kids. I got older. As big a jerk as he was, he always made money. After a while I gave up and played it safe. You did too. Why did you give up so easy?"

"Let's see—you left me and they kicked me out of the band; my heart was ripped out and my world was destroyed. I thought about sticking around until the album was finished; most of the tracks were mine. Then Mickey got high and accidentally erased the master tape. That was it for me, I gave up."

"You gave up—that's the story of your life."

"I'm glad you've had this opportunity to pour fresh salt on an old wound. What happened back then has haunted me my entire life. Hardly a day goes by that I don't think about it. Now you're telling me that it was even worse than I thought it was. You know what—who cares? Nobody acted like a hero, including me."

"Especially you."

"What difference does it make now? Did you really need to give me an update? It's over."

"It's not over, that's why I'm telling you all this. But I think I made a mistake. You're still the same old Will."

"It's not over? What do you mean? You said something about the accident upstairs, is that what you are talking about?"

"If I tell you, you're just going to walk away like you did before. You always played it safe, why would you change? I don't know why I thought this would be any different than last time."

"I *am* different. I told you, Padrig's death got me thinking about things. I've done some crazy shit in the last twenty-four hours. I quit my job to come here."

Jacqueline looked him up and down, shaking her head. She started to say something, then stopped.

Someone was opening the showroom door.

"Jacqueline?"

"It's my sister-in-law," Jacqueline whispered. "Get in the coffin."

"What?"

"Get in the coffin."

"Actually, it's a casket…"

Will felt his arm and elbow being gripped strongly; a moment later he was being forcefully guided toward an open casket. He took the hint, swung his leg over the side, and climbed in. He turned on his back in time to see the lid swing shut, plunging him into darkness.

It all happened so fast, he didn't have time to tell her he was somewhat claustrophobic.

He knew immediately what had caused him to shiver a few minutes ago. While the abstract thought of death was unsettling, the physical reality of being trapped in a padded box was terrifying.

In the stillness of his casket hideout, Will could hear Jacqueline call out to her sister-in-law and the conversation that followed. Jacqueline explained that she needed a few minutes to herself, her sister-in-law insisting on staying with her. As their conversation continued, Will found himself growing less concerned about who was going to win the debate and more concerned about how long it would take.

He was running out of air.

Will fought the rising tide of fear and began reviewing limited-air-supply movie scenes in his head. He remembered a variety of cave-ins, locked vaults, damaged submarines, and drifting spaceships and the universal lessons they taught: remain calm and breathe slowly to conserve oxygen. It hadn't been that long; the shortness of breath he was feeling was probably just a symptom of his barely contained panic.

He slowed his breathing down and tried to refocus on the conversation going on outside. It sounded like Jacqueline had made her point and convinced the sister-in-law to leave.

But she wasn't leaving.

Will felt another wave of panic ripple through his body as the sister-in-law recited every cliché she knew about losing a loved one.

She knew a lot of them.

He began to wonder if they would be saying these same things about him shortly, which led him to the obvious question: would he rather die than endure his second major public humiliation in the last twenty-four hours? The answer was not as clear-cut to Will as he hoped it would be.

He didn't want to die, but he also didn't want to pop out of a casket, scare an innocent woman, and face an angry mob of mourners. He decided to wait a bit longer.

More time passed; how much he wasn't sure. He noted with pride that he had conquered his fear. Unfortunately that meant that the shortness of breath he was experiencing was because he was, in fact, running out of air.

Will was still debating his next move when the lid swung open, the light blinding his eyes and Jacqueline's rapid-fire words filling his ears.

"They lied to you. The tape was never erased. They kicked you out of the band so they could keep it for themselves."

"What? Who are they?"

"Padrig and the record producer, Sam Rainier. Mickey must have been in on it too. He didn't erase it accidentally; they stole it."

"Do you mind if I get out of here before we continue this conversation?"

Will climbed out of the casket and asked the only question that came to mind, a question as logical as it was depressing.

"After all these years, what difference does it make if they erased it or stole it?"

"I just found out about it a few weeks ago. Padrig told me about it, he kept calling it his gold record."

"I don't get it."

"When the economy went to hell, we lost a lot of money in the market. Then GM went bankrupt and he lost them as a client. His business was failing and we were going broke. He made it sound like this was going to make up for everything."

"The tape that we made way back when? Did he think it was going be a hit after all these years? What drug was he on?"

"He wasn't talking about releasing the album; he had some other angle he wouldn't tell me about. Then he got scared and started acting funny. When I heard about the accident, I kind of lost it. I spent the day crying, which, to tell you the truth, surprised me. After that I remembered the way he had been acting and it hit me—it wasn't an accident. He was murdered."

"Have you told that to the police?"

"Yeah. They were patronizing as hell. The doctor had given me some Valium, and the police thought it had wacked me out. They said they would look into it, but it was obvious that they weren't going to do a damn thing."

"So what do you want me to do?"

"You're a reporter, right?"

"I used to be. Now I'm a PR guy, or I was until I quit."

"Whatever. You know how to find things out. Find out what happened to my husband."

Will hesitated for a moment. What she had said about him was true—he wasn't a risk-taker. He hated conflict and confrontations, didn't like taking chances or dealing with uncertainty. He was pretty sure he wouldn't like to be murdered either. But in the last twenty-four hours, something had emerged from the shadows of his hopes and fears that was even more frightening to him. It wasn't the possibility of ending; it was the ending of possibilities.

Nothing scared him more than anything.

"Where do I start?"

"I told you everything I know. Mickey knows what happened back then. He's still around. Go talk to him. Get him to tell you the truth about what they did to the tape."

"Then what?"

"I don't know. You're the reporter, do whatever reporters do. Find the facts. Uncover the truth. Then call me. The number is in the phone book, P. Wagner."

"If what you're saying is true…"

He didn't finish the sentence. He wanted to ask her what would prevent the people who killed Paddy from killing him but decided he didn't want to hear her answer—most likely it would be "I don't know" or, worse, "I don't care."

"If it's true, then you've done at least one good, brave thing in your life."

She grabbed him and gave him a long, lingering kiss, then was gone.

Chapter Eight

Meet the Killer

Will knew exactly where to find Mickey Hayes; so did nearly everyone else who lived in metropolitan Detroit. After struggling for decades in relative obscurity as a chef, Mickey opened his own restaurant at the turn of the century. *Taste Detroit* became a hit, drawing business people from downtown for lunch and urban hipster wannabes from the suburbs for dinner.

Finding him was easy. Getting him to confess that he had screwed Will over thirty years ago—as Jacqueline said he had—would be a lot tougher.

After leaving a phone message saying he wanted to talk, Will got a text telling him to come to the restaurant the following day at three o'clock. He arrived at the slow time between lunch and dinner; when he pulled into the parking lot, it was nearly empty.

The parking lot was surrounded by a chain-link fence topped with serious-looking barbed wire. Beyond the fence, looking strangely out of place, row after row of carefully cultivated crops swayed in the breeze.

Taste Detroit was located in an old Gothic Revival house just off Woodward Avenue, the busy boulevard that divided the city into east and west sides. The original owner was a minor auto baron who made a fortune selling engine and chassis components to the city's rapidly growing collection of automakers in the 1920s, then lost it all in the Great Depression. Other than a footnote in the history books, his only legacy was his mansion, now the last house standing on a block once filled with beautiful homes.

Will climbed its steep stone steps and was greeted inside by a hostess standing behind a lectern in the massive entry hall. She picked up a phone and said his name, and a few moments later Mickey Hayes was clomping down the curved marble staircase at the far side of the hall.

"Of all the gin joints, in all the towns, in all the world…"

"I had to walk into yours."

There was an awkward pause when the two men met at the bottom of the stairs. They faced each other, grinning expectantly, but neither made a move or said a word.

After growing up as close friends, then spending nearly every waking moment together for several years in the band, they had only seen each other three times in the last thirty years—at an auto show charity preview, a hockey game, and some trendy, overpriced suburban restaurant. On all three occasions they had nodded and moved on.

Now, together at last after all these years, their knowledge of even the most basic introductory social skills seemed to have deserted them, frightened away by their shared history.

Mickey looked pretty much the same as he always had, except his long hair was now gray, and pulled back into a ponytail. Will mentally reviewed three decades of evolving handshake styles, trying to decide what would be appropriate.

It felt like a high-five moment, but their advanced age and the death of their friend argued against excessive exuberance. He considered the Roman Legion thumb grab, a sort of mid-air arm wrestling contest that was popular in his band days, but dismissed it as too old and unfashionable. He finally settled on the timeless and classic straightforward palm grip.

They held the shake for a moment, then Mickey pulled him into a man hug and whispered into his ear.

"It's been thirty years, man. Why the hell do you want to talk to me now?"

"This thing with Paddy," Will whispered back. "It shook me up, made me think. Life's too short to stay disconnected from old friends."

"This thing…you mean his death? That's a pretty big thing."

Mickey released him from the hug, smiled at him, and spoke out loud.

"We can talk upstairs in my office, but first let me show you around the place."

They walked slowly through the restaurant past the last few lunch crowd stragglers lingering over coffee or drinks. Mickey played the role of enthusiastic tour guide, mostly talking about what each room had been originally and what kind of rare marble or exotic wood it featured.

Taste Detroit was unusual in that it didn't really have a main dining room—with the exception of the entry hall, there were groups of tables in nearly every room on the main floor. There was a small bar to the right of the entry hall; beyond that the study and original dining room looked out onto Woodward Avenue. On the opposite side of the entry hall, the family room and great room had views of the parking lot and the field of vegetables beyond it.

A sign at the top of the basement stairs read *Lower Bar*. Down the stairs was a huge room filled with cocktail tables, a bar at one end, and a small, low-rise stage at the other. Upstairs on the second floor there were a few dining rooms that could be reserved for large groups. There also was a private screening room where Mickey and his friends could watch movies.

"What do you think of my movie room, Will? Remember when we were kids?"

"We spent every Saturday watching a double feature with a cartoon intermission at the Civic Theater."

"And during the week we would watch *Bill Kennedy at the Movies* or *Rita Bell's Prize Movie* on TV and try to stump each other with trivia questions. Think you can still stump me with a question?"

Will didn't answer.

The final stop on the tour was Mickey's office in the former master bedroom.

"What d'you think?"

They sat in the wood-paneled office, Mickey behind his desk and Will facing him in an overstuffed, brown leather chair. Everything in the room looked like it could have belonged to the original owner, except for the computer and multi-line phone on the desk and the framed Robert Crumb drawing on the wall behind it.

The drawing showed a stocky man in a suit punching a casually dressed thin man in the stomach and saying, "Don't criticize Detroit unless y' can back it up, chump!" Will knew it was time to begin his quest for the truth, but the violent image was an unsettling reminder of what could happen when people don't like what you have to say.

Mickey still had long hair and loved movies, but it was clear that he was no longer the easygoing musician Will remembered. He was more polished and accomplished, and there was also something darker under the surface, a wariness that wasn't there years ago. The tough questions could wait—it would be better to start with flattery and nostalgia.

"You have a beautiful place here, Mickey. But I don't remember you ever cooking anything, except for your 'special' brownies. How'd you end up owning a restaurant?"

"When the band split up, I was flat broke, with no job skills other than playing keyboards. I played out in clubs for a while, but eventually that slowed down. Finally one of the places I was playing at said they needed a bus boy more than a piano player, so I became a bus boy."

"That must have sucked."

"It did at first, but then I started hanging out in the kitchen, learning how to do stuff. I had a kind of Scarlett O'Hara moment one night, you know the scene right before the Intermission in *Gone with the Wind*?"

With no hesitation Will recited the line: "I am going to live through this, and when it's all over I'll never be hungry again."

"After that I put myself through the culinary arts program at Schoolcraft College busing tables and helping out in kitchens, and then I graduated and became a chef. I worked in a lot of fancy restaurants, and finally saved up enough money to buy this place."

"That's a great story, Mick. You must be very proud of what you've done."

"It wasn't an overnight success. People said we were crazy. We were offering fresh, organic food, locally grown—in Detroit. They were sure customers wouldn't get it, or wouldn't care, or would be afraid to drive to this neighborhood. That's how we came up with the name for the room downstairs."

"The Lower Bar?"

"Obviously it's in the bar in the basement, but it also stands for the low expectations people had for the restaurant, and for the city. But they were wrong."

Out a side window Will could see that the planted fields stretched the length of the block and beyond. He knew the story behind them, just like he knew the story behind the restaurant. But it seemed like a good idea to keep Mickey talking about himself and his success.

"Is that your garden out back?"

"It's not just a garden, it's a freakin' farm, man. When we first opened, I bought all my vegetables from the farmers at Eastern Market. Then, as we became more successful, I started buying up the other houses on the block. Most of them were vacant and falling apart, and I didn't want them turning into crack houses and ruining my business. When I had them torn down, I ended up owning a lot of empty land, so I started growing my own vegetables. Now I supply the restaurant myself and sell what I don't need at Eastern Market."

"Now that you mention it, I remember reading something about what you were doing in a *Time* magazine article a few years ago. You were one of the 'Detroit Fights Back' people, right?"

"Yeah, that was me. I was in a lot of stories about Detroit, but eventually I quit doing interviews. Now I hate those ruin porn perverts."

"Ruin porn?"

Will was very familiar with the term and what it meant, but he stuck to his strategy of keeping Mickey talking, this time letting him play the role of the hipster sharing inside information.

"You never heard of ruin porn? It's what the national media who come to Detroit are looking for. They take pictures of all the shit that is falling down around here—old buildings, abandoned factories, Michigan Central Station. God, they love going there. It's an old railroad station, there hasn't been a train there in twenty years, deal with it."

"I've seen those stories. They always seem to have a picture of an abandoned house that is falling apart with the Renaissance Center in the background."

"Yeah, it's like they have a checklist or something. They come here, shake their heads, then package up our misery to scare the rest of the country with or maybe make them feel superior. It's either 'Thank God we're not Detroit' or 'If we're not careful we could wind up like Detroit.' They take a complicated situation, simplify everything, and come up with easy answers. There's nothing simple or easy about Detroit."

"The *Time* article seemed fairly positive, at least the part about you."

"That's the latest thing. They got tired of talking about how bad everything was here, so they started looking for anything that was going right. After the *Time* article I was swamped with requests for interviews. It was just another brand of bullshit— 'The brave pioneers reinventing the city.' I kept talking to reporters from out of town because it was good for business, but after a while I got sick of it. They seemed so amazed that something good could happen here. Their stories went from condescending to patronizing, but we were still just a freak show to them. I finally told them all to go fuck themselves."

"Good for you."

As soon as those last words were out of his mouth, Will knew they were a mistake. Mickey wasn't a naïve piano-playing pothead anymore; he was a successful businessman who no doubt could sense when he was being played. There had been too much flattery and one-sided conversation. Mickey stiffened in his chair and eyed him warily across the desk.

"So what have you been up to, Will?"

"It's a long story..."

"I've got time. The dinner crowd won't be here for another two hours."

This was it—time to find out the truth about an event that had changed the entire trajectory of Will's life and haunted him for more than thirty years. He would start slowly, build up sympathy, stick as closely to the facts as he could, and hope he didn't end up like the guy in the drawing.

Time to start living the dream.

"When I left the band, I went back to school and got a journalism degree from Wayne State. I got a job at the *Detroit News* and worked there for ten years."

"You were like an investigative reporter, right? I used to read your stuff."

"Yeah."

"You got fired over the stripper thing with the cops, didn't you?"

"I wasn't fired, I quit."

Will was tempted to explain the entire story to Mickey, how he was set up and lied to, but that was another sad chapter of his life that wasn't relevant to the task at hand. He needed to stay focused. There were bigger things at stake here; it wasn't the time for a sidebar discussion.

"I went over to the dark side, as we used to say—I quit the newspaper business and went into public relations. Not as exciting or fulfilling but a lot more lucrative."

"Who do you work for?"

Once again Will decided to avoid any sidebar discussions. A small lie would keep his mission on track.

"I work for Technart Innovation Corporation; most people know us as TIC. We make parts for the Big Three."

"You're the PR guy there?"

"Yeah. I make excuses for them when they do something wrong and brag about them when they do something right."

"So you're a big-shot executive working for a major automotive supplier. Good for you. You heard about Paddy's death and decided to get in touch with your old friends. That's cool. But if it was such a big deal to you, why weren't you at the funeral?"

It was Truth or Dare time, like the movie that girl from Rochester Hills made back in the '90s. Time to decide whether he should tell the truth or dare to lie.

The truth was that after the bizarre casket incident, Will lost his nerve and skipped the funeral service. Unfortunately that didn't seem like what a person who sincerely wanted to reconnect with his old friends would do. He could make an excuse, say he was at his company's offsite meeting in Florida, but undoubtedly Mickey had spoken to Jacqueline at the funeral. If so, he might be caught in a lie.

"I went to the visitation, but not the funeral."

"Why not?"

"I don't know. I guess I felt it would be awkward. It was tough enough going to the visitation."

"I can dig it. Must have been strange talking to Jacqueline after all these years. What she did to you was wrong. No excuses, but she was wild and crazy back in the day. We all were."

Will sensed his opening and went for it.

"I think she still is, Mick. She told me something crazy at the visitation."

"What was that?"

"She said that you didn't accidentally erase the master tape of our second album—that you and Paddy and Sam Rainier stole it."

Mickey stared at Will for a long time without saying anything. Finally he reached under his desktop and pushed something, and the door behind them swung shut.

"I think it's about time I introduced you to the killer," he said.

Chapter Nine

The Loud Assholes

Will knew it was just his imagination, but he could have sworn the tough guy in the Crumb drawing was glancing sideways at him. They sat in silence for a moment, then Mickey got up and closed all of the curtains in the room. He didn't speak until he sat back down again.

"She's lying, of course. You were there, you know that."

"Why would she lie?"

"Because she's bat-shit crazy, that's why. She was always a little wacked out, and when Paddy died she lost it completely."

Will noticed Mickey was slowly opening a drawer as he spoke. He imagined a gun being pulled out of the drawer and felt a jolt of adrenalin. Will pushed the fear aside and tried to think about the situation in a logical way.

Despite what Mickey had said about meeting the killer, he did not believe that he was in any danger. Then he thought that was probably how people who are about to get killed reassure themselves. His mental debate ended when Mickey took a plastic baggie filled with dried plant leaves out of the drawer and set it on the desk.

"As long as you want to go back in time, Will, why don't we go all the way?"

"What do you mean?"

"If we're going to talk about what happened to the band, we need to get into the right frame of mind. We need to get high."

Will hadn't smoked pot in years and did not want to revisit the habit. His youthful experimentation had proven to him conclusively that marijuana wasn't very useful when it came to clarifying things. It was not a tool that sharpened minds, and the memories it jogged were rarely relevant or reliable. On the other hand, this could be some sort of test that he had to go along with to keep the conversation going.

He decided to push back a little and see what happened.

"You sure you want to get high? We used to drink a lot of beer too, remember? How about we go down to the Lower Bar and hoist a few?"

"You came here to connect with old friends, didn't you? This is the great connector."

Mickey held up the baggie and shook it.

"Remember when really good pot was named after the place it was from, like Maui Wowie or Acapulco Gold? This shit is killer, so I call it 'Dee-troit Killer.'"

Mickey emphasized the first syllable of Detroit when he said the name of his special pot, the way a rapper who needed an extra syllable or someone from out of town would say it.

"I collected seeds from the best pot plants from around the world and cross-pollinated them in the garden out back. It's a private stash I grow for myself and my friends. You're my old friend, aren't you?"

"Yeah, of course. It's just that I haven't smoked in a long time. I guess I'm a little paranoid. Remember the judge that got busted at Ford Field for smoking a joint at the Rolling Stones concert? I was at that concert. When I heard about what happened, all I kept thinking about was how horrible it would be to spend the night in jail in Detroit."

"You haven't changed a bit, Will—you still overthink everything. Just relax. If you don't want to smoke, you're free to leave. It was nice talking to you."

There it was, the ultimatum. Back in the day, Mickey's appetite for cannabis was legendary, as was his ability to function under its influence, earning him the nickname "Purple" Hayes. The chances of Will being able to outsmoke *and* outthink him were slim—which was probably why Mickey had suggested they get high. Still, if he wanted to keep the conversation going, he didn't have much choice.

"You got a bong for that shit or are you going to roll one?"

Mickey laughed and pulled cigarette papers out of the drawer. Casually and effortlessly, he rolled and lit a joint, took a deep draw on it, and passed it across the desk.

Will pinched the joint between his forefinger and thumb, brought the OK sign this formed to his lips, and inhaled deeply. It had been decades since he had smoked pot, but apparently it was in the same category as riding a bicycle or falling off a log. After a few initial coughing spasms, he found himself expertly drawing psychoactive smoke into his lungs.

After they had passed the joint back and forth across the desk several times, Will decided to test how his brain on drugs was doing by saying something.

"That Stones concert was in 2002. The last time I saw them before that was at Olympia in 1969. That has to be a world record for length of time between Stones concerts—thirty-three years."

"I remember that Olympia show. Paddy's older sister drove us. B.B. King was the opening act."

"That's when I became a huge B.B. King fan."

"We started the band right after that concert, remember? We were all so geeked, we started talking about it on the way home. We thought of the name that night—the Loud Assholes. What a great name for a band."

The name of the band began reverberating in his mind and Will began to laugh. Mickey took the joint back from him and began laughing himself. Will caught his breath and continued the story from where Mickey had left it.

"We kept the name until the talent show at Our Lady of Sorrows. Paddy was a wild man, but he was afraid of those nuns."

"They were mean, man," Mickey laughed.

"I wouldn't know, I was the only one in the band who went to public school. But I think I was an honorary Catholic because

I hung out with you guys so much. Or maybe that made me a dishonorary Catholic."

Mickey laughed again, then continued their shared story.

"Paddy put his own name on the entry form when he got us into the talent show, he didn't want to put our real name. We're about to go on stage when Sister Pat sees there's a bunch of us, so she asks Paddy what the name of his musical group was. That's how she said it—musical group."

Mickey started laughing at what he had just said and Will joined in. After several false starts interrupted by giggling, they composed themselves, and Mickey kept the story going.

"There's no way Paddy is going to say, 'We're the Loud Assholes' to Sister Pat. So he's looking around the gym, racking his brains to come up with something, when he sees a sign."

"A red sign above the door..."

"And he tells Sister Pat, 'We're the Exits.'"

It was an old story with a familiar punchline, but time and chemical enhancement turned it into the funniest joke in the world. They laughed for several minutes and then sat in silence. Will was busy trying to remember why he had avoided this wonderful drug for so long when Mickey spoke again.

"What year was that?"

"Back in '72."

"Like the Bob Seger song. That was the greatest time in the history of the world."

"That was the year *CREEM* magazine moved to Birmingham, remember? We drove there and hung out all day 'cause we heard Alice Cooper was going to be there."

"You have a good memory, Will. I forgot all that old stuff we did."

"Did you know *CREEM* coined the terms 'punk rock' and 'heavy metal' in the same issue? They made Detroit the center of the rock-and-roll universe."

"We *were* the center of the rock-and-roll universe. We had the Stooges, the MC5, Bob Seger, Mitch Ryder…Detroit rocked. They should have built the Hall of Fame here."

"Alan Freed came up with the name 'rock and roll'; he was a disc jockey in Cleveland, I think that's why they built it there," Will said.

"The hell with Cleveland, man. It's like cars—we didn't invent cars, but we gave them to the people. Same thing with rock and roll. We gave it to the people. We were the garage band capital of the world. Hell, we invented garages."

"Don't forget Motown. Their recording studio was in the garage. I loved Motown."

"Bands loved coming here because the audiences were so cool. Detroit was the J. Geils Band's second home. Remember how geeked we were that time we opened for them?"

"That was after you guys kicked me out of the band."

Mickey stared at Will for a moment before he replied.

"Oh yeah. I forgot. Bummer. I blame Jacqueline for what happened. She was like the Yoko Ono of the Exits."

"And I was Pete Best."

"Who?"

"Pete Best—the drummer who got kicked out of the Beatles just before they made it big."

"We weren't exactly the Beatles. We were never that big."

"No, but we were good and getting better."

Will realized he had a tough decision to make. He could keep trying to be friendly to Mickey and hope the truth would somehow emerge. Or he could take advantage of the moment, and the point they had reached in their conversation, to confront him again.

As he thought about his options, he also realized that the pot was making it even more difficult to decide anything. In addition, it had suddenly made the hurt and anger he had felt in his youth feel fresh and new again. No wonder he hadn't smoked in all those years. Mr. T was right about everything, he thought.

Don't do drugs. Pity the fool.

"We really should get together and jam sometime, Mickey. For old times' sake."

"I'd like that, Will."

"The tape was good, Mickey. The album could have been huge. What the hell happened?"

"You know what happened. I got drunk and high and wanted to listen to the master tape. I thought it was great. Somehow, when I listened to it, I erased it. I told you then, and I'll tell you now—I'm sorry. I've regretted it all my life."

"Tell me about it."

"I thought we could just go back and re-record it, but then all that shit with Jacqueline happened. The other guys in the band tell me they're kicking you out, and if I don't go along with it, they'll kick me out too."

"The other guys? You mean Paddy."

"Paddy was in charge, you know that. But Tommy and Rick said they agreed with him, they wanted you out."

"Tommy and Rick were idiots; they did whatever Paddy told them to do. I expected more from you. I thought you were my friend."

"We were all afraid we would get kicked out too if we didn't go along with it. We thought we were going to be the next big thing, and we'd all be rock stars. Sam Rainier kept telling us that and we believed him."

"Sam Rainier was a bigger prick than Paddy."

"Sam is a good guy. He didn't forget his friends, even after he made it big. He still keeps in touch with us. He even loaned me some of the money for this place. When the chips are down, he's there for you. He would never hurt anyone."

In the foggy recesses of Will's mind, an alarm bell went off. At first he couldn't figure out why. Then a thought began gradually forming—he hadn't mentioned anything about Paddy being murdered or connected the car crash to the tape in any way. So why did Mickey say Sam would never hurt anyone?

"Sam's in town, you know," Mickey said. "He's producing a movie they're going to film here. Some kind of science fiction thing set in the future, in what's left of Detroit. "

"That doesn't sound very flattering to the city. More like hardcore ruin porn."

"Whatever. I'm not a Goodwill Ambassador anymore, I'm just trying to make a buck. They're going to use my farm as one of the locations. I may even get to be an extra. They've already come by here to do some pre-production work. That's what they were doing at the Joe Louis statue the day Paddy died."

"Sam was there when Paddy crashed his car?"

"Sam wasn't there. It was an assistant director and a couple of set designers. They were trying to see if they could make the statue look like an old ruin, like the Statue of Liberty in *Planet of the Apes*. They put some dirt piles in front of it, which is what made Paddy's car go flying in the air and hit the fist."

"He hit the fist?"

"Yeah, the big fist on the end of the giant arm. What did you think he hit?"

"The newspaper said he crashed into the statue. I thought they meant the base."

"Sam has a lot at stake here. He's hired a local PR firm that's very wired-in and influential, and he has a lot of friends in high places. I'm guessing he pulled some strings to keep the details out of the papers and make sure the accident wasn't connected to his movie. That kind of bad publicity could threaten everything he is trying to do."

"But the arm is like ten feet up in the air."

"Six feet. Paddy hit the dirt pile, flew up, and the fist came through his windshield."

"The fist came through the windshield? That's what killed him?"

"It's too bad it happened, but Paddy would have thought it was cool. After all the crazy shit he used to do, it was an awesome way for him to go."

"Dying in a car crash?"

"Getting his lights punched out by Joe Louis."

Will was contemplating the intertwined levels of horror, irony, and cosmic comedy this news evoked when a buzzer sounded. He would have jumped out of his chair in fright if his brain had been able to process the information and sound the alarm in a timely fashion. As it turned out, all he could do was watch in total amazement as Mickey pushed a button on his phone and it began talking to him.

"Mr. Hayes, there are two men on their way upstairs to see you. I tried to stop them, but they insisted on going right up."

"Who is it?"

"The police."

Chapter Ten

Dazed And Confused

W ill wasn't sure if he was watching a bad movie or living a nightmare. In either case, he didn't like what he was seeing.

Two men in blue uniforms burst through the door to Mickey's office and walked straight to his desk through a haze of smoke. The policeman who led the way looked around the room, sniffed the air, and pronounced his sentence in a loud, commanding voice.

"Mickey Hayes, you and your companion are under arrest for the use of illegal narcotics."

Visions of being locked in a holding cell with a posse of Detroit criminals flashed through Will's head. It was a horror show that would not end well.

The man who announced their arrest now spotted the smoldering joint sitting in an ashtray on Mickey's desk.

"Officer Markowitz, we need to examine this evidence," he said.

He picked up the joint, took a long toke, and passed it to the other policeman. They passed it back and forth until there was only a small stub left. The first policeman crushed it out in the ashtray and made another pronouncement in a loud voice.

"Let the record show that this is some good shit!"

At this point the two policemen and Mickey began laughing uncontrollably, while Will tried and failed to make sense of this new reality. Eventually Mickey calmed down long enough to explain.

"Will, this is Sergeant Preck and Officer Markowitz from the Detroit Police. The Central District is helping out with security for Sam's movie. They've been by here a couple times to scout things out, make sure the neighbors don't freak out when they hear gunshots and explosions."

"We're not worried about the neighbors freaking out, Mickey—we're worried they might return fire with live rounds."

The police and Mickey began another round of hard laughter, and Will managed a weak smile at the thought of not spending the night in a Detroit jail. When the laughter stopped, the sergeant spoke again.

"We're all set here, Mickey. No sign of the POEs. We just came by to say hi."

"To get high, you mean."

More laughter.

"What can I say? We're always trying to catch the Detroit Killer."

After a few more minutes of jokes and banter, the police left, and Mickey explained how he had gotten to know his new friends.

"I thought my pot garden was pretty well hidden, way in the back of the lot, but the first time they came here to check things out, they stumbled across it. They came up to my office and busted my chops like they did just now, then started laughing and told me to roll a joint. It turns out they've got a lot worse things to worry about in this city than people smoking pot. They like to get high themselves."

"Yeah, but while they're on duty?"

"I don't judge, man. I'm just glad they're cool with it."

"They said something about the pose. Who's going to pose?"

"Not pose, POEs—P-O-E-S. They're some kind of radical environmentalist group that is pissed off that Sam is going to knock down a few old buildings to film his movie. They've made a few statements that sound like threats; the cops are taking it pretty seriously."

"I thought environmentalists liked nature."

"These ones like old buildings too. Go figure."

As Will tried to make sense of that and everything else he had just seen and heard, the two policemen made their way down to the front porch. Officer Markowitz walked off to get their squad car from the parking lot, leaving Sergeant Preck alone on the sidewalk to make a quick phone call.

"I followed our man like you asked. He ended up at *Taste Detroit* talking to Mickey Hayes...I don't know what they said, but they were getting along just fine, like old friends should... How do I know that? They were getting high together...Don't worry, I'm not going to do anything to him unless you tell me to."

Chapter Eleven

Guardian Angel

Will spent the next twenty-four hours recovering from his trip down memory lane and wondering how he was going to arrange a meeting with Sam Rainier. Even in the old days, they were never close. Now that Sam was a Hollywood producer, Will assumed that the odds of getting in to see him were the same as drawing to an inside straight at the casinos.

Not that he had ever tried anything that risky.

He had left Mickey's restaurant soaring on a chemical and emotional high. The thirty-year chasm between them had disappeared in a cloud of smoke, and Will found himself chatting comfortably with his old friend as if no time had passed. They had even promised to get together and jam after hours at *Taste Detroit*.

It wasn't until the next morning, sitting alone in his motel room, that he remembered why he had visited Mickey in the first place. He was trying to find out if the painful events that had altered the course of his life more than thirty years ago were uglier and more sinister than he already knew them to be. That wasn't even the worst of it—he also was trying to find out if the people involved had gone so far as to murder his former bandmate.

It was time to talk to Sam.

Throughout the day he made and abandoned several clever plans to get in touch with the busy producer. The lingering effects of reefer madness made him feel like a cross between a sitcom neighbor hatching a wacky scheme and a schoolboy working up the nerve to call a girl for a date.

Late in the afternoon his problem was abruptly solved when Sam's administrative assistant called *him* on his cell phone to schedule a meeting. This sudden and unexpected solution to the problem he had been struggling with all day made Will happy for a moment, then uneasy.

"Why does he want to see me?"

"Mr. Rainier is here in Detroit to make a movie. While he's here, he wants to get in touch with his old friends."

Will could have repeated the question but he didn't.

"Our offices are located downtown in the Guardian Building, Suite 2700. We look forward to seeing you tomorrow afternoon at two."

The Guardian Building was a beautiful Art Deco skyscraper located in Detroit's financial district. The massive vaulted ceiling of the lobby, covered in brightly colored mosaic tiles, inspired the building's nickname—The Cathedral of Finance. To Will it looked more like some kind of Jazz Age Mayan temple, a great location for the opening scene of an *Indiana Jones* movie where Indy was setting out on a grand adventure.

The security guard behind the desk led him to the elevator lobby, which featured a stained-glass portrait labeled "Fidelity." To Will it looked like an angry demon about to toss a big rock onto someone. The guard swiped a card in a slot, pushed the button for the twenty-seventh floor, and sent him on his way.

On the twenty-seventh floor, Will made his way to the outer office of Future Tense Productions. He was immediately ushered into a corner office and a moment later found himself trapped in yet another awkward man hug.

"Wow. Will Harkanen. This really blows my mind."

Sam Rainier had a deep tan that was offset by dazzling white teeth and razor-cut silver hair. He was wearing an expensive sport coat over a black tee shirt and jeans. He smelled like wood and leather.

"Good to see you, Sam. You're looking good. From the looks of this office, you're doing pretty well for yourself."

Sam released him from the hug and gestured toward a corner by the windows. They sat down in two high-backed chairs that were arranged around a low table made of inlaid wood.

Once again Will felt like he was on the set of an old movie, but this time he wasn't in a run-down, poorly lit detective's office. This was more like an expensive, well-furnished New York penthouse that Nick and Nora Charles would have felt at home in.

"How about a drink?"

"No, thanks."

"You sure? I've got a great single-malt scotch, Glenfiddich. I've been drinking a lot of it ever since Donald Trump banned it from all of his resorts. It's my way of giving the finger to that prick."

"I'm not sure I follow you."

"It's a long story. I'll give you the trailer version—I once tried to get financial backing from Trump for a movie I was doing. He strung me along forever, then said 'no.' So, years later, Trump wants to build a golf resort in Scotland—like they need more golf courses there—but one lone sheep farmer holds out and won't sell him his land. You with me so far?"

"Yes."

"Okay, so every year the people of Scotland vote for the Scot of the Year, and this farmer wins because he stood up to Trump. It turns out the contest is sponsored by Glenfiddich, and even though they had nothing to do with the voting, Trump declares war on them. So Glenfiddich becomes my favorite single-malt scotch."

Sam looked pleased with himself when he finished the story, and for a moment Will considered applauding. Instead they sat in awkward silence until Sam spoke again.

"Would have been a great movie too. You know the Hemingway story *Big Two-Hearted River*?"

"Yes."

"We were going to do a modern-day version. Instead of a World War I veteran going on a fishing trip on a river in the Upper Peninsula to forget about the war, it was going to be an Iraq war vet."

"Sounds interesting."

"It gets even better. Instead of sitting around moping and fishing, our vet gets attacked by a mysterious creature with two heads. Guess what the title was going to be?"

Will was pretty sure he knew but was afraid he couldn't say it without laughing, so he remained silent and shook his head.

"*Big Two-Headed Monster*! Awesome concept, don't you think?"

Will thought this might have been the only time in his life Donald Trump had demonstrated good taste, but he replied in a more self-serving way.

"That is an awesome concept, Sam. Too bad it didn't get made."

"It's the picture that got away—like the big trout in the story. We don't call them movies in Hollywood, by the way. We call them pictures."

"Good to know. Whatever you call them, I'm a big fan."

Sam gazed steadily at Will and seemed to be considering something puzzling. At last he smiled and spoke.

"Isn't this place awesome, Will? All this Art Deco stuff reminds me of old Hollywood. That's one of the reasons we decided to lease office space here."

"One of the reasons?"

"Originally we were just going to open a temporary office in this building as a publicity stunt for the movie we're making. Then when we saw how great it looked, we decided to sign a long-term lease. We're bringing Hollywood to Detroit, and this building was made for the part."

Will was aware of most of what Sam was talking about, although he hadn't heard anything about the movie until he talked to Mickey. But, as he had done with Mickey, he decided to play dumb and let Sam talk about himself. Hopefully it would soften him up a bit for the nasty accusation he was about to confront him with.

"You're bringing Hollywood to Detroit?"

"Don't you read the papers? We're trying to open a movie studio here in Detroit. Michigan has a tax incentive program to encourage filmmakers to shoot their movies here. We're trying to get Detroit to match the state's tax breaks. If they do we're going to build a state-of-the-art studio right here in the city."

"That sounds great. How's it going?"

"You know Detroit, everything is political theater. The mayor is pushing back on our proposal, but the city council is lined up pretty solidly on our side. Councilman Rogers has been a great champion for us."

Will grimaced when he heard the name but Sam didn't notice. Of course he read the papers, he knew all this. But his next question was sincere; he was genuinely curious.

"What's the movie you're making about?"

"I heard you used to work for the *News*. You're not a reporter anymore, are you?"

"No, why?"

"Because the media know we might be filming something here, but we haven't given them any details yet. We're going to hold a big press conference to announce it, and we hope to be able to officially announce the new studio at the same time. We'll do it right here in the Guardian Building, which will make it doubly cool."

"Why's that?"

"So you're not a reporter anymore? Because this is confidential."

"I'm on the other side these days, I'm in public relations. I know how to keep a secret. I promise you I won't tell anyone."

"The movie is called *The Guardian of Detritus*. It's set in a post-apocalyptic Detroit, only it's the government that destroyed the city. They turned it into a forest to help clean the air, or some kind of bullshit like that."

"Sounds interesting."

"To tell you the truth, I don't really care about the back story. I paid a lot of money for this script because it has lots of fighting and explosions. It's kind of like *Saving Private Ryan* meets *Terminator 2* meets *The Hunger Games*. It's going to be huge."

"That's really exciting. I'm glad things are going so well for you."

For a moment Will was afraid he had crossed the line with too much obvious flattery, as he had done with Mickey. But apparently people in the movie business had a higher tolerance for insincere admiration.

"Thank you. Things really are going well, and they're about to get better. This movie is going to make a fortune for us. And when we get the studio up and running, we won't be a small independent shop kissing ass and groveling for financing anymore. We'll be one of the big boys, with a studio of our own. People will have to kiss ass and grovel for *us*."

"Sounds wonderful."

Sam gave no indication that he heard what Will had said. He stood up slowly and looked out the window in silence. He continued looking straight ahead as he spoke.

"We're not just doing this for ourselves. I fell in love with Detroit years ago, when I first came here from Los Angeles to produce the Exits' second album. This is where my career took off, where I became Sam Rainier the hit maker, then Sam Rainier the music video maker, then Sam Rainier the movie maker. Building a studio here is my way of giving back to the people of Detroit."

With his public relations background, Will was certain Sam was reciting a sound bite he had memorized for the press conference he was planning. After a dramatic pause, Sam snapped out of his reverie and looked down on Will.

"Did I mention we're building the studio in an enterprise zone? It's a real shitty neighborhood the federal government is trying to revive. They're pouring money into it, and we're going to be getting some of those incentives too."

"You're going to get tax breaks from the city, the state, and the federal government to make movies here. Sounds like a great deal."

"It's a win-win for everyone involved."

Will recognized the phrase "win-win" from the years he had spent in the business world. It meant someone was about to get screwed big time.

Sam looked back out the window, but this time he looked out over the Detroit River toward Windsor.

"Did you know that from where we are right now, Canada is actually south of us?"

Even with a Hollywood executive, there was a limit to how dumb Will could play, so he answered truthfully.

"Yes, I knew that."

"Of course you do. You're a smart guy. If somebody told you Canada was north of us, even though it sounds like it could be possible, you wouldn't believe them. You know the truth."

Sam sat back down and looked across the table at Will.

"I heard you went to visit Mickey Hayes the other day, right out of the blue, after all these years. Told him some crazy story about the old days. Something Jacqueline Wagner told you."

The mystery of why Will had been invited to visit the busy producer had been solved. He tried to think of some way to make the conversation less painful and confrontational, but he couldn't. He was out of clever ideas for avoiding trouble. It was time to do something meaningful and see what happened.

"She told me that the master tape to the Exits' second album was never erased. She said that you, Padrig, and Mickey stole it."

"Do you believe her?"

"I don't know what to believe."

"You should believe the facts that you know are true. Mickey got wasted and erased the tape. End of story."

"Why would she say it was stolen if it wasn't?"

"I think you know the answer to that. I remember this like it was yesterday. She was a real wild one. She broke up the band, right? My understanding is that, when Paddy died, she kind of lost it. The police don't believe the crazy stories she's telling, why should you?"

For the second time in the last three days, an alarm bell sounded in Will's mind. Obviously Mickey and Sam were connected and talking to each other. But he hadn't told Mickey about Jacqueline going to the police, so how did Sam know about it? He decided against asking the question directly; he didn't want to tip his hand this early in the game.

Accusations and confrontations could wait. Right now it was time for some professional-grade Hollywood-style ass-kissing.

"I apologize if I've offended you, but I had to ask. After Paddy died I really felt a need to get in touch with people from the old days. But I wanted to remember the good times, not dredge up unpleasant memories. If anybody knows how crazy Jacqueline can be, it's me. It would be just like her to make up a story to mess with our minds and get us fighting among ourselves. I'm ready to forget about it and move on."

Will extended his hand in classic manly fashion and Sam grabbed it. As they shook, he looked Will in the eye and nodded.

"No offense taken here. Paddy's death has been tough on us all. If any good can be taken from it, maybe it's the fact that it's brought us back together again after all these years."

Sam released Will's hand but continued to maintain eye contact. After a moment Will looked away. When he looked back, Sam was still staring at him, and he had a slight smile on his face.

"I'm sorry if I'm making you uncomfortable, but I just had a wild thought. Can I ask you a question?"

"Sure."

"How'd you like a part in my movie?"

Chapter Twelve

Adult Language and Brief Nudity

Will had no intention of appearing in a movie.

He said this several times, but Sam appeared to be genuinely excited about his seemingly spur-of-the-moment casting decision.

He wasn't about to let it go.

"Ever since the first time I read this story, I've had a mental image of what this guy looks like. Our casting people went through hundreds of headshots and couldn't find what I wanted. I'm looking at you and a light bulb goes on—I'm talking to the Guardian of Detritus."

"I'm flattered, Sam, but I told you—I'm not an actor."

"Don't worry about it, we can get you a SAG card, no problem."

"I'm not talking about joining the union, I mean I'm not a performer: I don't know how to act."

"Acting is the most overrated skill in the world. If you can talk without looking at the camera, you can act."

Will was less flattered at this point and still not convinced.

"But it's the title character. Doesn't the whole movie revolve around him?"

"This movie revolves around gunfights, explosions, and hot women running through the woods half naked. Trust me, I've been doing this shit for a long time. I wouldn't ask you if I didn't think you could do it. We can introduce you at the press conference, local man playing the title role. It will be great publicity for the movie."

In the end Will agreed to think about it, mainly because if he didn't, Sam wouldn't let him leave his office. As it was, Sam insisted that he take a full script with him, along with a script treatment. Will knew what that was, but Sam explained it to him anyway.

"A script treatment is like an executive summary of the movie. We use it to get people who are too busy, too important, or too stupid to read a full-length script interested in a project. If you read it first, it will help you follow what's going on when you read the script."

After reassuring Sam several times that he would read the script as soon as possible, Will returned to his Economy Executive Suite at the Motown Motel, the place he had called home for the last three months. He threw the binder that held the treatment and script on the bed, grabbed a beer out the mini-fridge, and sat down in the room's overstuffed easy chair to think.

Despite his love of movies, he had no intention of playing a part in this one. For starters, he didn't like the idea of stepping out of his comfort zone and making a fool of himself. He had spent a lifetime adhering to an unwritten Code of Dignity. The one time he violated the Code was in Orlando, and it had thrown his life into turmoil and cost him his job. Sam's assurances that acting was easy did not seem like a good enough reason to violate it again.

There was another factor, as well—a vague uneasiness that being offered a part in the movie was some sort of quid pro quo for dismissing Jacqueline's story. Sam probably remembered what a movie buff he was, or maybe Mickey had reminded him. The offer was made right after Will said he wanted to forget about Jacqueline's accusations and move on.

Was that a coincidence or a bribe to help seal the deal?

The truth was, with or without the movie part, Will was beginning to doubt Jacqueline's story. He had covered more than his share of murder trials as a reporter, and they almost always involved money, infidelity, drugs, or alcohol. People didn't get killed over tape recordings that were accidentally erased thirty years ago. Sam and Mickey were successful and respected businessmen. What would they have to gain by killing Paddy?

Even the things that made him suspicious could be easily explained. Mickey said Sam was a nice guy who wouldn't hurt anybody because he gave him money to help open his restaurant. And of course Sam would have spoken to the police; someone crashed and died at one of the locations that was being scouted for his movie. They would have told him about the hysterical widow claiming it was murder.

Bribe or not, he was pretty sure he was not going to pursue his investigation any further. He was even more certain that he wouldn't take the part. His *Walk on the Wild Side* had ended badly. It was time to cut his losses and get back to normal, no matter how dull and grim.

Still, he knew that when he said "no," Sam would grill him about the script and why he didn't like it. He needed to at least read the executive summary so he could fake his way through that conversation.

He grabbed the binder off the bed, got another beer out of the refrigerator, sat down at the small metal desk that served as the room's "Executive Business Center," and began reading:

Script Treatment: The Guardian of Detritus

Writer—Frank Fitzgerald
Director—Alan E. Smith
Producer—Sam Rainier

© *Future Tense Productions*

In the year 2121 the city once known as Detroit is a subtropical rainforest filled with the decaying ruins of abandoned buildings. For fifty years it has served as a natural carbon sink, with millions of trees planted to absorb and store carbon dioxide from the atmosphere to help reduce global warming. This controversial project required the forced relocation of the residents of the city. Many felt the project was racist, because the majority of the population was African American. Others felt the city was targeted because of its historic association with the automobile, a significant source of carbon dioxide emissions through the years. This anger continues to the present time, and rebel groups have been formed.

People are forbidden from entering the 143-square-mile forest, which is now called Detritus. The exception is the Guardian, a public servant who is a combination forest ranger and police officer, tending to the forest and keeping out trespassers. It is a job made difficult by the Archivists, who search the ruins to preserve the artifacts of the past, and the Anarchists, who want to re-inhabit and rebuild the city and make it better than it ever was. They fight among themselves as both groups search for the lost statue of the arm of Joe Louis—to one group an important relic of a glorious past, to the other a symbol of the fighting spirit of Detroit that will inspire others to join them in building a brighter future.

As the picture opens the Guardian of Detritus has not been heard from in months, and a squad of elite Army Rangers has been sent to find him. They have been told that the Guardian may have been kidnapped by Archivists or Anarchists to help them in their search. In fact, as we learn in a montage set to songs in the public domain, he has gone rogue and is acting as an emissary of peace between the two groups, teaching them to get along while gradually coming to see their point of view as well. The Rangers arrive and a series of battles and chases ensue, causing violent deaths, explosions, adult language, and brief nudity. The Guardian makes his way through explosions and gunfire across a battlefield to negotiate a truce, but on his way back he is accidentally shot by one of the rebels he has befriended. He is found by the Rangers, injured and near death, outside a famous Detroit landmark TBD—the ruins of either the Lafayette Coney Island or the American Coney Island restaurant. He tells the sexy female platoon leader, whose uniform has been almost completely ripped off in the fighting, the location of the Joe Louis arm statue. He says that he has told the Archivists and Anarchists where the statue is located, and if they hurry the Rangers will be able to ambush the rebel groups there.

The Army Rangers follow the directions they have been given and end up at The Hand of God, a statue of a nude youth in a giant hand originally commissioned to honor C. E. Johansson, who revolutionized precision measuring of auto parts, making the moving assembly line possible. The Guardian has tricked the Rangers and dies with a smile on his face. In the final scene the Archivists and Anarchists meet in front of the Joe Louis arm statue, having been given the correct directions there by the Guardian. They are bumping fists à la Joe Louis and making plans to honor the past while building a new and better Detroit for the future.

When he finished reading the script treatment, Will set the binder down on the desk, got another beer, sat back down, and started laughing.

Maybe he was qualified to act in this movie after all.

Sam Rainier had begun his career as a record producer. When MTV went on the air in 1981, he started directing music videos to go along with the songs he produced. A few years after that, he was asked to direct a full-length feature film about a zombie rock band. He went on to direct several successful, low-budget horror films before becoming a producer. Over the years the films he produced had become slightly more mainstream and respectable, and a lot more profitable.

After reading the script treatment, Will suspected this movie was intended to be more thoughtful and high-brow, without abandoning the sex and violence that sold tickets. Global warming and racial politics would give the critics a bone to chew on; T&A and TNT would put butts in seats. It was *Apocalypse Now* meets *Mad Max* meets *Hot Tub Time Machine*, a cynical and pretentious rip-off.

Give the people what they want, he thought.

He grabbed another beer and began skimming through the script, looking for his lines. An hour later he set the script back down and started laughing again.

Whatever his motivation, Sam was not risking much by offering the title role to Will—the Guardian of Detritus only had four lines, each of them more stupid than the last. They were:

"All hail Detritus. What was, what is, what will be… whatever."

"Hold your fire, I'm going over there to try to smack some peace into them."

"It's too late for me; download these coordinates into your Locater if you want to catch the rebels."

"Can't forget the Motor City."

The last line was delivered by the Guardian just before he dies. Did they know it was a line from "Dancing in the Streets," a Motown song recorded by Martha and the Vandellas in 1964? Did they care? Could they not imagine that—intentional reference or not—a line this contrived and corny would surely cause the audience to laugh, not cry?

Will began to reconsider his refusal to act. However bad his performance was, there was no way he could hurt this movie— whatever wounds it received would be self-inflicted. He did a quick inventory of his life and found that, on further reflection, there was really nothing to hold him back. Whatever the hell dignity was, he had run out of it on stage in Orlando.

Good riddance.

He was without a wife for the first time in twenty-five years, out of work, and living in a cheap motel. His half-assed effort to recapture the passion of his youth was rapidly running out of steam; it was becoming more embarrassing than exhilarating. The mystery he was trying to solve for a damsel in distress was turning out to be either a cruel prank or a paranoid delusion. To top things off, an entire lifetime spent trying not to embarrass himself had ended with a butt-hole joke.

The good news in all of this was that he no longer had to agonize over what people thought about him—that issue was settled. So instead of sitting back passively and watching movies, maybe it was time for him to act in one. Why the hell not? He was turning that thought over in his mind when he heard a knock at his door, which caused him to start laughing again.

"Is that you, opportunity?"

"Open the door, asshole."

It wasn't opportunity, it was Jacqueline.

Chapter Thirteen

Motown Motel

"I see you're still playing guitar."

Will's cherry sunburst Les Paul sat in a stand in the corner next to a Fender Bandmaster amplifier head with a set of headphones plugged into it. He still played, but these days no one could hear him.

"How'd you find me?"

Will was sitting on the bed, Jacqueline in the easy chair. She was wearing a summer dress and sandals, one of which dangled precariously from her foot when she crossed her legs.

"How does anybody find anything these days? I started with an online search. It gave me your address and phone number in Northville. I called the number and your ex answered. She told me you had moved out months ago."

"You talked to Jane? What did she sound like?"

"She didn't sound very happy that I called."

"Did she say anything about me?"

"She said that your life was dull and uninspiring and that you were stifling her."

"She keeps saying that. I don't even know what it means. Anything else?"

"She said she had asked you to leave, but you had a cell phone, and she gave me a number that wasn't in service."

"That was my old cell phone from work. I had to turn it in and get my own phone when I quit. That's all she said?"

"She dumped your ass, Will, it's time to move on."

"So how did you find me? Jane doesn't know where I live."

"I remembered you signed the guest book at the visitation. Lucky for me you weren't embarrassed to write that your home address was at an Extended Stay USA. By the way, why do they call this one Motown Motel? It's in Novi, for God's sake—it doesn't get any more suburban than that."

"I think they call it that to attract out-of-town business people who are coming to Detroit. It makes them think they'll be near the city, but not in it—the hipness without the danger."

"So why did you come here?"

"Same reason. I was going to be cool and get a room in one of those rundown hotels downtown but I chickened out. I liked the name, it sounded funky and dangerous."

"Still a wannabe, huh? Paddy used to say where there's a Will there's no way."

"What do you want, Jacqueline?"

"I asked you to call me and you didn't. I want to know what you found out."

"I didn't call because I didn't find anything out."

"Did you talk to anybody?"

"I talked to Mickey Hayes and Sam Rainier."

"What did they say?"

As Will thought about his reply, he had a serious 'oh shit' moment.

He prided himself on being goal-oriented, but the goals he pursued had always been short-term and achievable—the low-hanging fruit. He had turned away from the things he really wanted, the goals that were difficult and uncertain. The most basic question—what do you really want to do?—remained unanswered.

Before he started burning his bridges in Orlando, he had promised himself that from now on, he would keep what really mattered in mind before he decided on a course of action. But, in this case, he wasn't exactly sure what really mattered to him or what he was hoping to do. Investigate a murder? Find out the truth about a painful incident from his past? Help an old girlfriend? Seduce an attractive widow? Follow his heart, regardless of the consequences, for the first time in his life?

In the end he decided that, whatever he was doing, he would stick to the truth with Jacqueline.

"They both said you were crazy."

"Do you think I'm crazy?"

"No, I don't. But I think you've been through a very traumatic experience. Maybe you misheard or misunderstood what Paddy said about the tape."

"I know what he told me. He said it was never erased; that they stole it."

"Mickey and Sam both say that isn't true."

"Then they're lying."

"Okay, even if they are lying, that doesn't mean Paddy was murdered. Maybe they're just embarrassed to admit they did something stupid thirty years ago. Why would anybody kill someone over some songs by a band that was never more than a local favorite?"

"I don't know. All I know is that Paddy was up to something involving the tape, then he got scared, then he was dead. I don't think it was a coincidence."

"I talked to the only other two people in the world who know what really happened to the tape, and they stuck to their story. There isn't a lot more I can do."

Jacqueline stood up, stepped out of her sandals, and sat down on the bed next to Will. She put a hand on his knee and looked into his eyes, on the verge of tears.

"I know Paddy wasn't a good friend. He wasn't a good husband either. But I'm not going to let this go and neither should you. Someone ripped you off and ruined your life. Don't you want to settle that score?"

"I'm not after revenge, if that's what you mean."

"Not revenge, just the truth. Don't you want to know what really happened?"

She wanted the truth. He would give it to her.

"Jacqueline, I'm sorry, but I'm going to have to tell you—"

She lunged forward and kissed him in mid-sentence, pushing him backward onto the bed. Her kisses were fierce, urgent, and overwhelming. She pulled herself on top of him and drew him closer, straddling his thigh. For what could have been an instant or an hour they lay together, trying to squeeze out whatever space remained between them.

Then Jacqueline lifted her head, smiled, and spoke.

"What were you saying, Will?"

Even in his delighted, distracted state, Will recognized what has happening. He thought back to the kiss in the coffin showroom. At the time he wasn't sure if it came from gratitude or affection or something more. But now he was fairly sure that her kisses were merely a cynical manipulation that would amount to nothing in the end. He knew he should be angry and upset, but all he could think was: well played, Jacqueline.

A few moments earlier he had made a commitment to telling the truth; now, once again, he decided to abandon it. There was some solace in knowing that it seemed to get a little easier each time he did it. Jacqueline had made the game of cynical manipulation a lot of fun.

He could play it too.

"I was starting to tell you my plan. I've figured out a way to stay close to Mickey and Sam, so I can find out more about what they've been up to for all these years. It might give me a chance to look through their files or maybe overhear something important."

"How are you going to stay close to them?"

"Mickey and I are going to get together and jam. Who knows, maybe we'll get the band back together again, do a tribute to Paddy."

"When you find out what happened, you might not want to do a tribute to Paddy. And some of the other band members might end up in jail. What about Sam? You weren't exactly close to him, even back then. Now he's a big-shot movie producer. How are you going to hang out with him?"

"He's in town to shoot a movie. I have a part in the movie."

"You have a part in a movie? You're not an actor, are you?"

"No. That's what I told Sam when he offered me the part, but he insisted."

"How much is he paying you?"

"I don't know yet. Probably not much. I was just getting ready to call him and accept the offer when you knocked."

Jacqueline started laughing, rolled off him, and sat up.

"Can't you see what's going on? He's trying to dazzle you with Hollywood glamour so you'll forget about what happened. It's a bribe so you'll leave him alone."

It was Will's turn to sit up and laugh.

"Wait a minute, someone is trying to entice me into doing what they want? What kind of sick person would do something so despicable?"

Jacqueline said nothing, so Will continued.

"I don't know if it's a bribe or not, but if it is, I'm going to play along with it. I'll pretend that I've forgotten about the tape, but I'll keep looking for clues."

"Sounds like a plan Velma and Freddy would approve of. Is the Mystery Van washed and gassed? Did you pack enough Scooby Snacks for Scooby Doo?"

"I know it's not much, but it's all we've got at this point."

"No, it's not. You could go talk to the police."

"You said you already did that and they didn't believe you."

"I have to admit, I was kind of out of it at the time. I might have sounded a little hysterical. Plus they were sexist as hell; condescending and patronizing because I was a woman. If you go back to them and tell them the facts, they might listen to you. All I want is for them to look a little closer into what happened. Didn't you used to deal with the police when you were a reporter? You might even know some of them. That would help, wouldn't it?"

Will couldn't lie about this one; she needed to know the truth.

"Not really. It might make things worse. You never heard the story of how my newspaper career ended?"

"I knew you were a reporter, but, to tell you the truth, I don't really read the papers that much."

"I quit the *Detroit News* in 1992. At the time I said I did it to take a job in public relations, but the real reason I quit was because of a series of stories I did about the Detroit Police Department."

"What kind of stories?"

"There was a rumor going around that the mayor had a wild party, with drugs and strippers, and one of the strippers got into an argument with a guest and got beat up."

"I remember that. It turned out not to be true."

"That's what they said. I said differently. I wrote a front-page story for the Sunday paper that outlined everything that had gone on at the party. My source was the stripper who was beaten up."

"What happened?"

"Word leaked out that the story was coming. The cops had me subpoenaed and hauled before a judge who was friendly to the department. I gave him a smartass answer when he asked me who my source was, and he threw me in jail for contempt of court."

"How long were you in jail?"

"Just overnight. I called my old college professor to defend me. His specialty was media law; he did work for a lot of local radio and TV stations and newspapers, including the *News*. He got me out of jail on Friday, and the story ran on Sunday. On Monday morning the *Free Press* ran a front-page story claiming my story was completely false, that there never was a party."

"How could they say that?"

"The stripper said I never talked to her, that I was lying. She told the *Free Press* she had never been to the party I described, that she didn't know anything about it."

"So she was lying?"

"Yes. Someone got to her and frightened her into changing her story. They had her wait until my story ran to go to the *Free Press*. They set me up and knocked me down. I was pretty much finished in the newspaper business after that; even my own editors didn't believe me."

"Why not?"

"No one knew the name of the stripper, they covered it up pretty good. But I did a lot of digging, found out who she was, and called her. She agreed to talk to me, but she was scared to death. The only way she would do the story was if we met in secret and I didn't use her name. She wouldn't even let me tape record her. I couldn't prove I had met with her."

"But you knew her name."

"When the *Free Press* story came out, she let them use her name. By Monday morning everybody in Detroit knew who she was; the fact that I knew her name didn't prove anything."

"So what happened?"

"I was suspended without pay for ninety days. The mayor and some of the cops who were involved threatened to sue me and the paper for libel. They actually threw me in jail on some kind of trumped-up contempt-of-court charge when I told them what to do with their subpoena."

"You were in jail? For how long?"

"Just a few hours. My old professor got me off the hook. They were public figures so they had to prove that I knew the story was false or that I had a 'reckless disregard' for the truth."

"But you had told the truth."

"That's not always as rewarding as they make it out to be. I thought about sticking to my story and continuing the fight, but I didn't. In the end they agreed to drop the case if I apologized and stopped my investigation. They put out the word that I was overzealous trying to get a big story, that I had misunderstood what the stripper had said, twisted her words to make them fit what I thought had happened."

"In other words, you pleaded stupidity and won. Good for you. What happened after that?"

"I tried to keep working, but it was too hard. There was too much history, too much second-guessing. So I got a job as a PR guy."

"Did you ever figure out who set you up?"

"I assume the mayor was giving the orders. But when he died a few years later, he was given a hero's sendoff—no one said anything about drugs or strippers. There were two other guys I'm pretty sure did the dirty work. One of them was the mayor's press secretary at the time, Bronson Rogers."

"The city councilman?"

"Yeah. He's done pretty well for himself since then. The other was a Detroit cop assigned to the mayor's security team. He did pretty well for himself after that too."

Jacqueline put a hand on his knee.

"I'm sorry all that happened to you, but it was years ago. I'm sure it's forgotten by now, and the people involved have moved on. I still think you should talk to them."

As much as Will disliked the idea of talking to the Detroit police, he did not want to discourage Jacqueline in her attempts to manipulate him. He liked this game.

"Who did you talk to?"

"I started with a traffic cop at the Atwater Street station house. He was the first one to show up at the site of the crash; he wrote the report that called it an accident. When he didn't believe me, I talked to his boss, and then that guy's boss. I finally ended up talking to the Central Precinct Commander."

"Do you remember his name?"

"Letner."

"Joe Letner?"

"I think so, why?"

"That's the guy I was telling you about—the cop who set me up and ruined my career."

Chapter Fourteen

Reporting an Incident

Jacqueline didn't leave Will's hotel room right away.

That gave him hope.

She stayed to hear his argument against going to the Central District police headquarters and to offer a rebuttal to every point he made.

That led to trouble.

"Letner hadn't even made sergeant when I knew him; if he's in charge of a district, that means he's a commander now. That's a pretty impressive career for a guy who was basically a redneck thug with a badge. They obviously took good care of him after he saved the mayor's ass."

"Whatever he did to you then has nothing to do with what happened to Paddy. He might even feel like he owes you one."

"Yeah, right."

"It can't hurt to have someone besides me ask them to reopen the investigation."

"It can if it's me."

In the end Will gave in and agreed to talk to Commander Letner. It wasn't Jacqueline's arguments that persuaded him; to his great shame and chagrin, it was the hope of further physical manipulation. He was disappointed when, throughout their discussion, she kept her contact to a minimum, only occasionally touching his knee or elbow as they sat side by side on his bed. Her attempt at emotional manipulation, on the other hand, was quite impressive.

"I'm sorry I was so rude to you at Paddy's visitation. I guess I was still mad at you after all these years. I was a stupid, romantic young girl. I really did want you to fight for me."

"I'm sorry I didn't fight for you back then. I'm sorry about a lot of things I didn't do."

Will was debating whether or not to make a move of his own when she got up, stepped back into her sandals, gave him a quick kiss on the cheek, and was gone.

Two days later Will walked through the front doors of the Central District police headquarters. It was a massive, gray concrete and smoked-glass building, located on Woodward Avenue about halfway between downtown and Mickey's restaurant.

He followed a police officer into an elevator and down a corridor, thinking about how ironic it was that ever since he quit his job, all he had done was go to meetings. The officer nodded to a secretary, knocked on a door, and there was Joe Letner, sitting behind a desk.

"Sit down."

He looked heavier and grayer. He did not look smarter or kinder.

"I was told you had a crime to report. I hope it doesn't turn out to be a false report like the last one. I'm sure you remember how much trouble you can get into when you make a false report."

"It's good to see you too, Commander. My congratulations to you for a very successful career."

"You said you wanted to talk about a crime, and you would only talk to me. Start talking or get the hell out of my office."

Will noted for future reference that Detroit cops didn't seem to enjoy insincere flattery as much as Hollywood producers.

"A few weeks ago you spoke to the widow of an old friend of mine, Padrig Wagner. Mrs. Wagner told you that she suspected her husband's death wasn't an accident, that he was murdered."

"That's what this is about? That's why you are taking up the valuable time of a Detroit police commander? You need to stop believing crazy bitches when they tell you a crime has been committed. That really hasn't worked out too well for you, has it?"

"Mrs. Wagner is not a crazy bitch."

"She came in here wacked out on sedatives, acting hysterical. I had a patrolman drive her home in her own car and another follow them to pick him up. That's two cops who could have been patrolling the streets and preventing crimes, and instead they were babysitting a hysterical Bloomfield Hills housewife with too much time on her hands and too much Valium in her bloodstream."

"But didn't you—"

"Let me finish. After I sent her home, I checked the report on Mr. Wagner's accident, and I spoke to the officer who was there on the scene. Mr. Wagner was alone in his car. He came out of the Cobo tunnel onto Jefferson driving at an excessive speed, lost control of the car, and crashed into the Joe Louis statue. There were more than a dozen witnesses. It was an automobile accident—end of story."

"Did you check the car? Maybe somebody tampered with the brakes or the accelerator or something."

"Just what I need—another concerned citizen who watches too much CSI. You want us to take the car to the lab and put it under the microscope? You think a criminal mastermind tampered with it? It doesn't happen that way in Detroit. We don't have any criminal masterminds here, just old-fashioned, hard-working bad guys. If somebody wants to put the thriller down, they give him a fo' sho'."

"What?"

"I forgot, you live in the suburbs, don't you? If somebody wants to kill someone, they shoot them in the head."

"It can't be that hard to cut a brake line."

"Mrs. Wagner said the same thing. Against my better judgment, I had someone look at the car. It was not tampered with. Do you want to read the report? Better yet, we still have the car in the impound lot. Do you want to examine it yourself?"

"No, thank you."

"Mr. Wagner left the office at five o'clock, he came out the tunnel at five-thirty. Take away the ten minutes it would have taken him to get to his car, and you still have him driving around for twenty minutes. Why didn't he crash sooner? Because there was nothing wrong with the car except for the loose nut behind the wheel."

"If he lived in Bloomfield Hills, what was he doing coming back down Jefferson?"

"He called his secretary from his car at approximately five-fifteen, and she reminded him that he had left some files he wanted to take home with him at the office. His office was in the Renaissance Center. Obviously he made a loop on the freeways and was coming back to his office to get his files. He was in too big of a hurry to get there and he paid the price. Is there anything else you want to waste my time with?"

Actually, there wasn't. As much as Will hated to admit it, this time Letner was right—no crime had been committed. It was time to cut his losses and leave, but he couldn't resist giving some shit back to the man who had ruined his second career.

"I'm done here. I just wanted to make sure my dead friend—the man you called a loose nut—wasn't murdered. That will be of some comfort to his grieving widow—the woman you called a crazy bitch."

"Are you going to quote me in the paper, Harkanen? Is this another big scoop for you, like the stripper you said got beaten up, but who really didn't? Oh wait, I forgot—you quit being a reporter twenty years ago."

"Fuck you, Letner."

"Get out of my office, scumbag. Don't come back."

As Will followed the police officer back down the hall to the elevator, he tried to decide if the meeting had gone well or badly. On one hand, he was now certain Paddy's death was an accident. On the other hand, he had given the man who ruined his newspaper career another chance to take a victory lap. It was probably a toss-up, which is what he felt like doing with his lunch.

Back in his office, the Central District commander sat staring out the window. He had a nice view of the building a few blocks away that had served as General Motors headquarters for seventy-five years. Now it was a ward of the state, filled with government employees, but Joe Letner was not thinking about faded glory as he pulled out a cell phone and dialed a number.

"It's me, he was here... Fuck the phone company's records. If they look it up, you and I are still talking about movie logistics, it's official city business... I'm not going to do anything, at least not yet, I'll just have him followed... I told you, it was an accident, they were just trying to scare him... You've said that a hundred times, it's getting old... I promise you, we'll do it your way. Just remember, if that doesn't work, we'll do it my way... dead or alive, either way works for me."

Chapter Fifteen

Phony Excuses

W ill had arrived at a familiar place: he was going to give up.

As much as he hated and mistrusted Joe Letner, there was no arguing with his logic. Paddy had crashed his car at a busy intersection in front of witnesses. It was tragic and bizarre but it wasn't criminal.

Letner had no reason to cover up a crime; he didn't even know Paddy. And Will himself didn't really believe the car was tampered with, that was just an idea he'd thrown out in desperation. Paddy had driven his car for twenty minutes before he crashed, making a big loop on three different freeways to get back to Jefferson. A car that had been tampered with couldn't have made that loop. Besides that, they had inspected it and found nothing.

He was certain that Paddy had not been murdered, which also threw the rest of Jacqueline's story into doubt. Why would Paddy, Mickey, and Sam steal the band's tape and say it was erased? They could have just given him his songs and kicked him out of the band. Will remembered most of what they recorded, and he could still play some of it; in all the years since then, he had never heard anything like it.

The only conclusion he could reach was that, despite her denials, Jacqueline must have misunderstood what Paddy had said about the tape. His death was a shock to her, she was taking sedatives, she probably wasn't thinking straight. She had imagined something that wasn't real.

Coming to this conclusion was easy—sharing it with Jacqueline would be much harder.

Will knew that the right thing to do would be to meet with her in person to tell her. He also knew that he couldn't do the right thing. Her use of sexual charm to get him to do what she wanted was obvious and insincere, to the point of being insulting. It was also very effective.

As much as he relished the idea of her trying to persuade him once again, he knew he couldn't say what he needed to say to her in person.

He called her from a Starbucks.

"What did the cops say?"

"I spoke to Commander Letner."

"And?"

"He was certain that Padrig's death was accidental."

"You believed him? The cop who ruined your career?"

"After you talked to him, he looked into what happened personally. He read the report, he talked to the officer who was on the scene, he even had them check the car to see if somebody had tampered with it."

"They hadn't even thought about that until I talked to them."

"He double-checked everything and did everything by the book. He obviously didn't want anybody second-guessing their conclusion."

"Anybody? You mean me, right? I'm the only one who thinks they're wrong. Except for you. You think they're wrong, don't you?"

It was another moment of truth for Will. As much as he wanted to stay in Jacqueline's good graces and continue playing her games, he also felt he owed her something more. It was time for the truth.

"I'm sorry, Jacqueline, but I don't. I think Padrig died in a car accident."

There was silence on the phone. Will started to congratulate himself for making sure they weren't having this conversation in person, then realized how very much he would have enjoyed being physically persuaded by her right now.

"So you believe the guys who destroyed your life and not the woman who loved you?"

She had left out the part about her dumping him and breaking his heart, but he let it go.

"I believe the facts. The police were very thorough. There is nothing to indicate anything happened other than a car accident."

"I've done a lot of things wrong in my life, Will. This is something I need to get right. I can't do it myself, I need your help. Please."

There was a quiver in her voice as she said the last word. Real or not, to his great dismay, Will found it more compelling than the most passionate embrace. His keep-your-distance phone call strategy had failed.

As a former reporter, he knew that reaching a dead end in an investigation didn't mean you had to stop—it just meant you had to back up and pursue the truth from a different direction.

"If Padrig was going to cash in on the tape, he might have had a copy of it himself. Have you looked through his stuff?"

"I tore the house apart but I didn't find anything."

"It wouldn't necessarily be a tape. He might have transferred it to a CD or an electronic file."

"I went through everything he had—tapes, CDs, computer, iPod. I listened to all of them. There wasn't anything I didn't recognize or couldn't identify."

"You said he seemed scared. Did he say anything to you? Did you hear him talking on the phone to anyone? Did he leave any notes or e-mails that talked about the tape?"

"No. He had an office in our home. I went through everything in it—calendar, files, e-mail—I didn't find anything."

Will felt a muted flash of recognition and the familiar feeling of knowing he was supposed to remember something he couldn't remember. This was happening more frequently to him as the years passed and he progressed from being an old fart to being a really old fart. Usually whatever he couldn't remember would pop up later at a random moment. He supposed that when he became a really old fart, he wouldn't even remember that he couldn't remember. He wished he could go back to...

There it was.

"Did you check his office at work?"

"No."

"Is his office still there?"

"Yes. Two of his employees are negotiating with my attorney; they want to buy the business. But no one has touched his office since the crash."

"Letner said Paddy called his secretary after he left the office, and she reminded him that he had left some files there that he had wanted to take home. That's why he was on Jefferson; he was going back to the office."

"You think the tape is in the files?"

"Or a CD or a flash drive copy. It could be—it's worth checking."

"Can you check it for me?"

"Why me? Can't you do it?"

"His secretary doesn't like me."

"Why not?"

"We had a disagreement. I said she was having an affair with Paddy and she said she wasn't."

"That's it?"

"Well, actually, I ran into her at the Rattlesnake Club, called her a skanky bitch, threw my drink in her face, and wrestled her to the ground. So I don't think she would be too happy to see me. She would be much more cooperative for you. Obviously she likes older men."

"Thanks."

"I'll have my attorney make the arrangements; you can go to the office and see what's there."

"I'm not sure I'm the right guy for this. If there is something going on, wouldn't it be less suspicious if your attorney searched the office? I'm too tied into the—"

"Did I mention that I am completely naked?"

Will laughed.

"Let me know what time I'm supposed to be there."

Chapter Sixteen

The Office

The central atrium of the Renaissance Center always made Will think of the movie *Blade Runner*. It was a massive, concrete-and-glass cavern that would serve well as a public space in a dystopian future.

He made his way along one of the circular walkways that connected the hotel tower in the middle of the complex to the four office towers that surrounded it. Even though he was familiar with the building, he walked slowly. The interior of what everyone called the Ren Cen resembled a three-dimensional chessboard, with the different levels connected by circular staircases and escalators.

It was easy to get lost, which he promptly did.

After he walked past the same tee shirt kiosk for the second time, he realized that he had walked completely around the circle. He doubled back, found a walkway he had missed, and made his way to the lobby of the tower he was looking for. A glass elevator rocketed him upward, bursting into daylight before stopping at the floor that held the offices of Wagner and Associates.

Sue Ursell sat at a desk in a small lobby that was overcrowded with abstract sculptures and paintings. She was in her mid-thirties and extremely attractive, and she did not seem happy to see him. The most logical explanation for her attitude was that she associated him with the woman who had dumped a drink on her and wrestled her to the ground. Despite what Jacqueline had told him, he was pretty sure being an old guy didn't help either.

He wondered how Paddy had managed to seduce her; his best guess was that money—the world's most powerful aphrodisiac—had something to do with it.

"How can I help you, Mr. Harkanen?"

"On the night he crashed his car, Mr. Wagner was coming back to the office to pick up a file he had left here. I'd like to look at that file."

"No, he wasn't."

"I beg your pardon?"

"He wasn't coming back here on the night of the crash."

"The police said he was. They said he called you from his car, and you told him he had forgotten a file that he wanted to take home."

"I did. But he said he didn't need the file and wasn't coming back."

"Did you tell the police that?"

"Yes, but they didn't seem too interested in what I had to say about it. They said he must have changed his mind."

"But you don't think he changed his mind."

"No."

"Why not?"

"I worked with Mr. Wagner for many years. It was part of my job to know what he thought and how he liked to do things; that's what good secretaries do. He hated driving in rush-hour traffic. He told me in no uncertain terms he didn't need the file and he wasn't coming back. He was not an indecisive man. Once he made up his mind, he wouldn't have changed it. He was not on his way back to the office that night."

"Then what was he doing driving down Jefferson Avenue?"

"I don't know."

It seemed like a minor detail, a difference of opinion that didn't change anything. But the years he had spent as a reporter had taught Will to pay attention to small irregularities in a story. They were like loose threads: if you kept picking at them, sometimes they unraveled everything.

"I'd still like to see the file if I could."

"Certainly. Follow me."

She grabbed a set of keys from a drawer and led him down a hallway, unlocking the door to an office that featured more abstract art as well as a sweeping view of the city. As he looked around the room, she unlocked the top drawer of the desk in the center of the room and took out a manila folder. When he walked to the front of the desk, she handed it to him slowly and formally, as if she wanted to fix the moment in her mind.

He set the folder on the desk and opened it up to find a stack of newspaper clippings. As he flipped through them, a common theme quickly became apparent—they were all about the movie business in Michigan. There were articles and editorials about the tax incentives the state was offering, feature stories about movies being filmed there, news analysis of the impact the movie business was having on jobs, recaps of opinion polls on the subject.

Toward the bottom of the pile, the articles and editorials began to focus specifically on Sam Rainier and Future Tense Productions, and his efforts to get further tax incentives from Detroit to build a studio in the city. These stories portrayed the project as controversial, dividing the city council and the public into two evenly matched sides. Some saw the studio project as a boost for employment and reputation; others insisted it was a waste of taxpayer money in a city that was broke. The clips included an op-ed from Councilman Rogers extolling the benefits a movie studio would bring to Detroit.

The final clip was a *Free Press* columnist talking about the rumors Sam Rainier was secretly scouting locations for a new blockbuster action film that would be made in Detroit. The details were sketchy but the columnist promised to keep her readers posted as she learned more. She also asked anyone who saw the movie crew around town or knew anything else about the film to e-mail her. Her e-mail address at the bottom of the column was circled in pen.

When Will turned this clip over, he saw the last item in the folder, a single piece of paper filled with some kind of poem that didn't make sense. It read:

It's Up to You and Down to Me
Change the Game
Dare to Be
Detecting a Pattern
Technodelic Dream
Notown Nightmare
UFO of U
Space Alert
The Things U Due

"Do you have any idea what this is supposed to mean?"

He handed her the paper, and she looked at it for a moment before shaking her head and handing it back.

"Is this everything that was in the file? There weren't any CDs or cassette tapes, anything like that?"

"That's everything."

"Has anyone else seen this file?"

"No."

"Didn't the police look at it?"

"No. I told them about it, but they weren't interested. They said the file explained why Mr. Wagner was on Jefferson Avenue that night, and that was all they cared about. They didn't care what was in the file, they said it was immaterial."

"Does anyone else have access to this office?"

"I am the only one with keys to Mr. Wagner's office and his desk. When I'm not around, I keep those keys locked in *my* desk drawer. Since he passed away I've been in here a few times to take care of business, but this is the first time I've unlocked the drawer and taken out that file since the night of the crash."

Will had reached another dead end but this one felt different. The previous dead ends he had encountered had left him feeling sheepish and chagrined, as if he were on a fool's errand. Even though he couldn't think of anyplace further to go at the moment, this time it felt like there *could* be somewhere further to go. He didn't know where that place was yet, but he knew where to start looking.

"Would you mind if I made a copy of these words?"

Chapter Seventeen

Renaissance Man

When he left the offices of Wagner and Associates, Will decided to take another lap around the Ren Cen atrium for old times' sake. In spite of its cold and confusing interior, designed in the appropriately named Brutalist style of architecture, he felt a great deal of affection for the complex. It had played a major role in the city's life, as well as his own.

Built by Henry Ford II to help revitalize downtown Detroit after the 1967 riots, the Renaissance Center was now the iconic centerpiece of the city's skyline. It also was reportedly the place where the mob had buried missing Teamster boss Jimmy Hoffa during its construction in the mid-seventies.

A Detroit defenestration.

Since 1996 the complex had served primarily as the world headquarters for General Motors, complete with a showroom-like product display on the ground floor of the central atrium.

For Will it was the place that had launched both his career and his marriage. Years ago he had spent the first night of his honeymoon at the hotel in the Ren Cen. Before that, as a reporter for the *South End,* Wayne State University's student newspaper, he had written a story about the first tenants in the Ren Cen. The story helped him get a student internship at the *Detroit News*, where he eventually was hired as a reporter.

Will made his way from the elevator lobby toward the lighted glass walkway that circled the atrium, suspended two floors above the ground by steel cables. He was trying to remember the name of the law firm that had been the Ren Cen's first tenants and where they were located. He knew there were four names—Something, Green, Green and Something—and they were on the twentieth floor. If he could remember what tower they were in, he would go up and see if they were still there after all these years.

He walked around the circle, weaving his way through the handful of office workers straggling back from a late lunch or using the circular track for a fast-walk workout. Halfway around the circle he glanced backward and noticed someone walking a short distance behind him. What he glimpsed unleashed feelings of paranoia and guilt.

It was a young black man wearing an oversized, wide-brim Tigers baseball cap pulled down low on his head and sunglasses that created blank spaces where his eyes should be. He was slowly gaining ground on Will, making him feel vaguely threatened, which in turn made him feel stupid and racist. It was broad daylight, there were people around, and Will was not a person who gave in to stereotypes and prejudice.

He kept walking and tried to think about other things as the footsteps came closer. He had just remembered the name of another one of the law firm's partners when he felt something poke him in the back.

"This is a gun. Don't be stupid or I will shoot you. You're going to walk with me now. Get ready to turn left when I tell you."

A blast of adrenalin made it hard for Will to think and breathe. For nearly sixty years he had lived without incident in a city with the highest murder and violent crime rate in the country. All that time he had imagined himself streetwise and savvy, but that had changed in an instant—he realized now that he had just been lucky. He had no idea what to do other than what the young man with the gun in his back told him to do.

"Turn here."

They turned onto a crosswalk that led back toward one of the office towers. His assailant led him around a corner to a quiet space between three massive walls of roughly cast concrete— the favorite building material of the Brutalists.

"Put your hands on the wall, spread your legs."

Will assumed the criminal suspect position he had seen so often on TV, and the man standing behind him began patting him down. For a brief moment Will was pleased when the man searching him felt the wallet in his back pocket but did not remove it—he was carrying $300 in cash he had just withdrawn this morning. Then a wave of pure fear went through him.

If this wasn't a robbery, what was it?

"Turn around."

Will turned to face his attacker, who was pointing something at him from inside the front pocket of his jacket. In the last remaining part of his brain that wasn't paralyzed with fear, Will reviewed his options and decided he had none other than to stand there and hope for the best. The person standing in front of him was holding a gun, and if Will didn't cooperate, he would be shot and killed.

With his free hand the young man reached into Will's sport coat and checked his inside pockets, grabbing and releasing the folded paper with the copy of the poem from Paddy's file. He patted down Will's chest and front pockets, then pulled back.

For a moment they stood looking at each other.

Then the gun began ringing.

The young man pulled his hand out of his pocket, raised a cell phone to his ear, and started talking.

"Yeah… I'm checking it out now… He's here too… Not like last time, I know… I got shit so far."

Will reviewed his options again and added one to the list—he could run. His attacker had either forgotten about the charade of the gun in the pocket, or he was so confident in his ability to intimidate or injure his victim that he hadn't bothered to maintain the pretense. Either way Will had a chance—a small chance—of getting away.

He wouldn't have to run far; the main circular walkway was only one hundred feet from where they were standing. If he could make it that far, someone would see them and come to his rescue. Unfortunately his attacker was still right in front of him.

If he tried to run from this distance, he wouldn't make it five feet.

"I'll check him again, but I'm not going to find anything. What… Do what… Shit, I can't hear you, man. Hold on."

It was at this point that the first of several miracles occurred—the young man on the phone turned around and walked several steps away from the concrete wall and continued his conversation. Once again Will couldn't be sure if this move came from stupidity or arrogance. The only thing he knew for certain was that his chances for escape wouldn't get any better.

So he ran.

It felt strange to be running at full speed through a public space. The only other time he had done it as an adult was when he almost missed a connecting flight in Chicago. He started to feel embarrassed, then remembered he was running for his life. Fear quickly pushed aside any other emotion.

As he ran he listened for footsteps behind him, but he heard only laughter. A second miracle had occurred—his attacker wasn't following him, he was laughing at him. As Will rounded a corner onto the crosswalk, he heard the young man casually and ominously finish his phone conversation.

"I got to go, he's running away. I'll take care of him."

Will reached the glass walkway, turned left, and kept running. It soon became obvious to him that the last of the lunchtime stragglers had made it back to work. He kept running, hoping that one of the exercise walkers he had seen earlier was somewhere ahead of him.

He heard footsteps behind him and glanced back to see his would-be mugger running after him. It was odd; he was running with exaggerated arm movements and did not seem to be going very fast.

But he *was* gaining ground.

Will rounded a corner and was heading toward one of the towers filled with GM employees. He thought about running down one of the crosswalks and heading for an elevator lobby; he was pretty sure GM would have a security guard there to check IDs. But he wasn't certain, and this being the Ren Cen, there was always the possibility he would make a wrong turn and be trapped in a dead-end space.

He kept running.

It occurred to him that he hadn't run this far and this fast in decades. As if in response to this thought, he suddenly felt his legs cramping up. He quickly corrected his thinking—he hadn't really run too far, and he wasn't going all that fast. This knowledge wasn't really helpful; his lungs began to burn as he desperately tried to suck in more air.

Another GM tower came up on his left and he passed it by. The young man who was going to take care of him was slowly getting closer. The fact that he hadn't caught up yet should have pleased Will but instead it puzzled him.

He was old and out of shape. Unless the young man chasing him was *really* out of shape, he should have covered the ground between them by now. Another miracle? He doubted it. And another thing—why hadn't anybody seen them and tried to help? Maybe they had but didn't want to risk getting involved. But didn't they have security cameras in this place?

He realized he was passing the crosswalk from which he had started his getaway. With a glance backward, he also realized his pursuer, still swinging his arms wildly, was gaining ground. It suddenly occurred to Will what was going on.

His mugger was pretending to jog.

It was a plan that hovered somewhere between crazy and brilliant. A young black man running full speed after an older white man would attract attention. A couple of fellows jogging slowly around the circular track would not. No doubt the office workers here did it all the time. There was another advantage to this plan—by the time his attacker caught up to him, Will would be completely out of breath and unable to defend himself. He wasn't sure what would happen after that, but whatever it was, he assumed it would be very unpleasant.

When he glanced back again, what he saw reinforced this assumption: another young man had joined in the chase. His second pursuer was a skinny white dude with heavily tattooed arms who looked vaguely familiar. For a moment Will felt an irrational sense of relief, his white guilt assuaged by the diversity of his attackers.

Then he came to his senses, looked back again, and saw that they were gaining on him.

With great effort Will calmed the voices of panic that were starting to scream in his head and tried to come up with a plan of his own. A moment later he cursed himself for ignoring the obvious—he should start screaming for help.

But just like in a bad dream, when he opened his mouth to scream, nothing came out. After a moment he finally managed to gasp out a weak "hey" that was barely audible. He was too winded from running to draw attention to himself.

The easy and obvious plan was eliminated; it was time for a crazy and brilliant plan of his own. Looking ahead around the curve, he thought he saw it.

Coming up on the right, a crosswalk on the floor below him passed directly underneath the glass walkway. Two of the steel cables that helped hold up the walkway, spaced a foot apart, were attached directly above one side of the crosswalk below.

It was about a twelve-foot drop to the first floor crosswalk, with another twelve feet to the ground floor below that. Will could use the cables to climb over the railing and drop to the crosswalk. He was pretty sure it led directly to the hotel lobby; he could make it there quickly if it looked like his pursuers were crazy enough to jump down after him.

The only drawback to the plan would be if he missed the crosswalk—that would turn his twelve-foot jump into a twenty-four-foot jump. He dismissed this as extremely unlikely. The cables were off to one side of the crosswalk, but it was at least ten feet wide. There was no way he could miss it.

Will used the last bit of energy he had to speed up and get to the cables. He grabbed them, swung a leg up, and began to climb on top of the railing. The approaching footsteps grew louder and faster; he looked up briefly and realized the flaw in his plan. He had assumed the young men would continue at the same slow jog pace they had maintained throughout the chase so as not to draw attention to themselves. That would give Will enough time to climb up one side of the railing and down the other before he jumped.

This assumption was dangerously wrong.

His original pursuer had begun running at full speed and he was very fast. Will tried to speed up his climb, but his foot slipped and he came down hard on his butt, legs on either side of the railing. Ignoring the shock of pain that ran up his spine, he swung his inside leg over the railing. He dangled by his arms for a moment, then found a narrow steel plate to stand on where the cables were attached to the walkway.

There was no time for calculations or second thoughts; the footsteps had arrived. He braced himself, crouched, and jumped. As he did, an arm came over the railing and grabbed at him. It failed to catch him but succeeded in altering the trajectory of his jump. Instead of the middle of the walkway below, Will found himself plummeting toward its railing.

He hit the side of the railing with his knee, grabbed at it with both hands, then fell backward into darkness.

Chapter Eighteen

Henry Ford

Will lay on his back with his eyes closed, assessing his situation.

His butt hurt.

His knee ached.

His head was throbbing.

Whatever had happened to him couldn't have been good.

He knew he was in a hospital because an intercom announcement calling for a doctor had woken him up. But the story of how he got there was still a little vague, floating around in bits and pieces in his mind. He wanted to put those pieces together before he opened his eyes.

A few recurring images danced at the edge of his awareness. He was running—being chased by someone. It was on a track… no, it was inside an office building. The Renaissance Center. He was being chased…and he tried to jump down to the walkway below.

He must have missed.

Suddenly everything came together. He remembered waking up in an ambulance, then watching the ceiling tiles fly by overhead as they wheeled him into the hospital. Doctors shined lights into his eyes and asked him questions, and they put his head in a big white machine. Later on two uniformed police officers asked him more questions. The nurses wouldn't let him go to sleep for the longest time, but when they changed shifts, they told him it was okay, so he did.

"You dumb shit, what the hell were you thinking?"

The words came out of him before Will knew he was speaking. The charade of being asleep was definitely over; he opened his eyes and saw a nurse standing in the doorway.

"Oh good, you're up. How are you feeling?"

"My head hurts."

"I'm not surprised, that was quite a fall you had. Are you feeling nauseous?"

"No."

"How about your vision, are you seeing okay?"

"As good as I ever have."

"Good. Nausea and blurred vision are symptoms of a concussion."

"What time is it?"

"It's almost noon."

"Almost noon? I must have slept a long time."

"We kept you up pretty late. With a head trauma you want to make sure the patient is all right before you let them go to sleep."

Head trauma. That would explain the horrible headache. He must have hit his head when he fell. From where he jumped, it was a miracle that he didn't split his head wide open.

"Where am I?"

"Henry Ford Hospital. They took you here by ambulance from the Ren Cen."

"Am I free to go?"

"Not yet. The doctors want to check you one more time before you leave. They're doing their rounds now, it shouldn't be too long. You need to stay in bed until they clear you. If you need to go to the bathroom, there's a bedpan on the table."

"I'll wait, thanks."

"One other thing—there are some police officers in the waiting room who want to talk to you. If you feel up to it, I can tell them to come down."

Will was certain he had talked to the cops the night before, but he didn't mind talking to them again. It would be nice to have them on his side for a change.

"Sure. I'd be happy to talk to them."

A short time later two police officers came into the room. One sat down in a chair and pulled out a notebook, the other stood at the end of his bed. Their faces were so grim it took Will a moment to recognize them—it was Preck and Markowitz, the cops he had shared a joint with at *Taste Detroit*. Will was happy to see them, but they didn't seem to share the feeling.

"Hey, how you guys doing?"

There was no response. Will tried again.

"Remember me? We met at Mickey's restaurant the other day."

They were staring at him but neither one spoke.

"I have a question for you."

Again no response, so Will kept going.

"I'm a little fuzzy about what happened last night. Did I talk to the police?"

The two exchanged glances and finally Preck, who was standing at the end of the bed, replied.

"You did. But you left out a few details. We're here to fill in the blanks and wrap things up."

"So you caught the guy?"

"What guy?"

"The guy who was chasing me."

"Someone was chasing you?"

"Yes. Didn't I tell them that last night?"

Markowitz flipped his notebook a few pages backward, then spoke.

"You told the officers someone was jogging behind you."

Preck took it from there.

"Are you changing your story?"

"I'm not changing my story. Like I said, I am a bit fuzzy about what went on last night. I don't know what I said then, but I'm telling you now…I was being chased."

"Who was chasing you?"

"An African American male, early twenties, about six-foot-two, two hundred pounds. He was wearing a Tigers cap and sunglasses."

"That's a very accurate description. You seem to have come up with a lot more details overnight."

"You sound like you don't believe me."

"Why was this young man chasing you?"

"He tried to rob me. He stuck a gun in my back and led me back to an out-of-the-way spot by one of the office towers. Then his gun started ringing, and it turned out it was a cell phone. So I ran."

"He robbed you with a cell phone?"

"He had it in his pocket. It looked like he was pointing a gun at me."

"Did he take anything?"

"No."

"So he robbed you but he didn't take anything."

Will understood why they might be skeptical; this story didn't make a lot of sense. But there was something else going on here. He was not getting the sympathetic victim vibrations he had expected. These two cops were not his doobie brothers, they were hostile interrogators. He needed to start being careful about what he said.

"I got away from my attacker before he could take anything."

"How far did you run?"

"I ran from the office tower to the central walkway, then I did a lap around the atrium."

"And your would-be robber chased you all that way?"

"Yes. And another guy joined him toward the end."

"So you're changing your story again? Now you say two people were chasing you?"

"I'm not changing my story. I'm telling you another guy started chasing me."

"Can you describe him?"

"He was white, early twenties, with tattoos on his arms."

"How old are you, sir?"

"Fifty-eight."

"Do you work out a lot? Are you a runner?"

"No."

"So I'm going to assume these two young men could have outrun you if they wanted to take your money. You ran a long way before you climbed over the railing—how come they didn't catch you?"

Will had an answer for this question—the first young man pretended to jog so he wouldn't draw attention to himself, and when his partner joined him, he did the same thing. But, given the skepticism these two seemed to have for his story, he doubted that they would believe him. And he was certain that his theory about why he was robbed—that it was related to the missing tape and Paddy's death—would be ignored or ridiculed. At this point it seemed like the best he could hope for was to at least get them to believe he was a victim.

"The first guy did catch me, right as I jumped."

"He was trying to stop you from jumping."

"That's crazy, he was trying to grab me so I didn't get away. He knocked me off balance or I would have landed on the walkway below like I planned."

"That's not what the witnesses say."

"What witnesses? There wasn't anybody else there."

"There was a group of office workers behind you doing their afternoon power walk—whatever the hell that is—and they saw everything that happened. They said there were two young men jogging ahead of them. One of them saw you trying to jump and ran to stop you, but he didn't get there in time."

Will was beginning to feel like Cary Grant in *North by Northwest*—the authorities refusing to believe his story and instead insisting on their own version of events. He was certain he hadn't seen anyone else behind him. There was no way he could have missed them.

"How many workers are we talking about?"

"There were six of them. It's some kind of exercise club that walks every day on their afternoon break."

"I was looking for someone to help me. How could I have missed six people?"

"It's your story, you tell me."

"Wait a minute. How long had they been walking before they saw me?"

"They had just started, why?"

"The walkway is circular. I could see these guys chasing me, but if they had just started walking behind him, they would have been around the corner."

"So?"

"So that's why I didn't see them."

"Well, they saw you. They said you climbed up onto the railing, then slipped and fell. The jogger that was ahead of them ran to help you but he was too late. He felt really bad about it."

"You talked to him?"

"The office workers did. His story matched what they saw."

"Where is he now? I'd sure like to talk to him."

"We don't know who he is or where he is. He left before the police arrived."

"What about the other guy? The guy with the tattoos?"

"There's no mention of anyone with tattoos in any of the reports. You're the only one who's said anything about him."

"I can describe him and the guy who tried to rob me to one of those sketch artists if that will help you find them."

"Mr. Harkanen, you don't understand. We're here to gather facts about what happened, and we will follow those facts wherever they take us. Right now the only criminal those facts point to is you."

"Me? What did I do?"

"Reckless behavior, to start with. Then throw in destruction of property."

"Destruction of property? What are you talking about?"

"You messed up the roof of that Escalade pretty bad."

"What Escalade?"

"The one you fell on when you jumped. You landed flat on your back on its roof. That Escalade isn't there, we wouldn't be having this conversation. Your brains would have been splattered all over the GM showroom floor."

"I don't remember landing on an Escalade, but if I did it was an accident. I was jumping for my life."

"Were you? That's a funny way to try to save your life, jumping from two stories up."

"What do you think I was trying to do?"

"I don't know what you were trying to do. But, over the years, there's been a lot of guys who have done stupid things in the Ren Cen. Climbing walls, walking on railings, jumping from one walkway to another. They're usually younger than you; most of them are drunk or high. Sometimes they are showing off to their girlfriends, sometimes it's a bet with their buddies."

"Are you saying I was doing it for fun?"

"I don't know why you were doing it, but I know what it's called—reckless behavior. It's against the law."

"I can't believe this. You should be looking for the guy who tried to rob me."

"The guy who didn't take anything? That six eyewitnesses saw jogging slowly behind you, then running to try to stop you when you climbed up onto the railing?"

"He left before the cops got there. Isn't that suspicious?"

"He talked to the office workers and a security guard and told them what happened. The Ren Cen staff were already doing a trauma assessment on you, they were on the radio talking to the EMS team that was on its way. The young man wished them good luck and left."

"Did the security guard get his name?"

"No."

"He didn't even get the guy's name? What kind of security guard is he?"

"There was a lot going on, he was busy helping to save your life. We have the names of all the office workers who saw you jump. If the Ren Cen or GM decide to press charges, that's all the witnesses we'll need."

"Press charges? Against me? That's crazy. I'm the victim in this thing, I should be suing them. The lousy security in that place almost cost me my life."

"That is your decision to make, sir. Based on the evidence I've seen, I wouldn't recommend it. Unless you have anything else to say, I think we're done here."

Will thought again about sharing his theories on why he was attacked, and why his attackers chased him slowly. But if it wasn't a good idea to share them at the start of their conversation, it was definitely a bad idea to do it now. They already thought he was crazy; talking about what he believed was happening would only confirm it in their minds.

"I have nothing more to say."

Markowitz closed his notebook, stood up, and walked out of the room. Preck followed him out, then turned around and walked to the edge of Will's bed. He leaned down to give Will one last bit of advice.

"By the way, if you're thinking about telling someone about what happened at Mickey's place, I would strongly recommend against it. If you did, you would be dealing with a whole 'nother level of ugly, you know what I mean?"

Without waiting for an answer, Preck turned and walked away.

Chapter Nineteen

Hitsville, USA

When the police left his room, Will turned on the TV and settled in to wait for the doctors to come. The TV remote control also had a call button for the nurse, which he pushed. He didn't want to be a nuisance, but he also didn't want to sit around all day in the hospital.

His nurse poked her head in the doorway a few minutes later. "Did you need something?"

"I was just wondering when the doctors will get here."

"It shouldn't be too long now, they're just down the hall. They may even get here before your lunch tray does."

"Lunch?"

"Your wife ordered lunch for you."

"My wife was here?"

"She was here all night. She went down to the cafeteria a little while ago to get something to eat. They were supposed to page her and let her know that you had woken up. I'm going to go check to make sure they did. I'll be right back."

When the nurse returned, she confirmed that his wife had been paged and began checking his vital signs and writing them down in his chart. Will spent several minutes wondering why the wife who had casually tossed him aside after twenty-five years of marriage was now so concerned about his health. He hadn't even bothered to change his will yet—if he died she would get everything, instead of nearly everything. He was beginning to allow himself the slightest hope that she had changed her mind about him when Jacqueline burst into the room.

"Darling, you're awake. I was so worried about you!"

She rushed over and gave him a long, soulful kiss before he could say anything. As he lay in stunned silence, she asked the nurse if they could have a moment alone. The nurse finished writing in his chart, said the doctors should be in soon, and left.

Jacqueline sat down on his bed and punched him in the arm.

"What the hell did you do? I was so scared."

Will started to respond but Jacqueline didn't stop.

"I tried to call you last night to see how it went at the office, and some nurse answered your cell phone. She asked me if I was a relative, and when I said 'no' she wouldn't talk to me anymore. So I called back five minutes later and told them I was your wife. They told me what happened and where you were, and I came right here. I figured the only way they would let me stay with you was if I kept pretending to be Jane, so I did. I spent the night here."

"You spent the night here?"

"I slept in the chair. You talked to me a few times, but you were pretty out of it. Remember?"

Will searched through the fog of last night and vaguely remembered talking to his wife but quickly dismissing the conversation as an impossible dream. Better to leave out those details to avoid another punch in the arm.

"I remember."

"All you kept saying was you ran around the Ren Cen. What happened?"

Will waited a moment to make sure she actually wanted him to speak this time, then told her the complete story of his office visit and what happened afterward. When he finished, she punched him in the arm again.

"What the hell were you thinking, jumping off that walkway? You could have been killed."

"I thought it was the only way to get away from the guys who were chasing me."

"Have the cops caught them yet?"

"The police don't believe me, they think I'm some kind of nut who tried a crazy stunt that went bad. And they think the guys behind me were innocent joggers I'm trying to pin the blame on. They're not even looking for them."

Jacqueline said "shit" but did not punch him.

Instead she stood up, went to the window, and stared out of it for a long time. When the silence became too uncomfortable for Will, he tried to fill the void.

"That's a nice view, I can see downtown from my bed here. If you look to your far right, you can probably see the Motown Museum. It's a white frame house with blue trim, with a sign on it that says 'Hitsville, USA.'"

"Oh, yeah, I can see it."

"That's the original Motown headquarters. Berry Gordy lived upstairs and the recording studio was downstairs."

"Have you ever been there?"

"Many times. It's one of my favorite things to do."

"I lived here all my life and I've never been there. Will you take me there when you're out of here?"

"Sure."

Jacqueline continued staring out the window for another minute, then turned back and sat down on the edge of his bed.

"I want you to stop, Will."

"What?"

"I want you to stop trying to figure out what happened to Paddy."

"But you wanted me to. You asked me to."

"And now I'm asking you not to."

Her hand flashed forward and Will flinched, but this time she didn't punch him. Instead she grabbed his arm and squeezed it softly.

"Please," she said.

"Jacqueline, the whole time I've been looking into this, I wasn't sure if there was really anything to look into. Now I'm sure there is. The guy chasing me proves it."

"It could have just been a random robbery. That does happen every now and then in Detroit, you know."

"If you really thought that, you wouldn't be asking me to quit."

"Fuck you."

She dropped his arm and went back to looking out the window.

"The guy who mugged me didn't take my wallet. He wasn't looking for money, he was looking for something else."

"What?"

"I don't know, but my guess is the same thing I was looking for in Paddy's office—a tape reel, a cassette, a CD, something that could have music on it."

"All you found was a file with some newspaper clippings in it."

In his haste to tell her what had happened before she punched him again, he had failed to mention the poem.

"There was one other thing. Where are my clothes?"

"In the closet by the bathroom, why?"

"I'm not supposed to get out of bed. Can you look in the inside pocket of my sports coat? There is a piece of paper I want to show you."

Jacqueline found the paper and handed it to Will. He unfolded it, read the poem again, and handed it to her.

"This is some kind of poem or riddle or something that Paddy had in the file. Do you recognize it? Do you know what it means?"

She looked at it for a few minutes, then set it on the table next to him.

"I've never seen this before. I have no idea what it means."

She sat back down on the bed and grabbed his arm again.

"Will, Paddy screwed around with this shit and he died. I don't want that to happen to you."

"Paddy didn't just die, he was killed. We both know that now."

"All the more reason to stop."

"Even if I wanted to stop, I'm not sure whoever is behind this would let me. But I don't want to stop. I've stopped all my life, every time things got uncomfortable. All I have for playing it safe for all those years are regrets. That tape represents the dreams I had as a young man. They stole them from me and I want them back. I'm not stopping this time."

"You asshole, don't you get it? You're not the only one who has regrets. I don't want to lose you again."

"I don't want to lose me either. It's not going to happen."

"Bullshit!"

As if on cue, a distinguished-looking older doctor walked into the room, trailed by a group of wide-eyed young residents. Will immediately thought of James Earl Jones in *Clear and Present Danger*.

"Mrs. Harkanen? I'm Dr. Jonas, these are Doctors Valaquez, Prasad, Mandel, and Young. I hope the two of you don't mind having this small crowd observe us, they are all neurology residents."

Jacqueline and Will both shook their heads 'no.'

Dr. Jonas jumped into the exam as if it were a foregone conclusion, explaining what he was doing as he went along. He asked Will a series of simple questions—name, birthdate, what day is it, where are you—and had him follow his finger back and forth. He checked his pupils with a small flashlight, then looked at his chart and discussed its contents with the residents.

"Mr. Harkanen, we're going to let you go home, but I want you to do a few things for me when you get there."

Dr. Jonas explained the precautions that Will and his wife would need to take for the next few weeks to make sure he was okay. He asked if they had any questions, and they again responded with a 'no' headshake. The residents began to shuffle out of the room, and Dr. Jonas turned to leave. Then he stopped, looked at the piece of paper on the table, and turned back to Will.

"It looks like you're into techno. Nothing too loud for the next few days, okay?"

Chapter Twenty

Techno Google

After he was released from the hospital, Will went straight to Motown Motel, turned on his laptop, and googled "Techno." He was familiar with the basics—he knew it was a form of electronic dance music that originated in Detroit in the late '80s—but he needed to know more.

The doctor at Henry Ford Hospital, who was about the same age as Will, had given him his first clue. He explained that Paddy's note was not a poem or a riddle, it was a list of techno songs.

"I used to listen to 'The Electrifying Mojo' on WJLB back in the day. He played everything from Kraftwerk and Tangerine Dream to Parliament Funkadelic and Devo. He used to play mixes by Juan Atkins and some of the other Belleville boys, the guys who created techno. After that I heard 'Strings of Life' and I was hooked. These songs are all later stuff from other artists, but it's all Detroit Techno."

Although he had nodded his head in agreement, Will didn't really understand a lot of the references Dr. Jonas had made until he got home and looked them up on his laptop. After he gained a better understanding of how techno had started, he began looking up the songs on Paddy's list.

At first the only common denominator he could find was that they were all hit songs from the early to mid '90s. None of them sold as many copies as a mainstream pop song, but by techno standards they were wildly successful, doing especially well in Europe. They were recorded by various artists, so there was no link there. It took several more hours of research before Will stumbled onto a connection—all of the songs were produced and distributed by Rain Man Records.

A few more clicks and he had the ultimate link—Rain Man Records was owned by Sam Rainier.

Will stared at the computer screen for a long time, trying to figure out the meaning of this new information. He couldn't figure out how it connected to what happened to Paddy—or if it even was—but it made him uneasy.

He was startled out of his thoughts by Bob Seger singing "Back in '72."

"Will Harkanen."

"Hi, Will. This is Phil Salzman, I'm with Salzman-Green-O'Malley Communications Consultants. We're the PR firm handling the publicity for Sam Rainier's projects here in Detroit. Did you get my e-mail about the press conference?"

In fact Will had checked his e-mails between Google searches and stumbled onto the lengthy note from SGO Communications Consultants about the upcoming press conference. It came complete with attachments that included an agenda, a list of invited guests and news media, two press releases, talking points, and a run-of-show with a detailed minute-by-minute description of the program.

He hadn't read any of it except the bolded section of the e-mail that showed the time, date, and location of the press conference—it was being held next week in the Guardian Building.

"Yeah, I got it."

"Great. I just wanted to make sure that you did and see if you had questions."

"No."

"Great. There are a few things I want to go over if you have a minute."

"Okay."

"First, I want to make sure you saw in the agenda that we are having a meeting with all of the participants two hours ahead of the press conference. We want to make sure everyone is on the same page and understands the messages we want to get across."

"The messages?"

"They're in the talking points document we attached. I hope you had a chance to read them."

"I had a chance," Will said without elaborating any further. The complete sentence would have been, "I had a chance but I didn't take it."

"Great. Then you know our main focus is to talk about the economic benefits and excitement the movie will bring to Detroit. When the conference is over, we're going to set you up with a couple of reporters to do sidebar stories, human interest stuff, local man gets thrill-of-a-lifetime. For those you can repeat the talking points and add that you are honored and humbled, and that Sam Rainier is a great guy."

"Okay."

"Great. I understand you work in public relations, so I'm sure you can handle it. One caution—I'm told you had a little bit of trouble with the Detroit police years ago."

"That's one way of putting it."

"I don't think it will come up in the interviews, but if it does, just say how happy you are that Sam Rainier has given you a chance not only to redeem yourself, but to help others as well."

"I see. How does that work?"

"By taking this part, you are going to be helping Detroit move forward. This movie, and the studio Sam is going to build here, will do great things for the city and its people. You know, from the talking points."

"Got it. Anything else?"

"Just a heads-up—there may be protesters trying to crash the press conference."

"What kind of protesters?"

"Nut jobs, if you ask me. The biggest group is a bunch of hippie slackers who want to preserve all the old, rundown buildings in Detroit. They call themselves the POES."

"I've heard of them. They're some kind of environmentalist group, right? Not sure what the name means."

"POES is short for 'Principals of Entropy.'"

"Entropy? That's the theory that over time everything falls apart, right? So they're fighting to clean up Detroit and save the environment."

"They're not environmentalists. They're opposed to anyone who wants to get rid of the blight and improve things. They spell principals with a p-a-l. They are *supporters* of decline and degeneration. They want to promote the city like it's ancient Rome and get tourists to visit the ruins here. They call it 'entro-tourism.'"

"Entro-tourism?"

"It's like eco-tourism, only instead of visiting what nature has created, you visit what mankind has destroyed. Ecology, entropy, whatever. Like I said, nut jobs."

"You said they were the biggest group of protesters—who are the others?"

"There aren't any other organized groups, but there's a loose coalition of people who are opposed to building a movie studio in Detroit. I'm sure you've followed the debate in the media—there are a few members of the city council who are trying to stir up trouble for political reasons."

"I've heard about that."

"They say the city is giving away too much in land and tax breaks. They are stuck in the past and don't want to move forward. Some of their supporters might show up for the TV cameras. I wouldn't worry about it; I'm just giving you a heads-up."

"I won't worry about it."

"Great. One last thing—I guess this should have been first now that I think about it, very insensitive of me. How are you?"

"How am I?"

"I understand you had a bad fall and hit your head. Everything okay?"

Will knew that he should act nonchalant so he wouldn't arouse any suspicion about what he was up to, but his paranoia and anger won out.

"That just happened. How do you know about it?"

There was a long pause. Will assumed the communications consultant was using his PR brain to come up with an appropriate answer. The fact that he was hesitating told Will there was good reason for him to be paranoid.

"You know Sam, he has friends everywhere. I'm sure somebody mentioned it to him. He knew I was going to call you about the press conference, and he asked me to pass along his concern and best wishes."

Like all great PR responses, it seemed to Will that this one was at least partially based on the truth. Whether there was a darker and more sinister truth involved remained to be seen.

After a few more "greats," their phone conversation was over.

Will thought that was great.

Chapter Twenty-one

It's the Same Old Song

Will spent the rest of the afternoon in amateur detective mode, trying to figure out what the hell was going on.

It was a lot like being in professional reporter mode, which was something he was familiar with and good at. The years he had spent working for the newspaper had given him tremendous respect for facts and taught him clever ways to seek them out. But he had learned to trust his feelings as well and the unexplainable instincts that often guided you to the truth.

He had feelings about what happened and he had facts, but they didn't match or add up.

Elaborate theories that seemed absolutely certain on a gut level got blown away by a single undeniable fact. Carefully constructed factual scenarios were knocked down by vague instincts he couldn't dismiss.

He didn't have squat.

Jacqueline said Paddy, Mickey, and Sam Rainier had stolen the master tape of the album the Exits were working on years ago, and because of that Paddy thought he was going to get money from Sam Rainier. Mickey and Sam denied everything. Paddy had a file filled with old newspaper clippings and a list of techno songs. The techno songs were produced by Sam Rainier in the 1990s.

Paddy was dead.

The police insisted that Paddy's death was an accident. But when Will went to examine Paddy's file, he was mugged by someone who patted him down but didn't take his money.

Will's head hurt.

He kept going over everything he knew and felt, but the more he thought about it, the less sense it made. There must be something he was missing, a connection that linked things together and made them understandable. Something so obscure it would take real genius to figure it out or so obvious that he was overlooking it.

The tape and the list. They were both about music. What else? He could still remember the melodies from the tape after all these years. He even fooled around with them on his guitar every now and then when he was feeling sorry for himself. For many years he used headphones when he played to avoid irritating Jane; now he did it so he wouldn't get kicked out of his motel room.

No one could hear him play his music but himself.

With that thought Will realized he hadn't listened to any of the techno music on the list. It was not a big deal—he wasn't really a fan of techno music—but he supposed he ought to listen to it anyway. If nothing else it would help him kill some time while he tried to figure this thing out.

Will went to his desk and in a few minutes had downloaded the first song on the list, *It's Up to You and Down to Me,* onto his laptop. He clicked on the "Play" button and pulled a writing tablet out of a drawer. While the music was playing, he was going to write his thoughts about what had happened down on paper. Maybe things would make more sense if he wrote everything down.

The music was actually pretty good—repetitive, soothing, almost hypnotic. It might even help him figure things out, give his brain more alpha waves or whatever it was that made your mind more creative.

He started by writing down the names of everyone involved, then the undisputed facts. He was about to write a list of the facts that were disputed when a change in the music caught his attention.

At first he wasn't sure what it was that made him stop writing and look up. Then he realized a new sound had been added to the mix—a looping guitar solo that flowed over the relentless electronic beat. He was pleased that something he liked and was familiar with had made it into the grab bag of rising and falling sounds. Then he realized why the solo was so familiar. In that moment he felt as if the chair he was sitting in was falling through the floor.

The guitar solo he was listening to was his.

When he recovered from the shock of recognition, Will downloaded the rest of the songs on the list and listened to them.

It wasn't always as obvious, and in some cases he wasn't certain, but in the end he was pretty sure that all nine of the songs on the list included bits and pieces of sound from the Exits' lost tape. Mostly guitar solos that he was familiar with because they were his, but also some bass lines from Tommy Werzbicki and a funky little Rick Casey drum riff that turned up on two different songs.

He knew that sampling—taking parts of existing recordings and using them in a different song—was a common practice in electronic and hip-hop music. But these artists had taken their samples from a master tape that was supposed to have been destroyed more than thirty years ago.

The mystery hadn't been solved; if anything, it had become even more confusing. But at least now he had more facts to consider.

Jacqueline was telling the truth about the tape and about Paddy being up to something. Mickey and Sam had lied. There was a direct connection between the missing tape and Sam.

He also had more feelings to deal with, including a growing sense of betrayal that went far beyond the already strong feelings of betrayal he had carried with him for more than thirty years. The only difference was this time, he was definitely going to do something about those feelings.

There was one other factor complicating things for Will: he had promised Jacqueline he would stop his investigation. When he was discharged from the hospital, she had given him a ride to the Ren Cen to pick up his Explorer. It was a short trip that seemed to take forever because Jacqueline spent the entire time pleading with him to stop trying to find out what happened to the tape.

Finally, just to get her to stop her relentless verbal assault, he agreed to stop trying to figure out what had happened.

"Thirty years ago?"

"Yes."

"Thirty days ago?"

"Yes."

She actually cried at that point, and when they got to where he was parked, she gave him a long, soulful, tearful hug. It was a wonderful moment, diminished only slightly by one small detail.

He had lied.

Will had spent his entire life playing it safe, and it hadn't exactly worked out. He was determined that, for once in his life, he was going to follow his passion and not worry about the consequences. He had been a great investigative reporter until things got too uncomfortable. He still had all the tools and tricks of the trade, and it was something he loved to do.

He didn't want to stop now.

So he decided to continue looking into what had happened but also add Jacqueline to the growing list of people that he had to hide his activities and intentions from. That had solved the immediate problem but hadn't brought him any closer to figuring things out.

Things had gotten a lot more intriguing but not any clearer.

Will was still trying to decide what his next step should be when Bob Seger called him to the phone and gave him the answer.

"Hi, Will—it's Baxter. Your divorce agreement is finalized. She's cleaned your clock like I said she would, but this is the absolute best we can do under the circumstances. If you want to sign the papers, you can come by my office tomorrow afternoon."

"I'll be there."

Chapter Twenty-two

Legal Matters

"You told me you wanted to settle immediately. You said you didn't care what it cost because you had a good paying job."

"I told you what happened, Baxter. The last time I talked to you, I *did* have a good paying job, but then I quit it."

"Once again you're stalling, Will. Do you still want to sign the papers or not?"

It was a good question.

Will had returned to Baxter Fineman's office in Old Main eager to sign his divorce papers and get on with his life. But when Baxter asked him casually how his trip to Orlando went, he got flustered and started talking about the movie *Office Space*. Baxter cut him off and demanded the real-life story. Will gave him the director's-cut version that left out the parts about murder and assault. It was still enough to unleash an incredulous and angry barrage of questions from his attorney that raised new doubts in Will's mind.

Under Baxter's intense cross-examination, Will began to question his whole follow-your-passion/embrace-life/no-more-compromises thing. It seemed like a great idea when he had a few drinks in him, but from a sober perspective it was stupid and self-destructive. He was broke, about to be divorced, unemployed, and in over his head with people who might be murderers.

None of those things were on his bucket list.

On the other hand, for the first time in years, it felt like he was doing something authentic and important. He suddenly realized he wasn't hesitating to sign because of the money.

"I don't want to sign the divorce papers, Baxter."

"Dammit, Will—"

"Let me finish. I don't want to sign the papers, but I will. I just figured it out—I wasn't having second thoughts because of the money. It's just the reality of what's happening; it's so final. When I sign those papers, a big part of my life will officially be over."

"And you'll officially be broke."

"I'll figure that out. I'll figure out what my new life is all about too. Give me a pen, let's do it."

Baxter slid the papers across the desk and handed him a pen. Will looked them over for several minutes, then signed on the lines that the stick-on arrows pointed to. When he finished, he thanked Baxter, and they shook hands in classic old-school style. He was about to ask a question when his attorney beat him to it.

"Did you tell your boss you were getting a divorce?"

"Yeah, why?"

"So they were aware that you were under emotional stress, in addition to what I will assume was a heavy workload?"

This time around his attorney's questions were quiet and thoughtful, not loud and sarcastic.

"Again, yes—why?"

"You were in the middle of a divorce, putting in long hours at a busy offsite business conference, when you found out an old friend had died. You shared a joke with a colleague in a bar and asked a two word question in a meeting and they fired you."

"That's my story and I'm sticking to it. Why are you asking me about it again?"

"I'm not an expert in this area of the law, but I'm pretty sure you could make a case for wrongful termination."

"Why would I do that?"

"You're broke. You need money. You may be able to get a cash settlement from your former employer—maybe even your old job back."

"I don't want my old job back."

"What about money? Would you like some of that?"

"Sure. But I'm not a lawsuit guy."

"You're talking to an attorney, you know. That sounds very judgmental to me, no pun intended."

"I just don't believe in going to court over every little misfortune in life. No one wants to take responsibility for themselves or their actions anymore. I made a mistake and I'm paying for it. That's how it should be."

"They made a mistake. They overreacted to a situation they helped create."

"I knew what I was doing—I did it on purpose, I wanted them to fire me. I don't want to go over all that again under oath in front of a judge."

Baxter started to explain how, regardless of his intentions, what happened could be attributed to stress, but Will cut him off.

"Let me ask *you* a question—what do you know about copyright law?"

"I know a lot about it. Anything specific you want to know?"

"What does the law say when you take a part of someone else's music and use it in your song?"

"Sampling is a murky area. If you have permission from the copyright owner, it's no problem. If not, here in the United States it's usually protected under fair use—if you're using it for a limited purpose: educational, commentary, parody, that sort of thing. It helps if you don't borrow too much, if you change what you use, or if you don't cause significant financial harm to the copyright owner. Why are you asking me this?"

It was a good question but not one that Will was ready to answer at this point—at least not honestly. He didn't want to drag Baxter into what was going on until he actually knew what was going on.

"I've been fooling around on the guitar, writing some new songs. I may even record some of them, maybe sell them online. I thought about doing a little sampling, throwing in some bits from songs I like."

"There are a lot of gray areas in the laws, but no one is going to bother you unless there's money involved. As long you don't sell too many copies of your songs, you should be all right."

"I don't think that will be a problem, but if I have a hit record, I'll hire you to defend me."

"I look forward to that. We're all done here, you're free to go. I'll let you know when Jane signs these, then your marriage will be officially over. The only other thing you need to do is contact your former employer."

"What for?"

"To let them know on a formal basis that you are getting divorced. They'll send you some forms to fill out and sign."

"I thought we were all done, why do I have to sign more papers?"

"Did you actually read the papers you signed or were you just pretending to? Jane is going to get half of your pension. There's a form you have to fill out and mail in to make that happen."

"I really don't want to talk to those people again."

"I suppose I could make the call and have them send you the papers."

"That would be great. Then all I have to do is sign them and give away half my pension. She gets my money now and my money later. I guess I really am all in."

"If you're talking about money, I think it would be more accurate to say you're all out."

"Baxter, you made a joke, way to go. When I say I'm all in, I'm talking about taking everything you have left and making a desperate, last-ditch effort to win."

"In that case you really are all in. Take care of yourself, Will."

Will thanked his attorney again, then made his way out of

what was still one of his favorite buildings in Detroit, even after all of the bad news he had received there lately. He plodded down the front steps and headed toward his aging SUV in the nearby parking structure. Will drove an old white Explorer, which lately had seemed very appropriate to him. As he circled down from the top of the structure, he slid a White Stripes CD into a slot and "Seven Nation Army" started blasting from his speakers.

"I'm gonna fight 'em off, A seven nation army couldn't hold me back,

They're gonna rip it off, Taking their time right behind my back."

As he drove away from the parking structure, a black Dodge Magnum pulled away from the curb and followed him down the street.

Chapter Twenty-three

Crossing the Line

When Will arrived at the Guardian Building two hours ahead of the press conference, the protestors were already there. As he looked at the angry mob circling in front of the main entrance, he found himself quoting Phil Salzman:

"Great."

From the sidewalk across the street, Will could see they were a diverse group; if he didn't know what they were protesting, he would have thought they were from central casting. For a minute he amused himself by guessing what their roles were: post-modern hippie, well-dressed minister, student, housewife, business person, factory worker. They walked slowly and in single file, forming an elongated circle that brought them back and forth in front of the lobby doors.

The signs they held were diverse as well, some hastily hand-painted, others professionally designed and printed: "No Handouts for Hollywood," "Preserve Our Past, Protect Our Future," "Our Tax Revenue—Gone With the Wind," and his favorite, "We're Broke, We Hate You, Go Home."

The one thing they had in common was their chant: "No business for show business," which they all kept repeating with a high level of enthusiasm.

He suddenly realized how much he did not want to cross that picket line.

The thought of being knocked unconscious again did not appeal to him, although he was pretty sure the protesters wouldn't physically attack him. There were too many cops around, and a couple of TV crews getting shots of the protest before they went inside for the announcement. But even if the threat of bodily harm was minimal, the fact was he just didn't like confrontations.

Will waited another minute for the light to change, then headed quickly across the street toward a gap in the picket line. He made it through that gap, but then had to wait for an opening in the second line. As he stood waiting between the lines, the protesters walking in opposite directions on either side of him began to offer their opinions on his character, appearance, and ancestry.

"Asshole!"

"Traitor!"

"Son of a bitch!"

"Scab!"

The last slur had nothing to do with what was going on; Will assumed it was just a habit acquired in a union town. He finally managed to squeeze through a gap in the second line and hurried into the spectacular Art Deco lobby, a lingering remnant of better days. A smiling young man in a sharply tailored gray suit stepped up to greet him.

"You must be Will Harkanen, you look just like your cast photo. I'm Phil Salzman, thanks for coming."

Will wanted to ask him where they got his photo from but decided now was not the time.

"Did you have any trouble finding the place? Did they give you a hard time crossing the picket line?"

"No one hit me."

"Great. The guard at the desk has a pass key to get you on the elevator, just tell him you are here for the press conference pre-meeting. That will be held in the conference room on the thirty-second floor. There's coffee and donuts, help yourself. The press conference will be in the auditorium on the same floor. I'll be up shortly and we'll get the meeting started."

Will made his way to the conference room, where people were milling around, getting coffee and donuts, and finding seats at a long mahogany table. At first he didn't recognize any of the people in the room, but when a group standing at the head of the table broke up, there he was: City Councilman Bronson Rogers.

Will circled the table slowly in the opposite direction, grabbed a cup of coffee from a credenza on the far wall, and sat down next to a middle-aged woman who was busily absorbed texting someone. When she finished a few minutes later, she looked up at him and smiled. She was impeccably put together, with perfectly arranged blonde hair, jangling gold bracelets, and a designer business suit that would have cost him a week's pay, if he still had a job. He was about to introduce himself when Phil Salzman appeared at the door.

"If everyone will please take a seat, we're ready to get started."

As people found seats around the table, Phil made his way to the front of the room. He stood in front of a lectern that sat in the corner of the room near the head of the table.

"For those of you who don't know me, I'm Phil Salzman, from Salzman-Green-O'Malley Communications Consultants. We are excited to be handling the media relations here locally for this exciting project. As you know, in two hours we are going to make the official announcement of the new movie Sam Rainier is going to film here in Detroit. That announcement is going to be tied to an update on the status of Future Tense Productions' efforts to build a studio in the city. But we also have a few surprises we are going to announce as well.

"The purpose of this meeting is to let you know what that 'new' news is going to be and to make sure we all are aligned on what our messages are and what we are going to say. To get us started, please welcome our host, the head of Future Tense Productions, Mr. Sam Rainier."

Sam apparently had been waiting out in the hallway; as he walked into the room, everyone stood up, clapping. He made his way to the front of the room, shaking hands and greeting people along the way. When he saw Will across the table, he smiled and gave him a Hollywood-style double finger point.

After much glad-handing and back-slapping, Sam reached his destination behind the lectern. He waited a moment for the applause to end; when it didn't he motioned everyone to sit down with both hands, as if he were a minister leading a church service. They sat back down quickly and waited in silence for Sam to speak.

By now Will had figured out this wasn't going to be the typical business meeting he was painfully familiar with. It apparently was going to be some kind of weird hybrid of business, show business, and televangelist revival meeting. Sam broke the silence like a rock star addressing a concert audience.

"Detroit!"

Everyone started applauding again.

"We are going to rock this town!"

The applause grew louder.

Sam motioned downward with his hands, and once again the room was quiet. This time when he spoke it was in a quieter, more conversational tone.

"I want to thank you all for joining us this morning. Before we get started, I want to introduce a few special people who are with us today."

Sam started with Bronson Rogers, spending several minutes explaining what a visionary saint the man was. After that he sped through a number of other introductions of various people involved in the movie and the proposed studio. The director's name was Alan E. Smith, and it turned out the woman sitting next to Will was one of the producers of the movie, Roxanne Williams. He even gave Will a few words of introduction; the part that stuck out was something about "incredibly brilliant gimmick casting."

As Sam continued, talking about Detroit and Hollywood and synergy, Will glanced over at Roxanne and saw she was looking at him. She smiled and he nodded and smiled back, somewhat unsettled by the attention being paid to him by this beautiful woman. He couldn't figure out why she was being so friendly, unless it had something to do with him being in a movie.

This could be a good gig.

Sam said something about bringing Phil back up to go over the details, but it was what he said next that regained Will's full attention.

"But before I bring back Phil, I want to tell you about the surprise we are going to announce at the press conference. As you know, we are going to make a movie, *The Guardian of Detritus.* And with the support of Councilman Rogers and others, we are going to build a movie production center, Future Tense Studios. But there is one other thing we are going to do that you haven't heard about yet, something really cool…"

Sam paused for effect, looking around the room, making sure everyone was focused on him, waiting in anticipation. When he was satisfied that he had their complete attention, he continued.

"Detroit put the world on wheels. It was the Silicon Valley of the Industrial Age, a boom town on the cutting edge of new technology. It was the Arsenal of Democracy that helped win World War II. It gave us the middle class, the Motown sound, and the best rock-and-roll audiences in the world. Future Tense Studios is going to repay the favor and settle the bill once and for all. How are we going to do that?"

Sam smiled and looked around the room before providing the answer.

"We are going to blow up Detroit!"

Chapter Twenty-four

Post-Apocalyptic Pre-Meeting

It turned out to be the best meeting Will had ever attended.

After Sam Rainier said they were going to blow up Detroit, he waited expectantly to bask in the glow of a standing ovation that never came. Instead there were muted groans, nervous laughter, and a smattering of confused applause.

Sam quickly invited Phil Salzman back to the lectern to run the rest of the meeting and share the details of what would happen. Will enjoyed watching the PR pro squirm as he tried to back away from the "blow up Detroit" statement without making his client look like an idiot for saying it.

"What Sam referred to so enthusiastically is a major problem in Detroit that Future Tense Studios is going to help correct. There are far too many abandoned buildings in the city that need to be demolished. *The Guardian of Detritus* is going to help make that happen."

It turned out that the final scene of the movie was going to feature a spectacular series of explosions that would totally destroy a five-block area of abandoned homes and businesses. When the smoke cleared, the bulldozers would roll in to remove the rubble, and the construction of Future Tense Studios would begin.

Over and over again, Phil stressed the fact that they should all emphasize how the movie and the new studio would help Detroit. Without saying it directly, he made the point that it probably would not be a good idea to hold a press conference to announce that they were going to blow up the city.

The rest of Phil's remarks covered the details of who would be speaking, what points would be made, and which reporters were expected to attend. It was mercifully short and, to Will's delight, ended on a high note: the introduction of the two stars of the movie.

Sam jumped back up to present them, grinning madly.

"There have been a lot of rumors about who will be playing the two lead characters in our movie. I'm happy to say those rumors were true. Please welcome the stars who are going to make Detroit forget about cars—Lexie Tisdale and Breed Larson!"

The two actors made their entrance Hollywood style, sweeping into the room waving and smiling. Will assumed they had been cooling their heels in the hallway until their names were called. It felt staged and hokey, but he had to admit it made things a lot livelier than a normal business meeting. And even though he had been around enough celebrities as a reporter to avoid being starstruck, he had to admit his level of interest and excitement went up along with everyone else's in the room.

Although they were decades apart in age, they were at similar junctions in their careers—the tipping point between continued stardom and used-to-be obscurity. They both were in desperate need of a successful movie to regain the momentum that, for different reasons, they had lost. Lexie was a beautiful young woman who had squandered away her early triumphs with a combination of bad movies and worse behavior. Breed was a veteran action movie hero who had made the mistake of growing older.

As they made their way to the lectern, Sam explained that the press conference would confirm the poorly kept secret that the two were joining the cast: Lexie as the Army Ranger platoon leader and Breed as the wise old peace-loving head of the Archivists. He called it a brilliant reversal of typecasting that would undoubtedly earn them both Oscar nominations. When they finally reached the lectern, they both said a few nice things about the movie and the city and got a big hug from Sam, who thanked everyone for coming and ended the meeting.

It was at that point things became really interesting for Will.

"Sam was right, you are perfect for the role of the Guardian. I am so excited that you agreed to be in our picture."

The meeting was breaking up all around them, but the woman sitting next to Will was touching his arm lightly, which held him in his seat like an iron shackle.

"I'm Roxanne, I work for Future Tense Studios. I'm the line producer for *The Guardian of Detritus.*"

Will knew this from Sam's introductions, but he was not about to complain about a little repetition at this point—he just wanted her to keep touching his arm.

"The line producer is the one who stays on location while the movie is filming, correct?"

"That's right. I actually help get things done, as opposed to the rest of the producers, whose job is to call from LA every day to complain that things aren't getting done. I'm looking forward to working closely with you."

"I have to confess I haven't done a lot of acting, but I'm excited about playing this part."

"Acting is easy. Come to work on time, know your lines…"

"And don't bump into the other actors."

"You know the Spencer Tracy quote, I'm impressed. What else do you know, Will?"

"Like I said, I'm not an actor, but I do know movies and movie history."

"That puts you miles ahead of most of the people who call themselves actors these days. I'm looking forward to working with you, Will Harkanen, and I want to get to know you better. Why don't you join me for lunch after the press conference? We can drink to a happy and successful future together."

The moment he agreed, she jumped up, gave him a hug and a kiss on the cheek, whispered "later" into his ear, and hurried away. It was the breathy whisper into his ear that made his head stop working properly. Will made his way slowly out into the hallway, in somewhat of a state of shock, and walked straight into Bronson Rogers.

"Will Harkanen, what a small world."

Small doesn't begin to describe it, Will thought. He added cruel, unfair, ironic, and disturbing, somehow managing not to say any of these things out loud.

"Councilman Rogers, I'm glad to see you are still supporting the performing arts."

"As usual, Will, I'm not sure I understand what you're trying to say."

"This is the second time you've helped create a fictional account of what happened in Detroit."

"I'm glad you haven't lost your sense of humor, Will—or your vivid imagination. I think we can both agree that this is a great day for the City of Detroit. Let's leave it at that, shall we? I'll see you at the press conference."

With that Rogers walked off, followed by a young man and woman who had been standing nearby, who Will assumed were aides. He watched them disappear around a corner. By the time he figured out he should follow them, it was too late: when he went around the corner, they were gone.

Based on his years of going to press conferences, first as a reporter and then as a public relations practitioner, he was certain there was some sort of VIP lounge nearby where the politicians and movie stars could relax until the press conference began. It was where the best food would be, and the most interesting conversations, and perhaps even a few adult beverages.

Unfortunately no one had told him where it was.

For several minutes he wandered the halls, hoping to find the room and crash the party, but he was unsuccessful. Finally he turned a corner and spotted a big guy in a dark suit standing outside a doorway looking grim. He was obviously a security guard, which meant this had to be the VIP lounge.

Will walked toward the guard and peered through the open doorway behind him. His plan was to spot someone inside that he knew, call out their name, and blow past the man in the doorway with a smile and a nod. But even before the guard moved forward to confront him, Will was stopped in his tracks by what he saw inside the room.

Breed Larson was sitting in an overstuffed chair, sharing a showbiz story with a group of people Will recognized from the meeting. Lexie Tisdale was stretched out on a love seat, texting. But it was what he saw behind them, in a far corner of the room, that made him freeze.

Sam Rainier, Bronson Rogers, and Joe Letner were huddled together and engaged in a quiet but intense conversation. Letner, in his police uniform, was doing most of the talking, between glances back over his shoulder at the room.

"Can I help you, sir? Are you a VIP?"

It was the guard, doing his job. Seeing three adversaries from his past conspiring together in the present had startled Will into forgetting his plan. The only thing that came to mind was a smartass reply.

"No, I'm just a P."

The guard looked unamused and ready to say something Will would regret. But before the situation could deteriorate any further, Phil Salzman materialized out of nowhere to smooth things over.

"Will, there's still plenty of coffee and donuts in the meeting room. Why don't you relax there until the press conference starts?"

Will was grabbed firmly by the elbow and swept down a hallway back to the room where they had held their meeting. Phil seemed anxious to get and keep him there, standing outside the door until he went inside.

During their walk Will recovered somewhat from the shock of what he had seen, reasoning that it was perfectly logical.

The movie was being filmed in Letner's precinct; he was no doubt involved in the security arrangements. But the instant and instinctive menace that Will felt when he saw the three of them together was hard to shake.

He was trying to figure out what to do next—whether or not he wanted to wait until Phil left and go back to the VIP lounge—when he spotted an old colleague from the *News* loading up a plate at the donut table. He couldn't remember his last name, but he was certain about his first name.

"I see you're taking full advantage of the free food, Tom. I'm glad some journalistic traditions are still being followed."

"Go to hell, Harkanen. I heard you were in jail or doing public relations, something horrible like that."

"Something like that. Last I heard you were on the Metro desk, covering the city council. What are you doing here?"

"Have you been hiding under a rock? This whole studio thing is a huge issue for the city council, the mayor, and the entire city. Detroit is broke and they're talking about giving huge tax breaks to a bunch of millionaires from LA. The *News* is horribly understaffed these days, they won't let us out of the newsroom to cover anything, but we've got three reporters here for this press conference—myself, Mary Barlett from Entertainment, and Ross Zellerman from Business."

"Sounds like the time Michael Jackson announced he was going to build a theme park in Detroit. We sent an army of reporters and photographers to cover this huge breaking story but nothing ever happened."

Will was about to add that he thought the studio project would end up the same way, but he remembered he was supposed to be working for the people who were trying to build it. He needed to keep his mouth shut. Tom finished stacking his plate with food and looked up at him.

"So what are you doing here?"

"Believe it or not, I have a part in the movie."

"You're working with Sam Rainier? Sam's new best friend is your old pal Bronson Rogers. Do you know how nasty those guys are?"

"I have a pretty good idea, but why don't you tell me."

"This whole studio thing is crooked as hell. Rainier is handing out kickbacks to everyone who will take them so he can get tax breaks from the city. Bronson Rogers is first in line for the biggest handouts. The city council is supposed to vote on whether or not to allow the tax breaks in the next few weeks. My sources tell me that Rainier is getting desperate; he's running out of money, and he really needs this studio deal to go through or he could go broke. He'll do whatever it takes to make it happen."

"I haven't read about any of this in the paper. If you know that's true, why hasn't it been in print?"

"We have you to thank for that. When you caved and gave up on your libel case, it scared the shit out of management. These days we can't print anything controversial unless we have at least two sources confirming any alleged misbehavior, and we have to be able to name them in print. That's not going to happen with these guys; they're too sharp to leave any loose ends, and everyone who knows anything for sure is afraid to talk on the record."

"So what *do* you have? Anything good you can use?"

Tom looked at him for a moment, then shook his head.

"You think I'm going to give up any information to you? You're working for them. These are bad people, Harkanen. They do bad things. If you're on their side, fuck you."

"And if I'm not on their side?"

"If you're not on their side, good luck. You're going to need it."

Chapter Twenty-five

A Few Bad Eggs

In his years of working as a public relations professional, Will had discovered one truism about press conferences: the last question asked was usually the one that did the most damage.

The toughest questions always came early, but they were also the most obvious—you could prepare and rehearse answers for them. Next came the more basic, easy questions: about background information or facts that filled in the details of the story.

After that the questions usually slowed down and wandered off into trivia or began repeating themselves. At that point the PR person typically stood up and asked for one more question before wrapping things up. That's when it came: a question that was so off-the-wall, weird, unanticipated, or unexplainable that it overshadowed the message the client was trying to get across and recast everything that had already been said in a whole new light.

A classic example was the time TIC held a press conference to introduce a new engine control module shortly after the 9/11 attacks. After a series of relatively painless and straightforward questions, Will called for one more and all hell broke loose. A reporter asked the engineer in charge if the module could be reprogrammed by terrorists to turn cars into bombs. Instead of simply answering "no" or "I don't think so" or even "I don't know," the engineer began trying to figure out how it might be done.

Out loud.

Before Will could get things under control and end the press conference, the discussion had ranged from how to make cars blow up to what processes TIC had in place to prevent deep-cover terrorists from being hired. One headline the following day summed up the conversation succinctly: "TIC Talk: Auto Supplier Says Latest Product Could Help Terrorists Make Bombs."

Will was hoping the press conference for *The Guardian of Detritus* and Future Tense Studios would prove to be an exception to the last-question rule.

Things started off well enough. Sam Rainier stayed on message, talking about how the movie and the new studio were going to help with the growing revitalization of Detroit. At no point did he talk about blowing up the city. Bronson Rogers was articulate and charming, talking about the jobs, investments, and excitement the movie industry would bring to the city.

Oddly enough, Lexie Tisdale and Breed Larson added a touch of reality to the proceedings. Judging by the questions that they asked, a lot of the people in the audience were having a hard time imagining a major motion picture studio in Detroit. The presence of actual movie stars—even slightly tarnished ones—made it seem more believable.

The Q&A session unfolded the way Will expected—tough questions followed by inquiries about basic background information and logistics. There was even a question about Lexie's current boyfriend that got everyone laughing. The Detroit media seemed pleased that one of their own had demonstrated a working knowledge of celebrity trivia; it proved that they were more than ready to provide serious reporting of foolish things.

For a subject that was supposed to be so controversial, things went remarkably smoothly. By the time Phil Salzman stood up to ask for one more question, Will had decided that the last-question curse probably wouldn't apply in this case. He figured it was probably just a figment of his imagination or something that only happened to him.

He was wrong.

Will was sitting in the first row, which had given him room to stand up, turn around, and wave to the crowd when Sam introduced him. By happy coincidence or intriguing intention, Roxanne Williams was sitting next to him. When Phil asked for the last question, he hesitated for a moment, then pointed at someone sitting a few rows behind them. There was a brief pause while the reporter waited for a microphone to be passed down to him. Then, loud and clear over the speaker system, came the question:

"Why are you destroying a neighborhood?"

After a moment of awkward silence, Sam spoke up. He was seated behind a long, narrow table on a slightly raised stage along with the rest of the press conference speakers. Each had a microphone in front of them; all but Sam now seemed reluctant to use them.

"We're not destroying a neighborhood. We are knocking down a bunch of old shacks so that we can build a business that is going to create jobs."

"How many of those jobs are going to go to local people?"

"As we said, we don't have a solid number we can share at the moment, but—"

"I think you have a number in mind, but you're too embarrassed to say it. You'll take our tax dollars and knock down our homes, but you won't give us anything in return except a handful of unskilled, minimum wage jobs. We'll be the janitors and you'll fly the people you need in from LA to fill all the skilled, high-paying jobs."

Sam apparently didn't have a response to this accusation; instead he took refuge in the message his PR man had drummed into him.

"We are going to help the city of Detroit by knocking down old buildings and creating new jobs."

"There are people living in those buildings: families, businesses, artists creating beautiful new works of art. The

Harmony House experiment is starting this summer right in the middle of the neighborhood you are going to destroy. This is the Heidelberg Project all over again."

From the look on his face, it was clear to Will that Sam didn't know anything about the Heidelberg Project. It also was clear that Sam's confident showmanship had completely deserted him; he began repeating his sound bite message but was mercifully interrupted by Phil Salzman.

"Excuse me, we made it clear that everyone asking a question has to identify themselves and who they are with. Can you do that for us, please?"

"If I answer your question, will you answer mine? Why are you destroying a neighborhood?"

"If you won't tell us who you are and who you are working for, we're going to have to ask you to leave. Can you please state your name and your media affiliation?"

Will knew a lot of the local reporters. He turned his head as slowly and discreetly as possible to get a look at who was asking the questions. Roxanne was doing the same thing next to him, only a lot less discreetly; she turned completely around in her seat and stared.

Over his right shoulder Will saw a young man with a microphone a few rows back: tall and thin, with thick glasses and slicked-down black hair, wearing a brown suit that looked like a Halloween costume. He also saw two security guards walking purposefully up the side aisle as the man answered the question.

"I'm Brown from the Sun."

It took a second for the crowd to figure out they had just heard a joke. When they did, the room exploded with groans and laughter. Phil's true but poorly worded reply brought even more laughter.

"There is no Sun in Detroit!"

He followed up with a statement that stopped the laughter cold.

"Whoever you are, you are not on the list of invited media—I'm going to have to ask you to leave immediately, or we will have security escort you out."

Along with everyone else in the room, Will turned in his seat to see what would happen next. The two security guards had reached the row where Mr. Brown was standing; they looked eager to have an opportunity to haul someone away. The local TV cameramen, who had been filming the people on stage from tripod-mounted cameras on a raised platform at the back of the room, now focused on the man with the microphone, hoping to get footage of someone being dragged away.

What happened next gave them much more than they expected.

Two men sitting on either side of Mr. Brown stood up and yelled, "The Principals of Entropy rule all systems!" After that they reached into their coat pockets and began throwing things at the stage. The objects they were throwing flew over Will's head; he heard them hit with dull thumps behind him as the people on stage began screaming.

Will ducked to avoid being hit. As he did Mr. Brown began chanting, "This deal stinks" into the microphone. By the third time he repeated the chant, Will was gagging from a horrible stench that rolled over him like a wave.

Then the gunshots began.

Chapter Twenty-six

Shots and Kisses

When the first shot was fired, Will instinctively jumped on top of Roxanne Williams, who had ducked down next to him. She toppled over onto her back with Will on top of her, emitting a soft "Oh!" when she hit the ground. Under the circumstances it was an unexpectedly pleasant sound, neither shocked nor scared.

She repeated the sound when a second shot rang out a few seconds later, at the same time pulling Will closer. When a third shot was fired a moment after that, she said it again and squeezed him tightly.

After that all they heard were the screams and footsteps of the panicked crowd trying to get out of the auditorium. Will looked up and could see Mr. Brown and the two men next to him standing very still with their hands in the air. All around them people were scrambling over chairs and each other to get away, with the exception of the two security guards, who were pushing through the crowd trying to get closer.

One of the guards had a gun pointed at the three men, and the other was yelling something at them. It was hard to hear above the chaos, but by reading his lips, Will figured out he was telling the three men not to move and to keep their hands up. Whether they could hear him or not, they were complying wholeheartedly. Since none of the three seemed to be wounded, Will figured the guard had fired warning shots into the ceiling to get them to stop throwing things.

If that was true, he thought, it was effective but extremely stupid.

He heard cursing behind him and once again was aware of the horrible smell that had filled the room. He looked toward the stage and could see the principals of the press conference coming out from beneath the table. On the wall behind them, there were a number of dark stains sprinkled with white flecks. When Sam stood up, he had a similar stain on the front of his suit coat. At that point Will realized what the protestors had been throwing.

Rotten eggs.

"I hate to spoil the moment, but I think it's safe to get off me now."

"I'm sorry."

"Don't apologize, you saved my life."

"Not really. Those were warning shots, they fired them at the ceiling."

"You didn't know that when they started shooting. You risked your life to save mine. I owe you a big thanks."

"You're welcome."

"Now will you get off me?"

Will got to his feet and helped Roxanne to hers. One of the security guards was putting plastic strips that served as handcuffs onto the wrists of the protestors. His partner held a gun on them with one hand and was speaking into a radio he held in his other hand.

The room had grown strangely quiet.

Reporters who had bolted in panic were returning, pulling out notebooks and cell phones and returning to the business of recording what was happening at the press conference, which had just gotten a lot more interesting. The TV cameramen, who had ducked when the shots were fired, had stepped back up to their equipment and were filming the security guards and their newly captured prisoners.

The footage they shot aired on the news that evening and went on to become a minor video sensation on the Internet. What made it especially interesting to web surfers was the photo bomb behind the guards and their prisoners: in the background observant viewers saw a couple talking briefly; then the woman grabbed the man and began kissing him passionately.

Chapter Twenty-seven

More Shots And Kisses

After lunch and drinks, Will had a confession to make to Roxanne.

"I know how to make an egg into a stink bomb."

The two had waited out the chaos of the aftermath of the press conference protest, given brief statements to the police—a man and a woman Will didn't know—then headed out on their lunch date. Will drove them a few blocks away to the Book Cadillac, the hotel where Roxanne was staying while the movie was being made. They got a table in a secluded corner of the hotel's dining room and tried to digest what had just happened to them along with their food.

"Are you going to share your stink bomb secret with me?"

"You take a needle and poke a hole in the end of the egg, then let it sit in a warm place for a week. Mickey Hayes showed me how to do it in junior high."

"Mickey was one of the guys in your band, right?"

"Yeah. How did you know that?"

"Sam told me all about the old days when he first came to Detroit."

An alarm went off in Will's head, slightly muted by the two Manhattans he had enjoyed with his filet mignon. He knew Roxanne worked for Sam Rainier, but up until this moment he had assumed it was his charm and good looks that had attracted this beautiful, high-powered Hollywood executive to him. He now realized the more glaringly obvious possibility—that Sam had told her to get cozy with him to find out what he was doing.

Roxanne must have noticed a reaction when she mentioned Sam, because she began asking him a series of rapid-fire questions about things he had explained while they were waiting to talk to the police.

"So tell me again, who were the guys who threw the eggs at the press conference?"

"They call themselves the Principals of Entropy. They want to preserve the old buildings in Detroit."

"Like the Archivists in *The Guardian of Detritus.*"

"I hadn't thought about it, but yeah."

"And what was the thing about the Heidelberg Project?"

"The Heidelberg Project is an outdoor art installation on the east side that was started by an artist named Tyree Guyton as a protest after the riots in 1967. He put polka dots on abandoned houses and old cars and made sculptures out of junk. The city spent years trying to tear the Heidelberg Project down."

"Did they succeed?"

"No. They finally acknowledged it was art that was important and valuable to the community. Today it's a big tourist attraction."

"So there are artists who are doing the same thing where we're going to shoot the picture?"

"I guess so. The egg man mentioned the Harmony House experiment, it's supposed to start this summer in the area that's going to be blown up."

"What's the Harmony House experiment?"

"Two artists, one black and one white, are going to live and work together with their families in a shared duplex home. The whole thing is some kind of performance art project itself, and a social statement. It's supposed to promote racial harmony in the city, which is great. Unfortunately when I hear that name, I think of the record store where I bought all my albums when I was a kid."

"A record store?"

"Used to be chain. Like a lot of things around here, it's out of business."

"Have you lived here all your life?"

"I was born in Detroit, raised in the suburbs. My grandfather came over here from Finland, he worked in the copper mines up in the U.P., the upper peninsula, then came to Detroit to work in an auto plant. My dad worked for Ford at the Rouge for forty years. Believe it or not, this once was the land of opportunity."

"It still can be, Will, that's what the studio is all about. Have you driven through the area where we're going to build it?"

"No."

"Well, I have. And I can tell you it's not a work of art. It's a disaster."

"Maybe the art is inside the buildings."

"Then why didn't they talk about it at one of the town hall meetings the city council had to discuss this project? Why start the discussion by shouting and throwing rotten eggs at a press conference?"

"I'm not sure why they did it. Maybe they went to the meetings and nobody listened, or maybe they thought this would get them more attention. They did get their message across, but now everybody is going to think they are a crazy fringe group."

"They *are* a crazy fringe group, Will. But don't worry, they're not going to shut down the picture. Sam is going to make this happen. He's a guy who gets what he wants."

"You're right about that."

Something in the quick and emphatic way Will responded made Roxanne pause for a moment and look him over. Then she smiled and waved the waiter over to their table.

"I'd like my usual after-dinner drink—for both of us, please. And the check as well."

Roxanne had assured Will that lunch would be on the studio's expense account—which is why he ordered two drinks and an expensive steak. But he wasn't sure he was ready for a mystery drink on top of all that.

"Can I ask what you just ordered?"

"I ordered us both a slivovitz."

"I'm familiar with the various types of alcohol, some would say too familiar, but I've never heard of... ah..."

"Slivovitz. It's a plum brandy, the national drink of Serbia. They serve it in a chilled shot glass. I was there a few years ago shooting a picture, and I fell in love with the stuff."

The waiter brought over two frosty shot glasses. They clinked their glasses together, Roxanne called out "Ziveli!" and they drank down a yellow liquor that burned Will's mouth and throat.

"So what does ziveli mean?"

"It's Serbian for 'let's live long.'"

"That's a nice sentiment. We all want to live long."

Roxanne looked at Will and seemed to be considering something before she spoke again.

"I like to think of slivovitz as kind of a Serbian truth serum. If I ask you a question, will you tell me the truth?"

"Sure."

Will didn't know why he had answered so positively and quickly, but he was certain he meant what he said. Maybe it was a truth serum.

"What have you got against Sam Rainier?"

Will didn't answer this question as quickly, but he still told the truth.

"I don't have anything against Sam Rainier."

"Then why are you obsessing about things that happened thirty years ago?"

"Sam told you about the tape?"

"Yes."

"I wouldn't call it obsessing. I'm just curious about what happened."

"Sam says that Mickey got high and destroyed it. He says you think he stole it."

"I don't know what happened. I'm trying to find out."

"I've known Sam for years, and I'm not going to defend him,

he can be a real prick. He's been known to lie, cheat, and steal to get what he wants. But my question to you is what difference does it make what happened to the tape? Either way, you're never going to get it back. If it got destroyed the way they say it did, you are wasting your time and pissing people off needlessly. If Sam did steal the tape, he would have to admit it in order to give it back to you. We both know that's never going to happen, right?"

"Right."

"I couldn't tell you why he gave you a part in this picture. He may think you're great for the part. Or maybe it's because he feels guilty about ripping you off. Or it could be to show you he has no hard feelings about your falsely accusing him of being a thief. Whatever it is, you should just enjoy the moment. The past is over."

Will wanted to explain to her why the past wasn't over, but first she would have to answer *his* question truthfully.

"I have a question for you. I want you to think about it carefully and answer it truthfully. Did Sam ask you to keep an eye on me?"

Roxanne answered his question as quickly and positively as Will had answered hers.

"Of course he did."

Maybe it was the drinks, or the company, or the unexpectedly candid answer. For whatever reason, Will now felt strangely compelled to share his suspicions with a woman he barely knew, who was working for the man he suspected.

"This isn't just about what happened in the past. A few weeks ago another one of the guys who was in the band died in a car accident. He was looking into what happened with the tape when he died."

"Padrig Wagner, stage name Paddy Wagon. Sam told me about him and about how you think Paddy may have been killed. He also told me about the police report, which I assume you've checked out. They said it was an accident."

"So Sam thinks I should just forget about it?"

"Yes."

"And what do you think?"

"I think you should quit getting high with 'Purple' Hayes and start focusing on doing a great job as the Guardian of Detritus. Pot makes you paranoid. Movies make you famous."

"That sounds like good advice."

Whether she was acting as a loyal employee or a crafty co-conspirator, Will decided he had shared enough information with Roxanne for now. Up to this point he hadn't told her anything that Sam didn't know or suspect, and he wasn't going to go any further at the moment.

Or so he thought.

"I have one more question for you, Will."

"What's that?"

"Would you like to come up to my room with me?"

They both were surprised when he hesitated and said nothing.

"Don't worry, not even Sam could get me to do *that* for him. I'm off duty now, I asked that question for me."

This time Will didn't hesitate.

"In that case I would love to come up to your room."

Chapter Twenty-eight

Ménage de Troit

In the morning Will and Roxanne put on the complimentary "available for purchase" bathrobes they found in the closet and ordered room service. They ate without talking, but to Will the silence wasn't awkward, it was intimate.

After breakfast they showered together, got dressed, and said their good-byes.

"I had fun, Will. See you at the movies."

"See you at the movies. All hail Detritus."

"What?"

"One of my lines from the movie. See you there."

"See you there."

Will drove home to his suburban motel room and spent the rest of the morning trying to get his head to stop spinning around like Linda Blair in *The Exorcist.* There was too much going on at once, good and bad. His clumsy attempt to incorporate more purpose and passion into his life was succeeding on a scale and speed that was overwhelming.

He needed time to think.

When he started on his little adventure, his idea of a walk on the wild side was quitting his job to attend the funeral of a former friend. Now he was trying to solve a possible murder, unravel a decades-old mystery, play a part in a movie, rekindle a romance, and perhaps prevent an entire city from being swindled by crooks. Not to mention starting an affair with a beautiful, powerful woman he knew virtually nothing about.

That alone was enough to start his head spinning.

It had been nearly a year since his wife left him. During that time he had gone on a handful of dates that made him feel awkward, desperate, and alone. He had concluded that dating, like military service, should be reserved for the young, strong, and brave—at his age it only served as a stark reminder of the comedy and tragedy of the human condition.

Plus he never got laid.

In contrast, his one-night stand with Roxanne had felt wonderful, natural, and fulfilling on many levels, not the least of which was great sex. It had been quite a while for Will, since before his separation, and the contrast between resentful late-stage marriage sex and first-time beautiful stranger sex was dramatic. The memory of last night's close encounter was one of the things that were making Will's head spin. Another was the question of whether or not proceeding beyond a one-night stand was possible or even advisable.

As much as he enjoyed the company of Roxanne, his night with her had also churned up unexpected feelings of guilt. His growing feelings for Jacqueline, which had gone largely unnoticed over the last few weeks, suddenly presented themselves front and center in his mind.

More spinning.

Leaving romance aside, there was still the murder, the mystery, and the movie to deal with. All of which was complicated by the fact that he had promised Jacqueline he would stop his investigation and then slept with the person who was assigned to keep an eye on him by the bad guy. It couldn't get much worse, but then it did.

Jacqueline knocked on the door.

Will opened it.

"I was in the neighborhood to have lunch with a friend; I thought I'd stop by to see how you were doing."

"I'm doing good. The headaches went away, I'm back to normal."

"That's great."

Jacqueline walked in and sat down on the bed. Will took a seat in the easy chair. He could sense something was wrong; she was holding back. Normally his "I'm back to normal" line would have been a great set-up for her, but she hadn't even bothered to insult him.

"I heard about what happened at the press conference for your movie yesterday. Were you there?"

For some reason this felt like a trick question to Will.

"I was. It was crazy."

"Who were those people throwing eggs?"

"They call themselves the Principals of Entropy. They're trying to stop Sam from building a movie studio in Detroit. They want to preserve the ruins."

"That's crazy."

"They claim there is some sort of artists' community back there."

Jacqueline studied him carefully before she spoke again.

"That sounds like the kind of bleeding-heart bullshit you would fall for. Tell me you're not going to start supporting them."

"I do have a soft spot for struggling artists, but I'm not sure preserving a bunch of old buildings that are falling down is going to help anything. It's probably a better idea to build a movie studio there."

"Probably?"

"I have to be honest with you, Jackie. I saw Sam Rainier, Bronson Rogers, and Joe Letner having an intense private discussion before the press conference started. I had a really bad feeling when I saw them all together."

"You saw the movie executive who wants to build a studio in Detroit talking to the city councilman who supports his plan and the precinct commander responsible for the neighborhood it will be built in. Why shouldn't they be talking to each other?"

"I figured that out myself later on, but my gut instinct was that they were up to no good."

"You told me you would stop poking around in the past."

"I know. I have. But I've learned a few things since I talked to you and they're bugging me. You need to know about them."

She sighed and shook her head.

"What?"

"The poem that Paddy had in the file wasn't a poem, it was a list of techno songs."

"Techno? You mean like electronic music? Paddy hated that stuff."

"There's more. The songs were all produced by Sam Rainier in the nineties."

"So?"

"All of the songs on the list have samples from the Exits' lost tape."

"What do you mean, samples?"

"Samples are parts taken from someone else's music. It's pretty common in rap and hip-hop, and in techno music too."

"All the stuff Paddy hated."

"So how did he figure out that Sam had stolen the tape and used parts of it on songs he produced years later?"

Suddenly Jacqueline looked stricken. She got up, walked around the bed, and went to the window. Will started to follow her, but she quickly walked back to the bed and sat back down. When she spoke again, it was in a low, soft voice.

"I think I know how he found out about it. If I tell you, will you stop messing around with this stuff?"

Will hated to lie to her but he had to know. Fortunately his PR background provided him with the loophole of semantics, which was not quite the same as lying.

"I'll stop messing around."

He made a mental note to himself: from now on he would take his investigation more seriously—i.e., stop messing around.

"Last year Paddy got some free tickets to Movement, the big electronic music festival in Hart Plaza, from a client of his that was one of the sponsors. He went just to make his client happy. When he got back he seemed bothered by something, but he wouldn't say what. Now that I think about it, it was around that time that he started acting funny."

"Funny?"

"Preoccupied. Secretive. He spent a lot of time alone in his office in our home. I thought maybe he had another girlfriend he was texting or talking to in there, but that wasn't it."

"How do you know?"

"How do all these assholes who cheat get caught? I checked his phone."

"So what did you find out? What did you want to tell me?"

"I never figured out what happened until just now. He must have heard some of the Exits' music in the songs at the festival."

"And after that is when he went home and spent months making his list and figuring out the connections."

"Yes. Now you know everything I know. Now you can stop."

"I'm guessing at first Paddy was just curious about what Sam had done. Maybe he was afraid someone else would figure it out, and the whole ugly business of the missing tape would resurface."

"You're not stopping, Will. You said you'd stop."

"I'm just thinking out loud. Sam and the guys in the band were the only ones who knew all the songs on that tape. Rick is dead. Sam and Mickey were in on the deal. That leaves Tommy and me. Not much chance of either of us figuring it out after more than thirty years."

"I don't like you thinking out loud, it's not going to do any good."

"There was something else that was motivating Paddy. At the funeral home you said that when he finally told you about the tape, all he kept talking about was how much money it was going to make him."

"But he never said how."

"I think I've figured it out. He was using what he knew about the tape to try to blackmail Sam."

"Okay, let's finish this and be done with it. Why would Sam care about something that happened that long ago? Why would anybody care? Paddy used to say that crooked deals were as much a part of rock and roll as electric guitars. Why would he think Sam would give him money to cover up something that wouldn't matter to anybody but a few old geezers who used to be in the band?"

"There's more to it than that, Jackie. I ran into someone I know from the *News* at the press conference. He told me this whole studio deal is crooked as hell, Sam is handing out bribes and kickbacks to everyone he thinks can help him. In the meantime the city council is getting ready to vote on whether or not to give him the tax breaks he wants."

"What does all that have to do with a bunch of old songs?"

"Everything is hanging in the balance for Sam and the people he is paying under the table right now. My guess is that Paddy thought even a minor scandal from the past would be enough to tip public opinion against Sam. Even if he didn't get into any legal trouble, he would still be called out as a crook. It might be enough to screw up the deal."

"So you think Sam killed Paddy to shut him up?"

"Sam or one of the people he is paying off."

Neither of them spoke again for what felt like a long time to Will. When Jacqueline broke the silence, her voice was once again loud and determined.

"I want you to stick to our agreement, Will. I want you to forget about all this and let it go."

"What about Paddy? Don't you want some justice for him?"

"We've both gone to the police and they've done nothing. I told you before, what happened to Paddy is over. Whatever happens, we can't bring him back. I don't want to lose you too, Will. Promise me this is over."

"Okay, I promise. It's over."

This time there were no loopholes to escape through. He went over and sat down on the bed next to her. It seemed like the time was right for a kiss, but when he reached over to make it happen, she pushed him back.

"Who was that woman you were with at the press conference?"

"What woman?"

"The one you were kissing on TV."

"You saw me kissing a woman on TV?"

"They were taking away the guys who threw the eggs. You were in the background kissing some woman very passionately."

He may have been lying about not pursuing the case anymore, he wasn't sure. But he knew it was important not to lie about this.

"She's one of the producers of the movie. I met her at the press conference. When we heard gunshots, I threw myself on top of her to protect her. She was grateful for that and she gave me a kiss."

"She looked *very* grateful to me. Did you sleep with her?"

"That's a pretty big jump to make, don't you think? Going from a thank-you kiss to sleeping together?"

"Did you sleep with her?"

Once again it was a moment of truth.

"Yes."

Jacqueline stood up, walked to the door, and was gone.

Chapter Twenty-nine

Montage de Troit

W ill wasn't sure if it was coincidence, fate, or conspiracy, but the first scenes he had to shoot for the movie took place at *Taste Detroit*. They were using the urban farm behind the restaurant as the location for the Anarchist settlement. An old crack house that hadn't been torn down yet, surrounded by rows of homegrown crops, would stand in as the group's headquarters.

Mickey's marijuana plants, which were hidden in a far corner of the lot, did not have a role in the movie. However, Mickey himself did—he was one of the Anarchist elders who would be talking to Will in the scenes they were going to shoot. It was the acting debut for both of them.

Will was excited to begin making the movie, but after everything that had happened in the last few weeks, he had mixed feelings about seeing Mickey again. If the opportunity presented itself, he was thinking about trying something out on him. It was an experiment that could help reveal the truth if it worked or perhaps get him killed if it failed.

There was also his promise to Jacqueline to consider. He knew he had feelings for her, and her abrupt storm-off proved she had feelings for him. He didn't want to do anything more that would jeopardize their relationship.

Will arrived on the set early in the morning, parked in the lot surrounded by barbed wire, and made his way into the restaurant. A sign on the porch indicated that *Taste Detroit* was closed to the public for the day.

A young woman with dark hair and thick-framed glasses greeted him in the entranceway and introduced herself as Connie. When he told her his name, she rushed him upstairs to a room filled with racks of clothing, where two people stripped him down to his underwear and dressed him in a camouflaged jumpsuit and boots. After that Connie led him into another room, and he sat in a chair while makeup artists sprayed and brushed him with fake sweat and dirt. Then she took him to Mickey's office to meet the director.

Alan E. Smith sat at Mickey's desk, looking like he had just found a fingernail floating in his coffee and ignoring Will's outstretched hand. He was dressed in black jeans, black boots, and a black tee shirt, with a large diamond stud in his left earlobe and a shiny head. Will guessed he had shaved whatever hair he had left so he would look like a hipster and not a middle-aged bald guy.

"So you're the *actor* who is going to play god?"

"Actually, I'm supposed to be the park ranger."

"The park ranger? I didn't see a character called the park ranger anywhere in the script. You are playing the Guardian of Detritus—G-O-D—god. Correct?"

"Yes."

"Let me make this perfectly clear: you are *playing* god on the set, but there is only one *true* god on the set, and that's me. Do you understand?"

"Yes."

"Ever act before?"

"No."

"Never acted before, that's terrific. Somebody must like you—but it's definitely not me. You are here against my wishes and against my will. Do me a favor and don't fuck up my movie. Do you have any questions?"

"Yeah. They told me I didn't need to memorize any of my lines for today. So what am I going to be doing?"

"Conifer will tell you."

"Conifer?"

"You *are* a quick study, aren't you, Mr. Harkanen? Conifer is the young lady you have been following around for the last hour, the one standing right next to you. Any other questions?"

"Actually I do have one other question. You're a director and your name is Alan E. Smith. I assume you've heard of the movie tradition about directors named Alan Smithee?"

Alan E. Smith now looked like he had found an entire finger floating in his coffee.

"Mr. Harkanen, I have a ton of shit to deal with today, I don't need any more from you. Conifer, will you please escort Mr. Harkanen out of my office and tell him what he will be doing today?"

Conifer led Will down the hall to what he assumed was a bedroom that had been converted into a conference room. They sat down at a massive wooden table in the center of the room that was covered in scripts, memos, storyboard drawings, and dirty dishes. He was dying to ask her why her parents had named her after pine trees, but instead he settled for a question that was a little more polite.

"You told me your name was Connie—I assume that's short for Conifer?"

She sighed and hesitated for a moment before plunging into what seemed like a well-rehearsed response.

"My parents both work in the movie business and they're big-time environmentalists. Twenty-seven years ago naming their daughter Conifer seemed like a good idea to them. I hate the name and call myself Connie, but people who know my parents still use Conifer. I share my name with a family of trees, it's very funny, and now you have a Hollywood weirdo story to tell your friends. Can we talk about the movie?"

"Sure."

Connie explained to Will that the scenes they would be shooting today would show the Guardian speaking to the

Anarchist leaders as a group and individually. She was bright and cute, in a Velma from *Scooby Doo* sort of way.

The scenes, which were listed in the shooting schedule they had given him, would be shot in various locations on the farm, including a house that in a later scene would be shot to pieces using squibs. The footage would be woven together in editing to form a montage of the Guardian's effort to reason with the Anarchists.

"Any questions?"

"A squib is a small explosive charge that looks like a bullet hitting something, right?"

Will knew about montages, squibs, and all things movie-related, but for some reason he felt like he had to prove he belonged on a movie set. Asking the question with the answer was his way of doing that, or maybe it was just his way of showing off.

"That's right. Near the end of the movie, the Army Rangers attack the Anarchists' headquarters and shoot it until it falls apart. They'll use the squibs for that scene."

"I have another question. If I am talking to the Anarchists, why don't I have any lines?"

"We're not recording dialogue for the montage, so all you have to do is *look* like you are talking to them. Say whatever you want, just make sure your expression is serious and intense. Can you do that?"

Will decided to practice on Connie before the cameras rolled. He grabbed the edge of the table, narrowed his eyes, and leaned forward.

"Connie, I swear by everything that is holy that I will maintain a serious and intense expression throughout the entire montage."

"Do me a favor, don't do that over-the-top shit in front of Mr. Smith. Just talk without smiling or looking at the camera, okay?"

"Got it. One more question—Alan E. Smith. What does the 'E' stand for?"

"Pretentious. Now let's go meet the other actors."

Connie led him down to the Lower Bar, where the actors and extras he would be working with today were waiting. There were about thirty of them, dressed in costumes that Will thought made them look like colonial farmers from outer space. They all had on loosely fitting shirts made from thick, rough cotton, dark pants that ended just below the knees, and triangular hats made out of some kind of shiny silver metal.

He was about to laugh when he saw Mickey standing at the back of the group glaring at him. Will couldn't tell if Mickey was glaring because he was mad at him or because he was wearing a serving dish on his head.

Connie got everyone's attention and introduced Will to the group, then explained that she would lead them out as a group for the initial shot. Later some of them would be paired with Will for individual dialog shots; she read those names from a clipboard, and Mickey was one of them.

After answering a few questions, she led them to the crack house, and Will began his career as an actor.

The work was easy and, for a while, fun.

The first shot was of two Anarchists taking a blindfold off Will; the explanation being that they would have covered his eyes before leading him to their headquarters. After that the entire group looked on impassively as he harangued them with an ad-libbed monologue.

Alan E. Smith sat under an umbrella in a canvas chair surrounded by eager assistants, saying the same five words over and over: roll camera, slate, action, cut. Occasionally he would huddle with one of the cameramen filming the scene, and they would reposition a camera.

Other than that he did nothing to direct any of them.

At first Will was self-conscious about what he was saying, but after awhile he got into it, passionately telling them about his favorite bands, his love of the Red Wings, the top ten movies of all time, and whether Lafayette Coney Island or American Coney Island was the best place to get a chili hot dog in Detroit. He was actually disappointed when the director announced that the group shot was over, and they were going to start shooting one-on-one dialogues. He was also so excited he couldn't resist asking for feedback.

"How did I do, Mr. Smith?"

"Congratulations, Mr. Harkanen, you are not the worst actor in the world."

Will took that as a compliment and used it for inspiration as the day dragged on and the work became more tedious. They moved to various spots on the farm throughout the day and filmed him talking with the other actors. It was awkward at first, but he soon discovered that he could carry on a normal conversation as long as both parties kept their expressions serious.

In this way he got to know a professor of dramatic arts, a Ford retiree, a middle school teacher, and several laid-off auto workers, along with a number of professional actors who would later have speaking parts in the movie. His confidence in what he was doing grew, but so did his uneasiness about the conversation he would have with Mickey.

They weren't recording the dialogue, and nobody was paying any attention to what was being said, just how it looked on camera. That gave him the perfect opportunity to try his experiment without anyone getting suspicious because he was talking to Mickey.

The plan was simple.

In his time as a reporter, Will had become good at sensing whether the people he interviewed were telling the truth or lying. It was fairly obvious to him that Sam was covering something up, but Mickey was a different story. He had seemed sincere when he told his story about what happened, but Will wanted to be absolutely certain.

If he confronted Mickey with the new evidence he had gathered face-to-face, he would be able to read him and know if he was telling the truth when he responded. Unfortunately this would also tip Will's hand and reveal how much more he knew. He didn't think Mickey would resort to violence, but if he told the other people involved about it and they realized he was still poking around in the past, who knows what would happen.

There was also his promise to Jacqueline to consider.

He agonized over the decision all afternoon, until they set up his scene with Mickey.

By that time they had moved the cameras into the crack house and were filming the dialogues in different rooms. They decided to do something different for Will and Mickey's shot, posing them by an open bedroom window on the first floor and setting up the camera outside to film them.

Even though the camera and director were fifty feet away, and the conversation would be private, Will decided to go slow.

"So how do you like acting, Mick?"

"This fucking bedpan on my head gets so hot in the sun, it's cooking my brain."

Apparently Mickey was upset with his costume, not Will.

"So your brain is being fried but not in a good way."

"You're a funny man, Will. Seriously, I wouldn't mind smoking a joint right now. It would take my mind off my brain. What about you, how are you doing?"

"I'm having a good time. I've been thinking about what you said about Sam the last time we met. You were right, he is a good guy. He set us up with a pretty good gig here."

"I owe him for a lot more than just being an extra in a movie. I wouldn't own this place if it wasn't for Sam. Hell, I wouldn't be alive if it wasn't for Sam."

"He saved your life?"

"The night I wrecked the tape, I was so fucked up I nearly died. Sam took me to the hospital, kept me from OD'ing."

In order to judge Mickey's reaction, Will knew he had to give him the facts face-to-face. From the other one-on-one scenes he had shot, he also knew that their scene together wouldn't last too long.

Time was running out.

"I didn't know that. The day I came here and we smoked a joint, you said Sam would never hurt anybody. Did you say that because he saved your life?"

"Yeah. Everybody thinks Sam is this ruthless bastard. But I know he has another side to him; that he cares about people. He saved my life, man."

"I guess there's a lot of things about Sam I didn't know. I just found out he was into techno music—did you know that?"

"Yeah, didn't you? It's not like it was a secret or anything. In the early nineties he produced techno records with Detroit artists. None of them did much in the States, but they were huge overseas. He used some of that money to make the jump from producing music videos to producing movies."

The afternoon sun was setting, casting a reddish-orange glow on the two old friends. Will didn't have much time left; he knew he had to follow his heart right now or play it safe and miss this opportunity. Whatever happened from here on, he wouldn't have another chance to relive this moment.

"Did you know that before he died, Paddy put together a list of techno songs that Sam produced? And that every one of the songs on that list has a sample from the master tape of the Exits' lost album?"

It took Mickey a moment to fully comprehend what Will was saying, but when he did, his response was immediate.

"That's bullshit! There's no fucking way, man. I wrecked that tape."

Mickey was either a great actor or completely sincere. Will had a few seconds to decide. If he was right, it might lead to the truth; if he was wrong, it might get him killed.

"I can prove it to you, Mick. But you got to promise me you won't say anything to Sam until I do."

Mickey stood staring at Will, saying nothing. After a few moments of silence, they heard the director yell cut.

"You two idiots are supposed to be talking. Fortunately we got some good stuff before you went on your break. This one's wrapped, everybody. Get the camera back inside, we'll do one more shot while the light is still good."

The crew outside began to scramble frantically to set up for the next shot, but Will and Mickey didn't move from their spot by the window. Will had the feeling Mickey was putting the pieces together in his mind. If he was, then he might be figuring out the two pieces that tied everything together—deception and death.

"What do you say, Mick? You want me to prove what I said is true?"

"Yeah. I want you to prove it."

Will heard a noise outside and stuck his head out the window in time to see someone disappearing around the corner of the house. He had no idea who it was or how long he had been there.

Chapter Thirty

The Conversation

Roxanne deliberately avoided showing up on location for the first day of shooting and asked Sam to do the same. Her explanation was that Alan E. Smith needed some time to establish his authority on the set. Sam's last-minute casting decision had challenged his leadership and hurt his pride; he would be further undermined if they spent the day looking over his shoulder.

She also felt that Smith was a miserable little shit whom she wanted to avoid as much as possible, but she didn't share that with Sam.

Instead she enjoyed a day of relaxation and indulgence. She had breakfast in her room, worked out in the hotel gym, and had a massage in the spa. After that she called the car service the studio was using and headed to the suburbs to shop and people-watch. She was enjoying a respectable cavatelli pasta with duck sausage in an upscale suburban restaurant when the head of security for Future Tense Productions slid into the seat across the table in her booth.

"Henry, how nice of you to join me for dinner. How did you know where to find me?"

"Where's Sam?"

"I asked first—how did you know where to find me?"

"Why aren't you answering your phone?"

"I turned it off so I could enjoy my day. Obviously that didn't work. You still haven't answered my question."

"I called the limo company, they called your driver. I thought maybe Sam would be here with you."

"As you can see, Sam is clearly not here. Perhaps you should call his office or his cell phone."

"His office doesn't know where he is and neither does the limo company. He's not at his house, and he's not answering his phone."

"You know how Sam operates, Henry. Sometimes he takes time out to 'audition' young actresses—I believe that's the correct euphemism. He probably has his phone turned off so no one will interrupt the important work they are doing. What is it that you want to tell him?"

Henry Cavett's lucrative career as a security man in Hollywood was built on a foundation of cynicism and mistrust. His most primitive survival instincts told him not to share what he knew, but he also was acutely sensitive to office politics, and he knew that Roxanne had a special relationship with Sam.

"Sam asked me to keep an eye on the new guy in the movie when they started shooting today."

"The new guy?"

"He's a local, met Sam years ago, he's playing the Guardian."

"Will Harkanen?"

"Yeah. I stayed close to him, out of sight, to check on what he did and what he said."

"And?"

"It was pretty routine until he talked to the burned-out hippie who owns the restaurant where they were shooting."

"Mickey Hayes. He's also an old friend of Sam's."

"So when they did their scene together, Harkanen starts talking about music and about a tape that was destroyed. He said something about proving it to the hippie, then he said don't tell Sam about it."

"And that's what you've been chasing around town to tell Sam about?"

"Yeah."

"First of all, how dare you interrupt me in the middle of my dinner. And for what? Some kind of bullshit banter between two actors that you don't even understand? Two actors who were on camera, being filmed, in front of an entire crew? And you think they were sharing a secret they didn't want anyone to know?"

"I don't know. They sounded kind of nervous."

"Two amateur actors who were doing their first scenes ever in a movie—I can't imagine why they would be nervous. It's a good thing you found me first, Henry. You know if you interrupted Sam during one of his auditions to tell him this crap he would fire your ass, don't you?"

Henry slumped back in the booth, the intensity and determination drained from his face. For the first time since he sat down, he looked concerned and indecisive. Seeing his reaction, Roxanne pressed on.

"Do me a favor, don't tell anyone about this. Don't embarrass yourself."

"What about Sam?"

"Leave that to me. I'll tell Sam what you heard, or what you thought you heard. It'll be better coming from me; it won't make you seem like such a fuckup. Now, unless you would like to piss me off any further, I suggest you get the hell out of here."

Henry apologized for his intrusion, thanked her for her help, and left.

Roxanne took another bite of pasta and washed it down with the pleasant pinot noir the waiter had suggested. She knew that the security chief was completely fearless when it came to breaking the law or physical violence. But she was counting on the fact that he was scared to death of offending any of the studio's senior executives, wanting desperately to keep his high-paying job.

She would use that fear to her own advantage.

It would be better for everyone if she was the one who told Sam what happened.

Chapter Thirty-one

It's Up to You and Down to Me

"I am trusting you with my life."

Will was all in on using Mickey to help figure out what had happened thirty years ago, not to mention thirty days ago. His former band mate had passed the truth experiment on the movie set—he was either a great actor or he really didn't know that the tape had not been destroyed. So Will had invited him to his motel room to find out what he *did* know.

But before he could start, Mickey had a question for him.

"You *live* in this shithole?"

"It's not a shithole, it's a nice, clean motel room. And yes, I do live here. I just got divorced. This is home for now."

"She must have taken you for everything."

"The rest of my stuff is in storage. But yeah, she did take me for everything."

"So why do they call this the Motown Motel? It's way out in the suburbs."

"Why does everybody ask me that? I don't own the place; I'm renting a room here. My guess is they think it will trick out-of-town business people into staying here—like it's conveniently located in the heart of Detroit."

"Yeah, that's genius. Out-of-towners are always eager to stay in the Murder City."

"I thought you were a Detroit booster."

"I am. I love the city. But ignoring its problems doesn't make them go away. So tell me again why you invited me here, Will. I liked your idea of getting back together and jamming, but I'm guessing that's not it. Whatever it is we are going to do here, why couldn't we do it at my restaurant?"

"Some of the crew from the movie are still there. If I am right about this thing, there are some very nasty people involved. I don't want them to know what we're doing."

"What *are* we doing?"

"I want you to listen to some songs that were produced by Sam Rainier in the nineties—more than a decade after the master tape for the Exits' second album was supposed to have been destroyed."

"It *was* destroyed. I destroyed it."

"Just listen to the songs, then we can talk about what happened."

They pulled chairs up to the desk in the corner, and Will clicked on the music file he had created on his laptop. He had edited the songs down to the places where the samples were, and the file played them all straight through. Neither one of them said a word while the music played, but Will noticed Mickey grimaced several times, as if the sounds were conjuring up ghosts from the past.

When the music finally stopped, Mickey shook his head.

"No fucking way, man."

"You heard it, then? Every one of those songs has a part taken from the album we were working on."

"This is some sort of trick. You're messing with me. I destroyed that tape in 1978."

"Did you? That's what I wanted to ask you about, Mick. Everybody said you destroyed it, but you were so wrecked they had to take you to the hospital. So the question is, do you remember doing it?"

"I didn't remember anything from that night. They told me I did it when I woke up the next day."

"Who told you?"

"Paddy and Sam."

"You can't remember anything at all from that night?"

"We were hanging out in the studio after a session. You had taken off to do something. I remember smoking a joint, and then

Sam broke out a bottle of scotch. The next thing I knew, I was waking up in a hospital bed."

"From what I remember, you could hold your liquor and your drugs. To tell the truth, you were sort of a legend."

"I never did figure out how that scotch could have put me in the hospital."

"Maybe it was more than scotch."

"What do you mean?"

"Maybe they put something in your drink to make sure you passed out—some Quaaludes or something."

"Why would they do that?"

"Jacqueline told me Paddy was jealous because most of the songs on the new album were mine. He felt like he was losing control of the band. I didn't really get along with Sam the way Paddy did either. My guess is he talked Sam into destroying the tape and kicking me out of the band, and they used you as the fall guy to take the blame."

"But now you're telling me the tape wasn't destroyed. And unless somebody recreated it note for note, it was sampled on a bunch of techno songs that Sam produced years later. So why don't we just go ask Sam what happened?"

"I already did that once. He told me the same thing you did, that Jacqueline is a crazy bitch who was imagining things. End of story."

"But you have these songs now. You can play him the songs and see what he has to say."

"It's not that simple. I think Paddy figured out Sam had kept the tape and used it years later. He was trying to blackmail him."

"With what? Some old songs nobody ever heard? Who gives a shit?"

"Sam's studio deal here is hanging in the balance; it could go either way. Somebody accusing him of being a crook and ripping off musicians might screw things up. My guess is Paddy was counting on Sam being worried enough about it that he would give him money."

"You're guessing about all this stuff. I still don't see why we just don't go ask Sam about it."

"Because Paddy's accident might not have been an accident. He may have been murdered."

Mickey grimaced again, then stood up and walked to the door. He stood there for a moment, then turned around and faced Will.

"You're tripping, man. You're just making shit up. Paddy lost control of his car and crashed. The cops checked it out, they said it was an accident."

"The cop who was in charge of that investigation is tied in to the people Sam is making deals with to get the studio built. Crooked deals."

"That doesn't prove anything."

"When I went to Paddy's office to try to find a copy of the tape, I was mugged. I ended up spending the night in the hospital. It could all just be paranoia and coincidence. But if it isn't and we confront Sam, we could be in danger."

Mickey was still standing in front of the door, but now he was shaking his head.

"That's bullshit, man. A car accident and a mugging don't add up to a murder. I think Jacqueline has gotten inside your head. You need to give this up."

"That's what she's been telling me. I don't think I can do that."

"Well, then just let me go ask Sam what happened. He may have drugged me and screwed you over but he didn't kill anybody. That's crazy."

"When you walked in that door, I said I was trusting you with my life. I really believe that. Please don't say anything to Sam or to anybody. Right now they think I believe what they told me about Paddy and the tape. Don't do anything to make them think otherwise. Give me some time to figure this thing out."

"If you really believe all this shit, why don't you just go to the cops?"

"I told you, I'm pretty sure the cop in charge of Paddy's accident investigation is in with the people pushing the studio deal. These are nasty people, Mickey. We were good friends for many years, I hope that still counts for something. Can I trust you not to say anything?"

Before Mickey could reply, Bob Seger starting singing "Back in '72" on Will's cell phone.

"Mick, it's my lawyer. I gotta take this, it might be about my divorce settlement. Just give me a minute."

Will turned his back and whispered into his phone.

"Baxter, I'm busy right now. Can this wait?"

"I won't keep you, it's just an administrative detail you need to handle. I called your former employer to have them send you the pension forms but they wanted more information. They wouldn't talk to me, they insisted on talking to you. Do you have the phone number for the HR department?"

"Trust me, I've got their number."

"Give them a call when you get a minute, and let me know how it goes. It should be routine, no problems."

"Thanks, Baxter. I promise I will call them as soon as I get a chance. I'll talk to you later."

When Will turned around, Mickey was gone.

Chapter Thirty-two

TIC Bites

Mickey's abrupt departure left Will with plenty of time to call the HR department at TIC. It also gave him plenty of time to consider whether or not he had just made the final arrangements to have himself killed.

His all-in attempt to revitalize his life was based entirely on trusting his instincts, and his instincts told him he could trust Mickey. He still believed Mickey wasn't in on the conspiracy, but he wasn't sure that Mickey believed there *was* a conspiracy. Because of that, he wasn't sure that Mickey wouldn't go straight to Sam to ask him about it.

And if that happened, Will wasn't sure that he would survive.

It was with that happy thought racing around in his mind that Will decided he may as well call HR and get it over with. He dialed the number, told the secretary who answered what he was calling about, and was transferred to the last person on Earth to whom he would want to speak.

"This is Marilyn, how can I help you?"

"This is Will Harkanen. We met at Disney World, you and John asked me about a joke Larry made. I'm calling about my pension. My lawyer said you needed more information, but you wouldn't let him give it to you."

There was a silent moment during which Will imagined she was rolling her eyes and shaking her head. He did not have to imagine her heavy sigh; he heard it loud and clear.

"There are a few more things we need to know to complete the process on our end. After that we will send you the consent forms to sign and return."

"I am happy to help, Marilyn. I can't wait for the company to give away half my pension."

"We are not 'giving away' half of your pension, as you put it. We are following the established procedures, and the law, to ensure this pension is distributed properly."

"Sorry—my bad. Fire away."

The additional information they needed was routine and simple, and he took the opportunity to give her his new address and phone number as well. They finished quickly and as much as he wanted the conversation to be over, he couldn't help asking what seemed like an obvious question.

"Is that all you wanted? Why didn't you talk to my lawyer? He could have given you all that."

"We are only authorized to discuss these matters with pension recipients."

"I understand. Just another dumb rule you have to follow."

Will knew that there was nothing to be gained by taunting her but he couldn't help it. As far as he was concerned, the HR staff at TIC weren't worthy of their title—they didn't seem human, and they certainly were not a resource.

"Your disregard for the rules is well documented. I trust you are happy with the results it has produced?"

Will didn't expect Marilyn would return serve on his taunt, and her smug dismissal of his struggle pissed him off. His first thought was to come right back at her with one of the several vulgar adjectives that came to mind. But that would be playing right into her hands, confirming her sense of bureaucratic superiority. He needed something that would get under her skin and cast a tiny shadow of doubt into her self-righteous little world.

Like an answered prayer, the thought came to him perfectly formed.

"I should caution you that anything you say could be used in a court of law."

"What are you talking about?"

"My lawyer is urging me to pursue a wrongful termination suit against the company."

"Wrongful termination? On what grounds?"

Will tried to remember what Baxter Fineman had said.

"I was under a lot of stress. Working long hours, traveling out-of-town on business, in the middle of a difficult divorce. I shared a joke with a colleague in a bar, and asked a two word question in a meeting, and for that I was fired. My lawyer says I had a breakdown because of you and then you fired me. He is very confident that he can either get me my old job back or win a large settlement if I choose to file a suit."

There was a long silence, during which Will assumed she was deciding the best way to apologize to him. Maybe she would beg for his forgiveness or even start crying. He would never actually sue them, but he definitely enjoyed making them—making her—sweat.

However, as was often the case with women, her response fell far short of his fantasy.

"Thank you for contacting us, Mr. Harkanen. We have all the information we need. This conversation is over."

Chapter Thirty-three

He Said, She Said

Roxanne finally got through to Sam on his cell phone late that night.

"Roxie, why in the hell are you calling me at this hour?"

"Because I know you stay up late, and I thought you might want to know how the first day of filming went."

"You're the one who told me to stay away from the set."

"I didn't tell you to stay away from your cell phone. Where have you been all day?"

"I was working with some promising new talent. You know the drill—I didn't want to be disturbed."

"I know the drill. Whoever it was must have been very talented if you haven't bothered to answer your phone until now. And in case you're interested, the first day of shooting went great."

"Roxie, you sound jealous. Does that mean there is still a chance you and I could get back together?"

"We never *were* together, Sam. We went on a few dates, that's all. It was a mistake."

"The kind of mistake I should make more often. Listen, I have some unfinished business here, okay? The movie is going fine, thanks for sharing. I will be on the set tomorrow. Anything else?"

There was something else but she wasn't sure how to approach it. For a moment she thought about hinting about what was bothering her, implying something was wrong and hoping he would take the bait. Then she remembered who she was talking to and, more importantly, who she was. Sam Rainier was not a student of emotional nuances, and she had not risen to the top in a cutthroat business by being subtle.

Her style had always been take-no-prisoners, straight ahead, no bullshit.

"I do have one other thing, Sam. You asked me to keep an eye on your old friend Will Harkanen, right?"

"That's right."

"So why did you have your security flunkey following him around on the set? Don't you think I can do the job?"

It was Sam's turn to hesitate before he responded.

"You said we shouldn't be on the set. I wanted to see how he did on his first day."

"I had it covered. I had eyes on the set. That's how I know it went well today."

"So we both had people watching things for us. What's the problem?"

"The problem is you didn't tell me you were bringing in someone else to see how Will did. Don't you trust me?"

"Of course I trust you. But tell me something, how did you find out Henry was watching Will for me?"

Once again a slight hesitation, then straight ahead.

"He tracked me down at a restaurant in Birmingham tonight. He was panicked because he couldn't get a hold of you."

"Why was he panicked? What was so urgent?"

Shit. Panicked was the wrong word to use. Sam would definitely check in with Henry Cavett after this. Straight ahead was definitely the only option left.

"He said that he heard Will talking to Mickey Hayes about the tape. It's not a big deal. I think he's just a loser who fantasizes that he would have been a rock star if the tape hadn't been destroyed. He can't shut up about it."

"You're right about that. I'm sorry I second-guessed you, I should have known better. See you tomorrow, Roxie."

"See you tomorrow."

After Sam hung up on Roxanne, he called Henry Cavett and spent five minutes talking to him. He made one more call after that.

"It's me. The son-of-a-bitch won't let it go… She said Henry overheard him talking to Mickey. I talked to Henry and it was even worse than she said… I agree, we have to stop him… You and those morons that work for you have fucked it up twice, we can't afford to fuck it up a third time. We're shooting at the Packard Plant the day after tomorrow. He'll be in my world, so we're going to do it my way… Shut up and listen—I have a plan."

Chapter Thirty-four

Forget the Past

W ill learned about the past, present, and future of the Packard factory from an assistant director named MacGuffin.

It was the future that concerned him the most.

"The Packard plant was considered the most modern automobile factory in the world when it opened in 1903. It closed in 1953 and has been abandoned ever since. In 2123 the Archivists are using it as a neutral site where they can meet the Guardian. That's why all of you are here; we are going to shoot that meeting today. This will be another montage sequence, similar to what we just shot with the Anarchist group. Any questions?"

"What's a montage?"

An older man in a Tigers jersey had asked the question, which made the crowd laugh and MacGuffin frown.

"I am going to assume you are joking and not answer that question. If you aren't joking, I would suggest you either attend the UCLA film school, as I did, or Google it tonight when you get home. If you don't know what the term 'Google' means, ask your grandkids."

When the second round of laughter died down, someone in the front of the crowd asked how big the place was.

"The main plant is three point five million square feet; the area around it includes a number of outbuildings and covers more than forty acres."

After a few more questions that centered on the timing, duration, food selection, and location for the lunch break—it would be served in a tent behind them—Will decided to ask a question. It was more personal in nature and non-lunch-related; still, he was surprised that no one else had asked it.

"Why am I the only one wearing a costume?"

They were standing outside a cluster of trailers on the edge of the Packard property. Will was in his camouflage jumpsuit, standing at the back of a group of people who looked like they had heard a police siren and wandered over to see what was happening. They were dressed in ordinary clothes, albeit with a clear Detroit theme: blue UAW windbreakers, Kid Rock T-shirts, Lions, Pistons, and Red Wings jerseys, Wayne State and University of Detroit sweatshirts.

The assistant director was standing on a small wooden pallet at the front of the group. He waited a moment, shook his head, and responded.

"These are the *Archivists*, Mr. Harkanen. Their mission in life is to preserve the past. As I explained a moment ago, it is the year 2123. All of these people are wearing period clothing from early twenty-first century Detroit. These *are* their costumes; they got them from the trailer behind you. Perhaps if you had arrived on time, you would have realized this. Any other questions?"

Will did have a question: he had been told to get there between nine and ten; he arrived at 9:45 and had suited up in one of the trailers in ten minutes. After that he had waited around for another hour before the briefing had begun. How was that arriving late? He decided not to ask the question; it would only give this jerk another chance to give a smartass answer. But his conversation with Mr. MacGuffin wasn't over yet.

In the brief time he had been working on the movie, Will had gotten along fine with the cast and crew. But the glorified gofers in the executive ranks were all following the lead of their director and treating him like something they had stepped in. It seemed like there was a small army of assistants and associates whose job it was to make him feel stupid and out of place on a movie set. He decided to ask another question, knowing the answer would put this puffed-up flunky in his place.

"Do you know the history behind the name MacGuffin?"

"My great-grandparents were Scots-Irish immigrants who came to America during the potato famine. And if I may anticipate your next question, as far as I know I am a bastard by reputation only. Now unless anyone else would like to waste more time inquiring about my family history, would you all please turn around and follow Conifer. She will show you to the set."

Will was standing at the back of the group. When he turned, Connie was standing behind him, smiling. She bobbed her head sideways and walked off toward the ruins. He followed closely behind her, thinking if somebody told him to 'go to hell,' he would keep walking in the direction they were headed.

The path they followed took them through a devastated landscape filled with the skeletal shells of concrete buildings. Will thought it would be a great place to make a movie about Berlin at the end of the Second World War, if the invading Allied forces had included a specially trained squad of wildly imaginative, sexually depraved graffiti artists.

As they rounded the corner of a smaller building, Connie slowed down her pace to let him catch up with her.

"You keep asking questions about names, Mr. Harkanen. Is that a thing with you?"

"What do you mean?"

"You asked about my name, Mr. Smith's name, and Mr. MacGuffin's name."

"I asked about your name to make sure I knew what to call you, Connie. I asked about Smith's and MacGuffin's names because they are part of the heritage of movie-making, something I'm not sure anyone cares about around here."

"How so?"

"Our director Alan E. Smith's name is very close to the name Alan Smithee. That's the name the studios used in the old days when a director lost creative control of a movie and didn't want his name on the final product. If you see 'Directed by Alan Smithee' in a movie's credits, you can be pretty sure it will stink."

"Do you think this movie will stink?"

"Hard to tell at this point. On a scale of 'Awful' to 'Great,' my guess is that it will be closer to *Plan 9 From Outer Space* than *The Godfather Part II*."

"You seem to know your movies. So do I. My parents used to have movie parties for their friends, and they would let me stay up late and watch them. There used to be a lot of funny-smelling smoke at those parties. I kind of remember them talking about MacGuffin one time, but I can't remember what they said. Was it a movie?"

"A MacGuffin is something in a movie, a person or a thing, that appears to be important at first but ultimately isn't—like our assistant director. The classic example is the embezzled bank money in *Psycho*."

"I saw *Psycho* when I was a kid at one of my parents' parties. They were hippies who didn't believe in rules or boundaries, so they let me watch it."

"They let a kid watch *Psycho*?"

"Yeah, and it scared the shit out of me. You know the scene where the woman gets stabbed to death in the shower? I was afraid to take a shower for years."

"You and everyone else who saw it. Films like *Psycho* are why I fell in love with the movies. The shower wasn't the only groundbreaking bathroom fixture in that movie, by the way. *Psycho* was also the first major motion picture that featured the sound of a flushing toilet."

Connie laughed and nodded her head.

"You're a nice man, Mr. Harkanen, and a pretty good actor from what I've seen."

"I haven't said anything yet. Not real lines, anyway, just nonsense for the montage scenes."

"I've seen the dailies. You have a presence on screen, which is a rare and valuable gift. Saying lines is easy; you just talk.

Don't think about it, and don't act, and you'll be great. Most importantly, don't let these assholes get you down. They're just jealous because you didn't have to kiss a mile of ass or sleep with somebody to get your job."

He was about to thank her and insist that she call him Will when she turned and spoke out again in a much louder voice.

"Okay, everyone, we're here. Please follow me inside and watch your step."

They followed her through a doorless opening into a cavernous concrete building, walking between rows of pillars that supported the high ceiling, past graffiti-covered cinderblock walls. The pillars converged in the distance at a spot where a part of the ceiling had collapsed. Thick slabs of concrete hung down from the floor above, held in place by iron reinforcing bars that had failed to do their job.

In the circle of light that shined down through the hole in the ceiling, Will could see the cameras and crew waiting for them, along with Alan E. Smith. He was seated in his director's chair, frowning at a clipboard, with several flunkies circling around him. Other than this small group of people, the vast space was empty, picked clean by decades of dedicated effort by several generations of scavengers.

When the actors and extras reached the set, one of the men who had been hovering over the director began herding them into place. As MacGuffin had explained, the first shot of the day would be similar to the first shot they did with the Anarchists— the Guardian would stand in front of the Archivists and address the entire group.

Someone helped Will climb on top of a pile of concrete rubble that was directly beneath the hole in the ceiling. They gathered the group in a semi-circle facing him, just outside of the light streaming in from above. There was a camera on one side of them and another behind the group, pointed at Will. When everyone was in place, they turned on lights that lit up the back of the group as well as a wall in the near distance behind Will. Then Alan E. Smith walked over to his camera, looked through its lens, and exploded.

"What the hell is that?"

It took several minutes of screaming and scurrying to establish what had angered the director—the lights had revealed fresh graffiti on the wall behind Will, and it was in the shot.

From what Will could tell from the various shouting matches going on around him, the art director had spent several days adding to the graffiti that was already on the wall to make it look more futuristic and less vulgar. To the multicolored block initials, couples' names in hearts, and gang signs, they added Chinese characters, symbols for chemical elements, and computer code, painting these new additions over the worst of the obscenities. But some unknown person had added something new to the mix, something unauthorized, something that really pissed off Alan E. Smith.

When Will finally turned around to see for himself what had caused this uproar, he felt a wave of fear flow through his body. It was a warning issued in dripping red letters:

Forget the past—or else!

The director was asking all the questions Will wanted the answers to: Who could have done this? How did they get past security? What did it mean?

The head of security was quickly summoned from one of the trailers on the edge of the property. But the man, whom the director addressed as Henry when he cursed him out, was as clueless as everyone else about what had happened. When he could get a word in between curses, Henry kept insisting that the set was secure.

At the end of their discussion, all they knew for sure was that sometime after Smith had given a final sign-off to the set yesterday, someone had snuck in and added these new words. Who did it, and why they did it, was a mystery to them all—

except Will, who had a pretty good idea who was behind it and what it meant. Mickey must have told Sam about the discussion they had, and Sam or one of his associates had left this message for him.

They obviously wanted Will to stop talking about the tape. The only question remaining was, "Or else what?" He really didn't want to know the answer to that one.

The flunkies were once again circled around the director in his chair, discussing their options. They could turn out the backlights so you couldn't see the wall, but that would make the shot look dull. They could paint over the new graffiti, but that would take time and money, with the cast and crew being paid to wait around and do nothing.

Or they could just leave it.

The assistant who suggested this was in the process of being savagely ridiculed by his peers when Alan E. Smith jumped out of his chair and cut them off.

"Everybody shut the hell up! I like it. This is neutral territory, no-man's land. The Anarchists hate the Archivists, they want them to leave. So they spray-painted a warning: 'Forget the past—or else.' It makes sense, it works, it will save us a shitload of time and money. Get everybody back in place, let's shoot this thing."

As the flunkies scattered and began herding the crowd back into place for the scene, they all commented loudly on what a brilliant idea it was. In a few minutes the cameras were rolling, and Will once again began sharing random thoughts with the group in front of him as they looked on in intense concentration. For a while he told them everything he knew about Packard, which he explained was the leading luxury car in America for half a century. After that he talked about the Tigers' chances for the season and the time his Uncle Ed took him to a 1968 World Series game against St. Louis.

Within minutes he was totally relaxed and really into it, having forgotten all about "or else."

That was a mistake.

After they took a short break to reposition the side camera, Will started telling the group about his old band, the Exits. He was explaining how they got their name when he heard a low rumbling sound above him. As he turned and looked up to see what caused it, he could hear the director yelling "cut" and cursing at him. At that point he saw what had made the noise.

A large chunk of concrete was falling toward him.

Chapter Thirty-five

Or Else

Other than a few rounds of golf in the summer and occasional visits to the gym, Will hadn't done anything physical in years. So his instinctive response to the block of concrete hurtling down toward where he stood both surprised and terrified him.

He dove backward without looking.

Will landed on his back at the front of the pile of rubble at the same moment the concrete block slammed down on the other side. He rolled down the slope backward, making a complete flip before plunging into the Archivist extras. Rolling like a human bowling ball, he knocked over several people, most of whom fell on top of him.

For a moment there was an eerie silence, then everyone in the pile on top of Will began cursing and screaming. He could hear the director and crew doing the same thing outside of the pile. As they gradually untangled themselves, the various voices grew silent until the only one speaking was Alan E. Smith, who kept asking the same question over and over.

"What the hell just happened?"

When he stopped asking, Henry, the security chief, spoke up.

"Okay, I'm going to need everyone to exit the building the same way you came in. Take your time, walk slowly, there is no need to panic. Let's move, people."

Will was still lying on his back as the people around him began to leave. One of the extras, a man in a Lions jersey, knelt down beside him, explained he was a doctor in real life, and asked if he was all right. It was a good question, one that none of the movie executives scurrying around had bothered to ask.

Will wasn't sure of his answer, so he did a quick assessment: his head and back were sore and his right knee hurt, but there didn't seem to be any serious damage.

"I'm fine, thanks for asking. Let's get out of here."

As they walked back toward the opening at the far end of the factory, Connie made her way through the crowd to Will's side and asked if he was okay. After she got the same reply as the Lions doctor, she made her way to the front of the group to help lead them out. Will walked along slowly, alone with his thoughts, fairly certain that someone had just tried to kill him.

The loud and animated conversation between the director and security chief, who were walking at the front of the group, did nothing to reassure him.

"I'm telling you, Alan, the location manager and the production designer both checked out the roof, and I looked it over after they did. It was solid. The section that collapsed fell years ago. Everything around that hole is as strong as the day it was built. There's no way anything could have broken off and fallen."

"Were you *not* there? Did you *not* see what happened? A piece of the fucking roof fell and almost killed one of my actors!"

The conversation ended there.

In his lifetime Will had been scared on many occasions: driving on ice in a snowstorm, asking a girl for a date, getting in a bar fight, giving a speech. But none of these things had prepared him for the level of fear created by the thought of someone trying to kill him.

He took a deep breath and let it out slowly, trying to silence the screaming in his head so he could think. He needed to figure out what to do, but it was hard to focus. The only next step he could manage at the moment was literal: putting one foot in front of the other as he walked toward the factory entrance.

Will took another deep breath, told himself to calm down, and tried to make a mental list of the things that he could do to save his life. The possible solutions came to him slowly at first, but before long his mind was crowded with ideas clamoring for attention and approval. Most of them were impractical or ineffective: buy a gun, get a bodyguard, move to a foreign country, go to the media with his story.

The best idea he had was to go to the police, but that obvious solution was compromised by the strong possibility that the cop who would handle the case was one of the people trying to kill him.

Speak of the devil.

As they approached the opening to the factory, Will could see a small group of people, a short distance beyond, walking quickly toward them. He recognized Police Commander Joe Letner, who had two uniformed officers with him. The groups met at the entrance.

"I'm Commander Letner, Detroit Police. Who's in charge here?"

"I'm Alan E. Smith, the director. We met at the press conference, remember?"

"Mr. Smith, we had a report of vandalism on the set, so we came right over. Can you show me where they spray-painted?"

Smith looked confused.

"Yes, I can. But don't you want to see where the roof fell in and almost killed someone?"

"What the hell are you talking about?"

At that point it seemed like everyone began talking at once. It took awhile for everyone to quiet down and even longer to sort out what had happened.

As Will understood it from listening to the disjointed conversation, Central District police headquarters got a call from someone complaining about the graffiti on the set. Because of the clout the studio had with the city, the commander himself had decided to take a team to the factory to investigate the incident. The police didn't know about the concrete slab falling until they arrived on the scene.

One of the other police officers asked the group if anyone had seen anything that looked suspicious. When his question was greeted with silence, the police huddled together briefly, then headed off with the director and security chief to examine the spot where the slab fell. Everyone else was told to return to the trailers and wait in the lunch tent for further instructions.

Lunch was scheduled for mid-afternoon, but after a near-mutiny by the actors, extras, and crew waiting in the tent, it was served early. They were just finishing up the meal when an army of suits marched into the tent. In addition to everyone who was on the set this morning, the army now included Sam Rainier and Roxanne Williams.

It was Sam who addressed the group.

"If I could have your attention, please. For those of you who don't know me, I am Sam Rainier, the executive producer of this movie and the head of Future Tense Studios. I want to apologize for what happened this morning and assure you that the safety of our actors and crew is our top priority."

Sam paused for a moment and looked directly at Will.

"I know this must have been terribly traumatic for you. The police have assured me that what happened was nothing more than an unfortunate accident. There was no foul play involved. So, as we say in the movie business, the show must go on. Mr. Smith tells me he has enough footage of the larger group for the montage, so we are going to dismiss everyone except for the Guardian and…what did you call them, Alan?"

"The Elder Council of the Archivists. There are five elders."

"The Elder Council of the Archivists. We're going to get some shots of the Guardian talking to the Elders in different locations around the factory. I've been assured that every one of these locations has been double-checked for safety. If you're not involved in these shots, you are free to go, but before you do we have one more surprise for you—a much more pleasant surprise than you experienced this morning. Here to film his first scenes as the leader of the Archivists, please welcome screen legend Breed Larson. Breed…"

The aging actor stepped inside the tent to enthusiastic applause, waving and smiling. As he strode to the center of the tent, Will's emotions reeled from anger to outrage to fear and back. The same movie executives who screamed hysterically over a poorly prepared latte were completely nonchalant about his almost being killed on the set. Still, he couldn't help but marvel at the enormous egotism it took to turn his near-death experience into an over-the-top act of self-indulgent Hollywood narcissism.

When the applause died down, what the aging action star said next made the moment complete for the crowd and completely surreal for Will.

"All right, Mr. DeMille, I'm ready for my close-up."

Chapter Thirty-six

Rendezvous With Slivovitz

As the crowd in the tent dispersed, Will tried unsuccessfully to get Roxanne's attention. She avoided looking his way and left quickly. He started to follow after her but was stopped by a sudden realization.

She was on Sam's side.

Will spent the rest of the afternoon filming soundless dialogue shots with various actors for the Archivist montage. He even got acting advice from Breed Larson when they filmed a scene together.

"Don't be nervous, Will. You're not talking to a big movie star; you're talking to the wise and kindly leader of the Archivists. Just relax, have fun with it, and don't worry—people are going to be looking at me when this is onscreen."

Will wanted to explain to Breed that playing dress-up and pretend didn't make him nervous; being a potential murder victim did. Instead he nodded, did the scene and the ones that followed, and somehow made it through the day.

In addition to being afraid for his life, he felt angry and sad about Roxanne. He had no illusions about them starting a great love affair, but he thought they shared a genuine affection for each other. It seemed obvious now that the night of lovemaking was intended to fool him into thinking she wasn't helping Sam. The idea of this friendly, funny woman being indifferent to his death was as chilling to him as the memory of the falling concrete.

It was late afternoon when Will made his way back to his SUV, which was parked on the far side of the trailers. The white Explorer had collected some dust in his absence. As he got closer to it, he could see that it also had collected something else—a note stuck under the windshield wiper. He looked around, picked it up, and read:

Slivovitz wants to talk to you tonight at 9 at the lunch spot. Please be careful!

A few things about the note were obvious to Will: Slivovitz was Roxanne, and the lunch spot was the restaurant in the Book Cadillac Hotel where they had shared a meal. Most obvious of all was the need for caution—he really didn't have to be told to be careful.

The only thing that wasn't obvious was whether or not the note was sincere. The meeting could be a trick or a trap. The only thing that argued against that possibility was the gut feeling he had that it wasn't.

He showed up at the restaurant at exactly 9:00.

She was waiting for him with drinks at the secluded table where they had lunch. He sat down and took a big gulp of his cocktail without saying anything.

"You prefer Makers Mark for your Manhattans, right? That's what I ordered you."

"I'm fine, Roxanne, thanks for asking."

"Are you mad at me?"

"I was almost killed today on the set, and you didn't even bother to ask how I was doing. You didn't even bother to look my way."

"I had to ignore you because I didn't want Sam to see us talking or being friendly in any way. I didn't want him to think I care about you. And, by the way, I did ask about how you were."

"That's bullshit. No one asked how I was except one of the extras who happened to be a doctor, and…"

"Connie? She told me you were fine. She also left the note on your windshield for me. Sorry about the intrigue but there are too many ways to track phone calls and e-mails these days, especially since my cell phone is provided by the studio."

"If you didn't want people to know you're talking to me, why are we sitting in a busy restaurant?"

"I'm the only one from the studio who is staying here. Sam is renting a home in Grosse Pointe, and everyone else is staying at the Westin in the Renaissance Center. We're hiding in plain sight; no one is going to see us here."

"And you trust Connie not to tell anyone? I thought she worked for Alan E. Smith."

"She does, officially. She also works for me unofficially. I trust her completely. She's my eyes and ears on the set when I can't be around. We keep it our little secret so that people speak candidly around her. I find it a great way to know what's *really* happening with the picture."

"So, did anyone tell her they were going to dump a rock on my head?"

"No, of course not. If I had known anything like that was going to happen, I would have warned you."

"That's nice to know. So the next time they try to kill me, you'll leave me a note?"

"They weren't trying to kill you, Will. I'm sure of that."

"How can you be sure? Did you ask Sam? Because from where I stood, it sure looked like they were trying to kill me."

"I was there when the police examined the set. They said it was an accident. A piece of concrete that broke off and fell."

"And you believe that?"

"No."

"So if it wasn't an accident, and they weren't trying to kill me, what was it?"

"I think they were trying to send a message. That's what the graffiti was for."

"And what was the concrete for?"

"To reinforce the message. To scare you."

"Well, it worked. But how is dropping a piece of the ceiling on me not trying to kill me?"

"They didn't drop it *on* you. It fell six feet behind you, at the back of the pile of rubble you were standing on. I think somebody pushed it off the edge, knowing that it wouldn't hit you but that it would come close."

"Somebody pushed the concrete off the edge—any idea who?"

"No, but I know that Sam was involved."

"How do you know that?"

"We were on the set with Alan yesterday, going over the shots he was setting up for today. Sam got really involved with the camera placement in the factory. He kept insisting that Alan keep the shot tight."

"So?"

"Sam never gets involved in the creative decisions on a picture unless he's directing it himself. And this afternoon, when one of the policemen asked Alan if they might have gotten anything on film that would be helpful, Sam jumped in and said 'no.' He told them that the camera was in too tight to show the hole in the roof. He seemed nervous as hell, which also isn't like Sam. That's when I knew you might be onto something with this tape thing."

For the first time since he sat down at the table, Will began to believe his gut feeling about Roxanne might be right. Despite all appearances and all logic, she was on his side. Unless she was pretending to be on his side in order to help Sam.

"So what are you going to do, Will?"

He didn't know if the question showed she was genuinely concerned about him or if it was a way to get information for Sam. In either case his answer was the same.

"I don't know."

"Why don't you just go to the police?"

"It's kind of complicated. I can't prove it but I'm pretty sure the police commander who investigated the so-called accident today is working for Sam."

"What makes you think that?"

It was another moment of truth for Will. She could use anything he said beyond this point to give Sam a complete picture of everything he knew or suspected. Or she could use it to help him figure a way out of this mess.

The Manhattan helped but something more than that kept him going. He felt like he could trust her.

"A reliable source told me that Sam has Bronson Rogers on the payroll. I saw the two of them huddling with Joe Letner—the police commander—at the press conference. I think the three of them are working together."

"Of course they are. The movie is being shot in their district, and the studio is going to be built there. Why wouldn't they be involved? You must have something better than that."

"Did it seem odd to you that Letner showed up so fast?"

"Someone called the police about the graffiti on the set. By the time they arrived, the concrete had fallen."

"So who called the cops? And why did they send the precinct commander and two officers to look at a minor case of spray-paint vandalism?"

"Sam called the cops. I was in one of the trailers going over some budget numbers with him when we got the word about the graffiti. He called the Central District headquarters immediately. Letner said it himself—this movie studio thing is a big deal to the city, so they sent their best and brightest to handle it."

"That's exactly what happened—they *handled* it."

"What do you mean?"

"I think Letner knew what was going to happen, and he got there fast with two handpicked cronies to declare it was an accident before anyone else could look into it. Just like they did with Paddy."

"I hate to keep arguing with you, Will. Believe it or not, I'm on your side. I know Sam and I know this business with the missing tape is bugging him. I have no doubt that he would bribe local officials, or even the police, if that's what it took to succeed. And I know he wouldn't hesitate to threaten or physically intimidate someone, I've heard him do it. But I can't believe he would have someone murdered."

"Then what happened?"

"I don't know, but it will take more than rumors and speculation to find out. Do you have anything more than that?"

Will thought about it for a moment before deciding that, once again, it was time to go all in.

He described the rest of the pieces of the puzzle as he understood them—how Mickey was tricked into thinking he destroyed the tape, the list of techno songs and how they were connected to the tape, his theory of how Paddy tried to blackmail Sam. He finished with two compelling and indisputable facts.

"Paddy looked into what happened to the tape and now he is dead. I looked into what happened to the tape, and I have nearly been killed twice. That's not speculation—that's what happened. If there is anything you can think of that would stop them from trying to kill me again, I would really appreciate if you shared it with me now. If not, it's time for me to leave."

When she didn't respond, Will started to stand up, but she waved him back.

"Please sit down, I'm thinking."

She signaled to the waiter for another round of drinks and didn't speak again until they were served.

"Okay, I might have an idea. Sam is a hoarder. He keeps old photos, movie props, CDs, DVDs, costumes, posters—anything associated with projects he's worked on."

"So?"

"He also is a compulsive note-taker. He writes down everything that goes through his mind: what he's doing, what he's going to do, random thoughts, creative ideas, whatever comes into his head. He types it on a laptop late at night and sends it up to the cloud or whatever you do these days."

"I'm still not following you."

"Isn't it obvious? You need to find out what's in those notes."

"You mean hack into his computer files, like *The Girl With the Dragon Tattoo*? Even if I knew how to do something like that, do you really think Sam writes about bribing people or dropping rocks on their heads in his journal?"

"Of course not, he isn't stupid. He probably uses code words, fake names, euphemisms, that sort of thing. But it's all there, I'm sure of it. There's got to be some sort of evidence you could take to the police, to someone other than Joe Letner."

It was Will's turn to sit and think. It was a crazy idea, the kind of thing that only worked in movies. On the other hand, he didn't have a lot of other options. And he did know someone who was good at these kinds of things.

"I might know a guy. I'll think about it."

"Would you like to come up to my room while you're thinking?"

For the second time that day, everything in his being agreed on what he should do next, including his gut feeling, but his head overruled them all.

"I would love to, but I can't. There's one other person I have to see before I do anything."

Chapter Thirty-seven

Gut Check

Jacqueline's home in Bloomfield Hills was in a subdivision, but the trees that surrounded it made it seem secluded. Will stood on the front porch, admiring how large and luxurious the house was and wondering if he had done the right thing.

He had headed straight to Jacqueline's from the restaurant, determined to get her approval for his next move. Now that he was there, it didn't seem like such a good idea. It was late, he was tired, and their last meeting had ended on a sour note. On the other hand, he really did want her approval, and something more.

He rang the doorbell.

Jacqueline came to the door a few minutes later, wearing a tee shirt and gym shorts. She did not look happy to see him.

"Will, what the hell are you doing here?"

"I need to talk to you."

"It couldn't wait until morning?"

"No."

"How did you find the place?"

"I got your address before the funeral. I was going to send you a condolence card."

"I never got a card from you."

"I know. Stuff happened and I never got around to it."

"That sounds like you, Will."

"Anyway, I used my GPS to get here. Is this a bad time? Did I wake you up?"

"No, you didn't wake me up, I was watching TV—and yes, it is a bad time. You can come in for a few minutes and say what you need to say. Then you have to leave."

She led him through a series of tastefully decorated and expensively furnished rooms to a small den where the local news was on the TV. They sat at opposite ends of a leather couch.

"So what do you want, Will?"

"I want to tell you two things, and I don't want you to freak out."

"That's a great way to start a conversation."

"First of all, I was nearly killed today."

"If you're trying not to freak me out, that's a bad way to begin. What happened?"

Will explained the falling concrete incident, the police reporting it as an accident, and his belief that it was intended as a message for him to stop asking about what happened to the tape. As he did, he couldn't help but notice that her tee shirt and gym shorts were all that she had on. He made a conscious effort to look her in the eyes when she responded to his story.

"So are you going to stop asking about the tape?"

"That's the second thing I wanted to tell you. I know I promised you I would stop, but I can't, not now. I'm going to find out what happened, Jackie."

He expected her to be unhappy with his decision. He didn't expect her to reach across the couch and slap his face.

"You son-of-a-bitch! You promised me you would stop!"

It took Will a moment to recover from this physical and verbal assault. He was losing count of the blows to the head he had taken recently. Whatever the number, it couldn't be a good thing. He needed to choose his words carefully and keep his guard up.

"I have new information. It gives me a way to get proof of what happened—to the tape and to Paddy."

"Where did you get the information?"

Will knew he had to tell the truth. He also knew that he had to keep his right arm slightly raised to block any potential slaps that came his way.

"It was Roxanne, the movie producer."

This time Jacqueline didn't hit him; instead she laughed. Somehow that hurt even more.

"The woman you kissed on the news? The one who seduced you? The one who works for Sam? You're going to act on information she gave you?"

"I know it looks bad, but I don't think she's on his side. She told me about a computer file he uses to keep detailed notes about everything he does. If I can hack into it, I can find out what he did and take it to the police."

"How are you going to do that?"

"I got a guy."

"You got a guy. Are you still obsessed with movies? Because that's what this sounds like—a movie with a really dumb plot that could never happen in real life. You said you had two things to tell me. You told me two things. I think it's time for you to go."

"Jacqueline, it's really important to me that I have your support for this. Please tell me you approve of what I'm going to do."

Her voice shook slightly as she replied.

"You want me to approve of some dumbass stunt that is going to get you killed? I can't do that, Will."

"Then let me tell you one more thing. I have feelings for you, Jacqueline. Strong feelings. I don't want to miss another chance with you."

She slid across the couch and embraced him for a long, lingering moment, then drew her head back and kissed him fiercely. He responded eagerly and she reacted to that, the intensity rising back and forth as they fed off of each other's growing passion. And then, suddenly, she was on her feet.

"It's time for you to go, Will."

From the tone in her voice and look in her eyes, he knew there was no use arguing or pleading. He took a few deep breaths before he stood up and started to leave. He didn't look back when she called after him.

"Will, if you love me, you will let this thing go."

Chapter Thirty-eight

Oh Shit

"Life is suffering. That's the first of the four noble truths of Buddhism."

Will's plan was not going as well as he had hoped it would. It had started out well enough: he found the phone number for the detective who had taken the photos of his ex-wife and set up a meeting. But he began to have doubts from the moment he arrived.

His GPS guided him to O'Cac's, a rundown bar in Corktown, an old Detroit neighborhood settled by Irish immigrants. He parked the white Explorer in an empty lot riddled with potholes, went inside, and asked for Murphy. The bartender directed him down a hallway in the back that led past the men's room to a staircase. When he climbed the stairs, he was greeted at the top by Murphy, who was clearly drunk.

"Welcome to O'Cac's. It used to be the Bier Haus, spelled b-i-e-r; it means beer in German. Some young hipsters bought it and changed the name."

From his brief time in the showroom, Will knew that, in English, bier was the word for the stand they set coffins on before a burial. He decided not to share that fact.

"Why O'Cac's? Is that the name of the new owner?"

"No. Cac means 'shit' in Irish Gaelic."

From the way he was feeling, Will had come to the right place.

Walking and talking with the careful deliberateness of someone trying to pass for sober, Murphy led him through a small room inhabited by a few threadbare couches into an office that was stunning in its disarray.

On the near side of the room was a large desk covered in newspapers, folders, paper cups, and what looked like a partially disassembled handgun. In the far corner there was a table and chairs, and a telescope strategically placed to be able to look out the front or side windows.

They sat at the table, and Will walked Murphy through the events of the past and present concerning the tape. Murphy's response did nothing to diminish Will's growing certainty that he had made a terrible mistake.

"It sounds like you're really pissed at this Sam guy. A wise man once said that holding on to anger is like grabbing a hot coal to throw it at someone—you're the one who is going to get burned."

"As I explained to you, Mr. Murphy—"

"You can drop the mister, my name is Murphy."

"As I explained to you, Murphy, Sam killed my friend."

"He *may* have killed your friend, you don't know for sure."

"And he tried to kill me or, at the very least, physically intimidate me."

"Do you know who the wise man was who urged his followers to let go of anger? It was Siddhartha Gautama."

"Who?"

"You may know him as Buddha."

It was at this point that Murphy began to explain the Four Noble Truths of Buddhism to Will. By the time he finished, there was one truth Will was certain of: there was no way in hell a drunken Buddhist detective could help him. He decided to engage Murphy in some small talk so he wouldn't feel insulted, thank him for his time, then leave.

"Baxter told me you became a Buddhist in Vietnam. How'd that happen?"

"Our attorney friend misspoke. I *fought* in Vietnam. I became enlightened in Cambodia."

Will waited for a further explanation. When none came, he asked again.

"How'd that happen?"

"I was an Army Ranger in Vietnam, what they called a lurp."

"A lurp?"

"Long Range Reconnaissance Patrol—LRRP—lurp. We humped it through the back country looking for bad guys."

"So how'd you end up in Cambodia?"

"The Special Forces were doing covert operations in Cambodia."

"Special Forces?"

"Green Berets. I know you heard of them."

Will was going to say something about *The Green Berets,* the John Wayne Vietnam War movie based on a pop song, but decided it would be a bad idea.

"One of the Special Forces teams got into some trouble, so they sent a few of us lurps into Cambodia to help get them out. We flew into a shit storm; our chopper got shot down as we were trying to land. I was standing in the open doorway returning fire. When we hit the trees, I got tossed out. I broke my arm and was messed up pretty bad, but I was the only one who made it out alive. Crawled through the jungle until I passed out. Some Theravedin monks found me and took me to their monastery."

"Theravedin monks?"

"It's the oldest surviving branch of Buddhism."

"So they taught you Buddhism?"

"The answer to that question is sort of a Zen thing—it depends on how you look at it. Baxter says they didn't teach me shit; I say they did, literally. There was one old monk who spoke English; I got him to teach me Khmer swear words, including shit. He taught me well, I still use them."

"Khmer?"

"It's the language they speak in Cambodia."

Will was no longer making small talk and looking for a chance to leave; he was genuinely interested in Murphy's story.

"So you're in enemy territory, you're badly wounded, and now you can swear in Cambodian. What happened next? How did you get out of there?"

"I was saved by the teachings of Buddha."

"Which they may or may not have taught you. I know all this ambiguity is supposed to help free my mind, but could you be a little more specific?"

"The monks didn't take sides in the war because they followed the noble eightfold path. Like I told you, the eightfold path is the fourth noble truth, which leads to awakening."

"I'm sorry, Murphy, I'm not up to speed on my Buddhist teachings. Would you mind walking me down that path?"

"One of the eight paths is right action, which is not doing something that would cause harm to others. In my case that meant not handing me over to my enemies. They set my arm, took care of all my other wounds, fed me, and gave me a place to sleep. I stayed with them three months until another Special Forces team came through the area. I don't know how the monks knew about them or how they contacted them without getting their asses shot off, but they did. The team came and got me out of there."

"Let me back up for a minute, because I have to admit I don't get the whole Zen thing about whether or not they taught you Buddhism in Cambodia. Did you learn it there or not? And if you didn't learn it there, where did you learn it?"

"That monk was a clever old bastard. When he was teaching me how to cuss, he kind of snuck in a few Buddhist teachings on the side. He must have known that they would stick with me and that I would need them someday."

"How's that?"

"When I got back to the States and I was going through rough times, I remembered some of the things he said. I went to the library and started reading about Buddhism. It got me through some bad shit, and I've been trying to walk the noble path ever since."

"So you're a Buddhist scholar."

"Oh hell, no. Your buddy Baxter knows more book stuff about Buddhism than I ever will. I just know what works for me. Sometimes I make up my own stuff. It's all good."

Will already knew the rest of the story from talking to Baxter. When Murphy returned from Vietnam, he joined the Detroit Police Department. After a legendary career and several broken marriages, he retired and became a private detective. As Baxter explained it, he was sloppy, fat, rude, and often drunk—and the best in the business at what he did.

Despite this high praise, the doubts in Will's mind would not go away. There were many more questions he wanted to ask, including what Murphy looked at through the telescope. But right now it was time write off this idea as a mistake, break off the conversation, and leave.

"It's been great talking to you, Murphy, but I've got to get going. I will let you know if I need your services."

Murphy straightened up in his chair. When he spoke, he didn't sound like someone pretending not to be drunk; he sounded serious and sober.

"You need my services. You just don't think a fat drunk who likes to ramble on about some ancient Eastern philosophy bullshit can help you. But you're wrong about that. I *can* help you. Buddha said there are only two mistakes you can make along the road to the truth. One of them is not starting; the other is not going all the way once you do start. You came here to ask me something, Will—what was it?"

Will was shocked by how accurately Murphy had read his thoughts and behavior. And the quote was uncannily appropriate: not going all the way with important and meaningful things was a lifelong bad habit he was trying to break. Baxter had never steered him wrong; maybe he just needed to trust his judgment about Murphy.

"Sam is a compulsive note-taker. He records the details of what he does every day and sends them off to a secured site in the cloud."

"Notes about what he does—like a diary?"

"Exactly. I'm pretty sure if we looked through his notes, there would be something we could use as evidence, something to show the police."

"So what do you want me to do?"

"Hack into his files and find out what's in there. Like in the movie *The Girl With the Dragon Tattoo.*"

Murphy slapped the table and started laughing. His laughter, which to Will felt like it went on for a very long time, finally ended in a coughing fit. This time when Murphy spoke, his voice was raspy.

"Baxter told me you like movies, Will, but this is reality. Do I look like a computer hacker to you? I'm not the girl with the dragon tattoo, I'm the guy with the draggin' caboose. I don't know ikuh about computers."

Will wanted to ask Murphy what he thought of the movie and also for a translation of what he guessed was a dirty word in Cambodian, but this was not the time for a cinema conversation or a language lesson. Instead it was time, once again, to end the discussion and leave.

"Well, Murphy, if that's the case, it was nice talking to you. I guess I'll keep looking for someone who can help me."

"Hold on there, Will. I said I couldn't hack into a computer. I didn't say I couldn't help you."

"How can you help me?"

"I can find out what this guy is up to and get you the evidence you need. But we're going to do it my way, old school. You okay with that?"

"Will you teach me some Cambodian swear words?"

"Sure, why not?"

"Then I say let's get going."

"Not so fast, Will. There's one other thing you need to know about my plan."

"What's that?"

"It could be dangerous."

"Well, isn't that a part of what you get paid to do?"

"Not dangerous for me—dangerous for you."

Chapter Thirty-nine

TIC Talk

Will was sitting in his easy chair, trying to make a tough decision, when the last person on Earth he wanted to talk to called.

"This is Marilyn from Technart Innovation Corporation calling. Am I speaking to Will Harkanen?"

"You are."

There was a long pause on the line. For some reason Will had a feeling she was gathering the courage to tell him something truly unpleasant.

"Mr. Harkanen, the senior management team here at TIC has reviewed the circumstances of your recent dismissal. I am…pleased…to inform you that TIC is reinstating you to your former position with the company."

"They want to give me my old job back?"

"Yes."

Will already knew the answer to his next question, but he couldn't resist asking it.

"Why?"

"The company may have been hasty in its decision. After a complete review of the facts, it was decided that the dismissal was unwarranted."

"So my threatening to take you to court and sue your pants off had nothing to do with it?"

"As I said, it was determined that the company may have acted in haste. The facts were reviewed and senior management decided to return you to your former position. We will complete the necessary paperwork this week, and you can return on Monday."

This good news made Will's tough decision easy, but not in the way he expected. In the past he would have jumped at the chance to get his old life back, especially when the alternative was risky and dangerous. But this sudden offer of a return to normal made him realize how much he loved his new life of passion and purpose.

Normal sucked. He would try Murphy's plan.

"I won't be there on Monday."

"I understand. If you need to take a few extra days to settle your affairs, that's fine."

"You don't understand—I'm never coming back. I don't want my old job. It turns out I didn't have a breakdown after all. I had a breakthrough."

"I see. You should know that I am authorized to offer you a substantial raise in pay if you return."

"I don't want your job, and I don't want your money."

"Please be aware, Mr. Harkanen, that your refusal to accept your former position will be taken into consideration by the courts if you decide to take legal action. It will make it extremely difficult for any litigation to be successful."

Following his instincts was a risky thing to do, but every now and then it led him to perfect moments of pure enjoyment.

This was one of them.

"You don't have to worry about a lawsuit, Marilyn. Tell the good folks at TIC I won't be suing them. I'm not taking the job because I have a life now—a crazy, scary, wonderful life. Do you know what I'm going to do?"

"It's none of my business or concern, Mr. Harkanen. This conversation is—"

"At the moment I have the title role in a movie that's filming here in Detroit, but I'm not sure that's a career path I want to follow for very long."

"Mr. Harkanen—"

"I've also been talking with some old band mates about getting back together, so I may be joining a rock band."

"We have nothing further—"

"But right now there is something else I am really excited about."

"This is not—"

"I am going to be a private detective."

Chapter Forty

Six Cups of Crazy

Will had explained that the plan sounded crazy to him, but Murphy had insisted that was what made it good.

"Playing it safe and following the rules will only get you so far in life. You have to add a pinch of crazy to the recipe to make it successful."

"A pinch of crazy? This is six cups of crazy. It's a felony."

Murphy laughed long and hard before he replied.

"I wouldn't worry about what happens if the cops catch you. I'd worry about what happens if the bad guys catch you."

It was good advice and Will followed it carefully when he returned to the Guardian Building to put Murphy's plan into action. He was relieved to see that Sam's office hadn't changed, but there were plenty of things left that could go wrong. Even if he executed Murphy's plan perfectly, there was no telling what might happen afterward.

He would find out soon enough.

"You said you had to talk to me in person right away, Will. In my business that's usually not a good sign. What's on your mind?"

What was on his mind was the plan, which was running over and over in an endless loop: Step one was to set up the meeting. Done. Step two was to get them both seated at the table in the corner.

"Do you mind if we sit down to talk?"

"Again, not a good sign. Your meeting, your choice—if you like we can sit at the table."

They sat down in the high-backed chairs next to the low table made of inlaid wood. Will could feel Sam watching his every move, trying to figure out where this conversation was going. That made him nervous, which actually helped make step three seem more natural.

"Do you have any of that single-malt scotch left?"

"You want a drink before we talk? That's a *really* bad sign. The only way I serve Glenfiddich is straight up or on the rocks— which do you prefer?"

"On the rocks is fine."

"Sounds good, I'll join you."

Sam walked over to a cabinet behind his desk and opened its doors to reveal an ice bucket, a set of crystal glasses, and an assortment of expensive liquor. When he picked up a set of silver tongs and starting putting ice cubes into two glasses, Will began step four.

Without taking his eyes off Sam, he casually reached into his left pants pocket and pulled out a square of black plastic about the size of a book of matches. While continuing to watch his host, he peeled a thin layer of plastic off one side. Then came the moment of truth: he leaned forward and pressed the square firmly against the underside of the table.

It stuck.

He returned the plastic film to his pocket, then watched Sam pour generous servings of Glenfiddich into the two glasses. When Sam returned to the table, Will was leaning back in his chair with a well-practiced smile. Sam handed him a glass and proposed a toast.

"Break a leg!"

Perhaps sensing the unspoken menace his toast implied, Sam added an unnecessary footnote that made it worse.

"It's a show business expression. It's *supposed* to bring you good luck."

They clinked their glasses together and drank. Will braced himself for the usual burning sensation that occurred when he poured whiskey down his throat. He was pleasantly surprised when a delightful mellow warmth made its way slowly to his stomach, spreading joy along the way.

This was great scotch.

For the first time since he walked into the office, Will began to think that Murphy's plan might actually work. Then he remembered that the hardest part was next. Step five: convincing Sam that he knew everything, without actually saying it.

"Okay, Will, we're sitting down, we've had a drink. You wanna tell me what this is about?"

"I want to thank you for giving me this opportunity, Sam. I've really enjoyed working on this picture. That's what people in the business call them, right? Not movies, pictures."

"That's right, Will. But we didn't have to take a meeting for you to tell me you're enjoying yourself. You could have just sent a fruit basket or, better yet, a bottle of scotch."

"That's not all I want to tell you. I've enjoyed working on this picture, and I want to make more. I want to be in the business. I'd like a three-picture deal with Future Tense Productions."

"I'm glad you enjoy working with us, Will, and I mean that sincerely. I've heard you're doing a good job, which is great. Win-win, there's nothing better than that."

This was not the reaction Will expected; in fact, it was the opposite. Step five was failing. He decided to keep pushing and hope for the worst.

"So you're going to give me a three-picture deal?"

"Will, before you go making these kind of demands, you really need to understand a few things. First of all, you don't go putting your friends on the spot by acting like an ungrateful prick. That's what agents are for."

Step five was back on track.

"Second, you don't make outrageous demands unless you have leverage. And you don't have leverage unless you can make someone a lot of money or cost someone a lot of money. Can you do either of those things for Future Tense Studios?"

"Maybe. I'm a good actor, you said so yourself. I'm also very knowledgeable."

Sam set his drink down on the table and locked his eyes on Will.

"What do you know about?"

"I know a lot about movies. As a matter of fact, I'm sort of an amateur film buff. I also know a lot about music...everything from classic Detroit rock to techno. I know stuff that nobody else does. My knowledge could be very valuable to someone."

For a moment Sam said nothing but continued to stare at Will. Then he jumped up so quickly Will thought he was being attacked. He started to raise his arms to block the first blows, but instead of attacking him, Sam wheeled and headed off to the liquor cabinet. He returned with the bottle of scotch.

"Freshen your drink?"

Before he could reply, Will's glass had been filled to the top. After that Sam topped off his own glass and sat back down, his face lit up like a Hollywood premier.

"You've got big cajones, Will, I admire that. And you obviously know a lot about the movie business, you understand how leverage works. I'm going to check with my people, make some arrangements. I'll get back to you, and we'll see about making a deal. How does that sound?"

"It sounds great."

"It *is* great—it's another win-win. But I want to be clear about one thing—if we pay you for your skills and knowledge, we expect you will share them with us *exclusively*. If you share them with someone else, we can make things very difficult for you. Do you understand?"

"I understand."

"All right then. Let's drink to your future in pictures."

They clinked glasses and drank, then repeated the process several more times. After handshakes and man hugs, Will left the office feeling calm and confident.

Murphy's plan was working perfectly.

As Will rode the elevator down to the lobby, Sam was completing step six in his office.

"It's me. The son-of-a-bitch *still* won't let it go. I think he's on to the whole thing, he's making connections... Because he talked about old-time Detroit rock and techno... Yes, it was my plan, but none of the dumb shit you did worked, either... They're both morons. One of them was just supposed to scare someone and he runs him off the road, the other shakes someone down for a tape and sends him to the hospital... I know what you want to do, but I'm not ready to put that option on the table... Because he's in the fucking picture, that's why—it would cost too much money to replace him. Tell those two morons to stay with him, but not to do anything to him... When I say you can, that's when. I gotta think about this, I'll call you later."

Chapter Forty-one

Rendezvous in Old Miami

Will answered the call as he was pulling out of the parking garage across the street from the Guardian Building.

"Don't come to my office, they might have a tail on you."

"A tail? You mean—"

"Have you ever been to the Old Miami?"

"Yeah. As a matter of fact, I used to—"

"Meet me there in a half hour."

Will was disappointed he didn't get to finish his story because it reminded him of his wonderfully misspent youth.

As a student at Wayne State University in the late '70s, he had been a frequent visitor to what was known then as the New Miami. Just down Cass Avenue from the university, the New Miami was the place where college students and street people came together to drink cheap beer and listen to great bands. At that time Cass Avenue was just embarking on a decades-long journey toward semi-gentrification and was still notorious for violent crime, drugs, and prostitution. After some disgruntled customers poured gasoline down an exhaust vent and lit it on fire in the 1980s, the bar went on a hiatus and then reopened as the Old Miami. In the years that followed, it became the adopted home of Vietnam veterans like Murphy.

"Catch Hell Blues" by the White Stripes, who had played their first gig just down the street, was playing on the jukebox when Will walked in.

"If you go looking for hot water…don't act shocked when you get burned a little bit. If you really want some hot water, I can help you find it."

It had been decades since he had been in the Old Miami, but it hadn't changed much—it still looked like the party basement of a frat house on double secret probation. The crowd was a mixture of fresh-faced students, grizzled vets, bikers, rockers, factory workers—all of whom would have made fine extras in *The Guardian of Detritus.*

Murphy was sitting at a table in the corner behind a tall glass of whiskey. He did not appear to be drunk, and he did not appear to be happy.

"You did a good job putting the bug in, it came in loud and clear. But you're not going to like what I heard when you left."

"What did you hear?"

"You want the good news first?"

"Sure."

"The plan worked. They think you know what happened and it scares them. As soon as you left Sam Rainier's office, he called someone and started talking about how you are making connections."

"Who did he call? Letner?"

"I'm not sure. They're smart enough not to use names, but I wouldn't be surprised if that's who it was."

"So I was right about everything—Sam ripped off our tape, then years later he let the acts he was recording take samples from it. Paddy knew about it and was trying to blackmail him, so they killed him."

"I'm not sure they killed him, at least not on purpose. From what I heard, they were just trying to scare him. It may have been an accident, like they've been saying."

"Whatever happened, Paddy ended up dead. Let's take the tape to the cops and let them figure it out."

Murphy finished what was left in his glass, then held up two fingers in a peace sign before he spoke.

"Not so fast, Will. There's enough on the tape to convince me that what you told me is true. But it's not enough to get the cops to do anything other than laugh us out of the station house. They're not going to help us unless we can deliver solid proof, especially if one of the bad guys is one of their own. We don't have that solid proof yet."

"So you believe me now—is that the good news?"

"No. The good news is that they aren't going to kill you."

"What's the bad news?"

"The bad news is they might change their minds."

On that happy note a waitress appeared with two more glasses of whatever it was that Murphy was drinking. Murphy raised one and nodded at Will to do the same with the other.

"No one saves us but ourselves. No one can and no one may. We ourselves must walk the path."

They clinked their glasses together and Will took a sip. It tasted like a distant cousin of the scotch he had enjoyed with Sam a short while ago.

"Buddha?"

"Jack Daniel's."

"I meant the toast."

"Yeah, that was the enlightened one. Buddha and Jack Daniel's, they make a good team, Will—like us."

Will wasn't so sure that either pair made a good team or good sense.

"Let me ask you a question, Murphy. If we are going to walk the path ourselves, where the hell is it going?"

"What do you mean?"

"I mean if we can't go to the police, what do we do next?"

"The bug is voice-activated. Its battery will probably live longer than either of us."

"That's comforting to know. What is it, some kind of black-market CIA thing?"

"I bought it on Amazon. It's linked to a voice-activated digital recorder in my office. Whenever someone talks in Sam's office, we'll have a recording of it."

"You still haven't answered my question—what do we do next?"

"Nothing. We sit back and wait for Sam to say something more specific that we can take to the cops or that we can use to figure out our next move. Go home, go make your movie. You should be safe."

Will took a serious swallow of whiskey and felt it make its way to his stomach. The whiskey did not make him feel any better about his situation and neither did the phrase "should be safe." He would have felt even worse about it had he seen his jogging partners from the Ren Cen making their way to the bar behind him.

Chapter Forty-two

The Battle of Detritus

The battle lines had been drawn. Each side was waiting expectantly for the fight to begin in earnest. The moment of truth had arrived at last.

It was time for Will to say something.

He arrived on the set an hour before he was supposed to, just to make sure the assistant director didn't give him any grief. They were filming on a block in the middle of the five-block area that would become the home of Future Tense Studios. The entire block was surrounded by a four-foot snow fence that had *Danger—Keep Out!* signs stapled to its red wooden slats every thirty feet, and a small army of security guards strolled along this perimeter.

Will pulled up to an opening in the fence in front of a large house at the end of the block. He had been told that the house would serve as a kind of multi-purpose production facility until it was time to blow it up. A sign in front of it read *Future Home of Future Tense*, and the trailers that were at the Packard plant were lined up in the backyard.

Henry Cavett was standing nearby with a walkie-talkie in his hand. Will rolled down his window and called out to him.

"Hey, Henry, why all the rent-a-cops? You expecting more concrete rain?"

Cavett quickly made his way to Will's car, then hissed a reply.

"We have reports that a number of violent radicals from the Principals of Entropy have been spotted hanging out around our film locations. We are taking precautions so they don't stage another attack."

"Good to know. I feel safer already."

Will gave his name to a security guard with a clipboard, who waved him over to the VIP parking area on the front lawn, and from there he made his way to one of the trailers. A short time later he emerged in costume and headed to a large tent where coffee and donuts were being devoured by a mixed mob of Anarchists and Archivists.

The tent looked out on a field spotted with random piles of rubble and loose debris as well as scattered clusters of trees and bushes. To Will it looked like a cross between a nature preserve and a city dump. Out of sight on the other side of this overgrown field, a row of old houses marked the far end of the block. At the end of this row, on the extreme opposite corner from where Will stood, was a white frame house that he had been told would serve as the studio's temporary on-site executive suite.

The apocalyptic landscape between the only two functional houses on the block was where the battle of Detritus would begin.

"You ready for this shit?"

Will turned to find Mickey Hayes dressed in his Anarchist costume, including the universally despised triangular metal hat.

"I've got my lines memorized, so I'm as ready as I'll ever be. I just wish I had a cool hat to wear like yours."

"Fuck you, Will."

"Good to know you're not still mad at me."

"Mad at you? What do you mean?"

"The other day you took off when I was talking on the phone to my attorney. I figured you were pissed off at me."

"Nothing like that. You laid a lot of weird shit on me, then you started talking on the phone. I needed some time by myself to get my head straight, figure out what I was going to do, so I split."

"So did you figure it out?"

"Yeah. I'm not sure I believe everything you told me, and I still think the easiest way to clear things up would be to ask Sam about it."

"So is that what you're going to do?"

"You asked me not to, and you're an old friend who I trust. So no, I'm not going to ask Sam about it."

Will was pleasantly surprised by how much better Mickey's decision made him feel. He wasn't sure if Mickey asking Sam about the tape would affect his "should be safe" status, but he didn't want to find out the hard way.

"Thanks, Mick, I owe you."

"Then why don't you come by the restaurant and buy an expensive meal? Afterward, if you still want to, maybe we can jam a little."

"I'd like that, Mick."

"And when you figure all this shit out, let me know. I'd like to find out if I wasted half my life feeling guilty about something I didn't do. Be safe, my friend."

After Mickey wandered off to join with his fellow Anarchists, Will made a run at the donut table. He grabbed a couple of glazed along with a cup of coffee, then found a seat at a table. He was taking his first bite when Connie sat down next to him.

"So are you excited to finally have some scripted lines to say?"

"Yeah, it should be fun. At least we'll be out in the open, so I don't have to worry about a hunk of concrete falling on my head."

"That's true. All you have to worry about are the explosions and gunfire."

"What do you mean?"

"Didn't you read the shooting schedule? The last scene we are doing today is the one with you running across no-man's land to talk to the Army Rangers. Lots of explosions, gunshots, and squibs going off. It's going to look awesome."

"I read the schedule but I thought they would have a stunt person do the running for me. Isn't that what they do?"

"Most of the time, yes. But Alan wants the scene to look as realistic as possible. He wants the audience to see it's really you running through the field. Besides, the budget on this picture is tight. It saves them money if you do the scene yourself."

"I'm glad I'm saving them money. That makes me feel a lot better."

"Don't worry, they'll walk you through everything. The stunt director will show you where to run so the explosions won't get you. The gunshots will be blanks. You should be safe."

There was that phrase again. Will desperately wanted to believe what she was saying and what Murphy had said. But the gut feelings he was using to guide his life these days were refusing to join in this chorus of reassurance. He should be safe—unless someone didn't want him to be.

"I do have to warn you about one thing, Will."

For a moment he thought about stopping her. He was pretty sure he was nearing his full capacity for bad news, and one more thing might be one too many. On the other hand, in his current circumstances, he couldn't afford to ignore any warnings.

"The word going around is that you are asking for a three-picture deal."

"Suppose that rumor is true. So what?"

"Alan and his little flying monkeys were already resentful of the way you got this job through your connection to Sam. The possibility that you might get a three-picture deal is really bugging them. They might be a little snippy with you today."

Connie was right about this second prediction.

When it was time to begin filming the first scene of the day, the assistant director and his flunkies gathered the Anarchists and Archivists together. They walked the group, which had been issued a variety of futuristic-looking weapons, a short distance to a half-demolished house surrounded by a large pile of rubble. When they arrived, they spent a considerable amount of time moving people around until everyone was standing in the right place. Then MacGuffin stepped up onto a box with a bullhorn to address the crowd.

"It looks like our prayers have been answered, god is with us this morning—and on time, even. Thank you for being so prompt, Mr. Harkanen. Do you have any more urgent questions you need answered today? No? Then let's get started."

MacGuffin then explained what the scene was about: the two opposing sides, who had been united by the Guardian, were facing off against the Army Rangers, who were waiting behind the houses at the far end of the block. The Archivist leader, played by Breed Larson, gives an impassioned speech before leading them into battle.

At this point two assistants helped Breed step up onto a pile of concrete blocks in front of the ruined house. The director, armed with a bullhorn of his own, made his way to the back of the crowd, just off camera, and asked a question.

"Are you ready, Breed?"

Will assumed the question was a polite formality; Breed did not.

"Not yet, Alan. Can we talk about my motivation in this scene?"

Will was standing a few feet to the left of Breed, on the opposite side of the crowd from Alan. But even from this distance, he could tell that the director would have preferred to discuss this question before they were joined by hundreds of on-the-clock actors and extras as well as a large crew of production workers being paid union scale wages. When he replied, it was easy to see that Alan was struggling mightily to keep his tone nonchalant.

"You are a leader urging his followers into battle. You are passionate, forceful, and dynamic."

"Okay, but what's that like, really? I mean, how do I convey that?"

It took a full minute for Alan to work his way through the crowd to Breed. When he finally arrived, he spoke in a quiet voice, but Will had no trouble hearing what was said.

"You are an actor; it is time to start acting."

"I'm just trying to get a feeling for what I'm going for here, Alan. Who is this guy?"

"He's the leader. Act like a leader."

"Okay, but how's that go? What note am I trying to hit?"

In the angry silence that followed, Will found himself fighting the urge to offer a suggestion. Alan was staring off into the distance, looking like he was counting to ten or maybe one hundred. When no one said anything more, Will couldn't stand it any longer—he spoke up.

"It's like the St. Crispin Day speech from *Henry V*. That's what you are going for."

"I'm not familiar with *Henry V*, Will. Was it a Broadway play?"

"It's Shakespeare. It has one of the most famous dramatic speeches of all time."

"Sorry. Must have missed it. Not a big Shakespeare fan. Maybe if it had been a movie."

"It *was* a movie—two great movies. With two of the most incredible performances ever captured on film, Sir Lawrence Olivier and Sir Kenneth Branagh, giving the St. Crispin's Day speech to their troops."

"Sorry. Not familiar."

Will was about to give up and join Alan E. Smith in complete disbelief and anger when he had one more thought.

"How about the battle scene speech in *Braveheart*? You must have seen that."

"The part where Mel Gibson gets all excited and starts yelling and then everyone shoots a moon at the other army?"

"Yes!"

"Of course I've seen that."

"That's the note you're trying to hit."

Breed narrowed his eyes and nodded his head, then spoke.

"Got it. Let's go!"

Amazingly he then proceeded to perform three flawless takes in a row, rattling off a long, complicated speech with great passion and precision. Each time he finished, the crowd gave a loud and prolonged cheer, after which the director yelled, "Cut." After the third take he announced that they had what they needed and congratulated Breed profusely.

Then it was Will's turn to say his first scripted line of the movie.

The director wasted no time in showing how he felt about Will helping him with his job.

"Okay, god, it's your turn. Far be it from me to tell such a talented actor and director what to do, but I would like to set the stage for you, if you don't mind."

"I would welcome anything you want to tell me."

"Isn't that special? How genuinely modest you are for someone who has achieved so much in motion pictures. In this scene Breed—who has become the de facto leader of both groups—has just completed his impassioned speech, and everyone is ready to go into battle. But you are their unifier and spiritual leader. When the cheering dies down, they turn to you to see whether or not you approve of the upcoming fight. You don't answer their question directly, but what you say tells them everything they need to know. What I need to know is this: are you ready?"

"Yes."

"God knows how this will turn out—but I don't. So let's do it."

The scene was simple and short: in the aftermath of the Archivist leader's speech, the crowd turns to the Guardian expectantly. He pauses for a moment, then says his line, and they all cheer again.

With the cameras rolling, Will could see everyone turning to look at him. He waited a moment, then said his line in a loud and commanding voice:

"All hail Detritus! What was, what is, what will be… whatever."

He knew they were all just pretending, but the roar that came when he finished his line filled him with a kind of joy that he hadn't felt in a long time. It wasn't just the cheering, although that helped. His life was a mess, he was in danger; an outside observer might reasonably conclude that he was having some sort of breakdown. But this was a moment of validation that made all of his struggles seem worthwhile. It was like the first drink of water after a desert journey—delicious, satisfying, life-affirming.

And short.

"That was *pure crap*, Mr. Harkanen. Can you do it again, and this time perhaps convey some infinitesimal amount of authentic emotion?"

Will repeated the line over and over again, in a brutal and boring *Groundhog Day* nightmare that left him hoarse from shouting. At last the director speculated out loud over the bullhorn that this would have to do and called an early lunch break. They returned to the food services tent, where the donuts and coffee had been replaced by sandwiches and soda.

Once again Connie joined him when he sat down to eat.

"Tell me, Will, why does everyone around here insist on calling it 'pop' instead of soda?"

"Because our parents taught us proper Detroit English."

"Thanks, I'm glad you cleared that up for me. Listen, I told you they might be a bit snippy with you, but what they did to you was really horrible. You nailed that line the first time and every time after that. Alan was just being an asshole and wasting time and money."

"Thank you for sharing that with me, I really appreciate it. But I would appreciate it even more if you told someone else about what happened."

"Don't worry, I already did."

"That's great, thanks. I'm not worried about my next scene—there's no way I can run across that field ten times."

"Well, the good news is once you say your line, you're only going to have to run across the field once."

These days when someone told Will the good news, it was inevitably followed by bad news. From the look on Connie's face, this would not be an exception to that rule.

"What's the bad news? And please tell me it's that I have to deliver the dumbest line in the history of the movies."

"Well, that's true—you do. But what I'm really worried about is that they might try to pull some awful practical joke on you."

"What do you mean?"

"You saw how nasty they were this morning. I wouldn't be surprised if they ran you close to an explosion just to get a reaction out of you."

"You mean deliberately injure me?"

"No, they're not that stupid. But they might want to scare you, make you panic and break character. They would get a laugh, and they could tell Sam you didn't have what it takes. You would get the blame for the delay, maybe even for making them hire a stunt double."

Will didn't want to tell her, but a scary practical joke was the least of his worries. There were people out there who might want to do much more than just scare him. He had every reason in the world to back out of the next scene. But he was not going to back out of the next scene.

In the past few weeks, the vague dissatisfaction he had felt from playing it safe all his life had snowballed into an avalanche of defiant disregard for common sense and convention. He couldn't stop now if he wanted to—and he didn't want to.

He was going to do the scene.

"Thanks for telling me this. I'll try not to look too scared when the explosions go off. It'll be great acting."

"I could be overreacting. The stunt director is a good guy and an old pro. He's not going to do anything that isn't by-the-book for safety."

"I feel better already."

To fill the hours before his next scene, Will waited inside the production office house in a makeshift actors lounge filled with couches and snack tables while various battle scenes were filmed outside. The sounds of explosions and gunfire did nothing to reduce his anxiety, which was reaching *High Noon* levels. Finally, in the late afternoon, he was called back outside to the spot where he had filmed his scene that morning.

The crowd of Anarchists and Archivists waiting there was smaller than it was in the morning, and those who remained were covered in dirt and soot. Will had two scenes to shoot: a dramatic monologue and an action sequence. Based on what happened earlier, he assumed it would be an afternoon of verbal abuse and physical danger, but he was wrong.

There was no verbal abuse.

"The powers-that-be have informed me that, as your director, I should accept a sub-par performance from you and not try to make you do better work."

Alan E. Smith had lowered his bullhorn and was speaking quietly to Will while the crowd of extras looked on. Will nodded but said nothing. Alan continued in a whisper that only the two of them could hear.

"I know you are the one who made the phone call and complained about my methods. That was a big mistake."

The director was wrong about who made the phone call, but Will thought it best not to correct him. Having one more item added to his list of transgressions was worth it if it helped him keep his hidden ally.

"I'm ready when you are, Mr. Smith."

The director got back on his bullhorn to bark out orders and set the scene. He yelled at the extras to take cover behind the rubble and the half-demolished home, and then yelled at his assistants to help those morons find better places to crouch behind.

When everyone was finally in the right place, he explained that the Guardian, dismayed by the mounting casualties on both sides of the fight, has decided to cross the battlefield and negotiate with the Army Rangers.

"There will be three cameras for these scenes. The one you see here will film you saying your line and running off. We'll do a crane shot to catch the action from the side, and there's also a camera on the roof of the production house that will follow your run from above. Any questions?"

Will decided not to ask if there would be any dangerous practical jokes included in these scenes. When the cameras finally rolled, he said his line with as much conviction as he could while trying not to laugh.

"Hold your fire. I'm going over there to try to smack some peace into them."

He was politely asked to repeat the line two more times, with no further comment. After the third take the extras in this scene were dismissed for the day; the final scene would feature Will and the extras playing the fighters who hadn't survived the battle. He was introduced to the stunt director, Jack Vincent, who literally walked him through the next scene.

"I used a football field chalker to draw this path for you. All you have to do is follow the line from one end to the other."

They were walking along the line, which zigzagged back and forth between piles of debris and patches of trees and bushes, making the run farther than he thought it would be.

"Won't the chalk line show up in the picture?"

"They'll take it out in post-production. I want to make sure you go exactly where you are supposed to go. There are going to be lots of explosions and squibs going off all over the place. The line is there to keep you safe—whatever you do, don't wander off it."

The line, which started on the other side of the pile of rubble where they had just been filming, twisted its way across the field to the houses at the other end. After they had walked all the way there and back, Jack asked if he had any questions.

"I'm not exactly a world-class athlete, and that's a long way to go with all the back and forth moves. How fast do you want me to run?"

The director, who was standing nearby, jumped in to provide an answer.

"I'm not really concerned about how fast you run, as long as you make it to the other side. Besides, when the explosions start going off, I'm sure you will find you have some extra adrenalin at your disposal."

In his brief time as an actor, Will had already learned that it took forever to get anything done on a movie set. But the waiting he endured while the final checks and adjustments were made for this scene was excruciating.

A small army of assistants carefully placed the extras who had not appeared in the previous scene at various spots around the field—they would be playing dead bodies. Others ran around shouting "roger," "check," and "copy that" into walkie-talkies. After what seemed like hours of last-minute preparations, the director was told everything was ready to go.

"Any final questions, Mr. Harkanen?"

Will didn't really have any questions, but he wasn't eager to begin, so he threw one out in hopes of starting a long discussion.

"How should I play this scene?"

"Be afraid."

The director emitted what sounded to Will like an excellent imitation of a Bond villain's evil chortle, then called, "Roll camera," "Slate," and "Action." Will began jogging along the chalk line, not thinking about acting at all but still managing to look very afraid.

At first nothing happened.

Will ran down the line at an easy trot, hearing only the sound of his breathing and footsteps. As he made his way around a rusted washing machine, the first explosion went off, some distance away. Not too bad, he thought.

After that the explosions began making their way closer and closer to him. Soon they were going off on either side of him, slamming his ears with concussive sound waves and throwing dust into his eyes. The explosions were joined by squibs, which popped along the ground or off of random piles of junk.

The squibs were getting closer too.

He could feel his fear rising, not so much from the logical calculations of who may or may not be willing to harm him but from the primal terror of being surrounded by deafening blasts and acrid smoke. But, along with the fear, there was another emotion that was growing stronger with every burst of noise and dirt—his anger.

He had turned back so many times in life, turned away from what he wanted most. He had let others do it to him, but far too often he had done it to himself. He told himself that this time he was not turning back.

Then he rounded a corner and the chalk line disappeared.

Will stopped and jogged in place for a moment, trying to think.

The smart thing to do would be to stand still until they noticed and stopped the scene. But if this was the practical joke Connie had warned him about, that would play into their game perfectly—they could blame him for ruining the scene and have a laugh at his expense.

On the other hand, if this was the work of some of his more serious enemies, not stopping and turning back could be a fatal mistake.

He looked around to see if the line continued beyond the spot where it was erased but he saw nothing. He was still struggling over whether or not to give up and play it safe when he spotted one of the dead bodies lying off to one side.

The dead body was pointing.

Will looked in the direction the corpse was indicating, and there it was—the line reappeared by a tattered red couch ten yards ahead and to the left. He tried to think back to his walk-through with Jack, but he couldn't remember this part of the trail. It had to be a straight line from where he was to where the chalk started again, right?

He didn't have much time to decide. They probably thought he had slowed down to catch his breath, but any second now they would decide he had stopped completely and yell "cut."

It was time to do something monumentally stupid.

He began running toward the couch.

The explosions, which had slowed down along with him, began speeding up again. They went off on either side of him, and squibs ripped a line to his right. He was covered by dust, but he was still on his feet.

He made it to the couch.

The rest of his run was as uneventful as a jog through a field being rocked by explosions can be. He followed the uninterrupted line back and forth until it looped around the last pile of trash and headed straight to the back of one of the houses at the far end of the block.

The line went through a gap in an old wooden fence and ended at a small, concrete-block back porch. Will didn't stop until he had reached the porch. The stunt director had told him that the explosions in the field would continue for a short time after he reached his destination and that he should stay there until they sounded the all-clear and came to get him.

Will sat down on the edge of the porch, panting hard. He could feel his heart racing and his hands were trembling. The adrenalin that Alan E. Smith promised had arrived in massive amounts. He was hoping it would gradually subside while he waited there, but that didn't happen because of what happened next: he heard a voice behind him.

"You're in great danger. We need to talk."

He jumped up and turned to see a young man standing in the open doorway. He was tall and thin, with thick glasses and black hair.

It was Brown from the Sun.

Chapter Forty-three

Brown from the Sun

"I know you—you're the guy from the…"

Will hesitated.

He was going to say the insane environmental group that is fighting to preserve urban blight, but he decided that insulting a fanatic with a track record of violence might not be a good idea.

"I'm the guy from the Principals of Entropy. My name is Cody Brown."

Will decided to stall until someone came to get him.

"Nice to meet you, Cody, my name is—"

"Will Harkanen. You're a former reporter for the *Detroit News* who quit and got a job in public relations after making false claims about the police department. We don't have much time; they will be coming to get you soon. I need your help."

Will had seconds to decide who was a bigger threat to him: the lunatic who had hurled rotten eggs at a press conference or the movie executives who had just tried to film him getting blown up.

The tie-breaker was how much this lunatic knew about him. Maybe he was a computer hacker who could help him get to Sam's secret diary.

"How do you know so much about me?"

"I heard your name at the press conference and I Googled you."

A computer user, not a computer hacker. But perhaps a better bet than the people who would arrive any minute and try not to act surprised that he was still alive. If nothing else, Mr. Brown did have a talent for showing up in places where he wasn't wanted.

"This place is surrounded by security guards. How the hell did you get in?"

"Downtown Detroit and the area around it are heated by steam from a central boiler. There are miles of tunnels under the city; most of them are more than one hundred years old. This block used to be a part of that system. There's an abandoned maintenance tunnel that you can use to get here. I'll tell you all about it later. Right now I just need to know if you'll help us."

"Why are you asking me for help? I'm an actor in this movie, I'm working for Future Tense Studios. Why should you trust me?"

"Because the enemy of my enemy is my friend."

"I get it that the studio is your enemy. Why would you think I'm their enemy?"

"Because I saw what happened at the Packard factory."

"The hunk of concrete that nearly fell on me? That was an accident."

"It wasn't an accident. I was on the roof that day. I saw the two guys who pushed the slab into the opening above you."

"You saw two guys? What did they look like?"

"They were young guys, one was black, one was white."

"Could you identify them if you saw them again?"

"Maybe."

"What were you doing up on the roof?"

"We've been spying on this movie, trying to find something that will help our cause."

"Any luck?"

"No. That's why we need your help?"

"First of all, I don't know if you're telling the truth or not, but even if you are, why do you care if they build a studio here or not? It looks like a wasteland."

"The block where they filmed today was pretty much trashed before they got here. But they used bulldozers and knocked down a lot of good houses to make that field you just ran across. And this block is surrounded by four blocks that are in much better shape, with nice homes and successful businesses. If the deal is approved by the city council, the studio will buy them out for pennies on the dollar. Those people won't have anywhere to go."

"I thought you guys just cared about preserving the ruins in Detroit."

"A lot of so-called ruins need to be preserved, for sure. You wouldn't knock down the Coliseum in Rome just because you don't use it anymore. But we also care about the people here too. This whole studio deal is a massive rip-off."

"So what do you want me to do?"

"You obviously have pissed somebody off who is connected with the studio. I know from personal experience how hard it is to sneak onto these sets. Those guys couldn't have dropped that slab and hightailed it out of there so fast unless someone was looking the other way."

"If you saw who did it, why don't you just go to the police?"

"Which ones? The cops who are trying to put me in jail for a year for throwing eggs or the cops who investigated the scene and declared it an accident?"

"Fair enough. But you still haven't answered my question. What do you want me to do?"

"You were an investigative reporter, why don't you investigate? We can help each other, maybe fill in some blanks. It looks like the city council is going to vote next week; we're running out of time. What do you say?"

"I don't know how much I can help you. But I got a guy."

Chapter Forty-four

Jacqueline

Will was on his way to Murphy's office to debrief and try to figure out what the hell to do next when his phone rang.

"It's me, Jacqueline. We need to talk."

"Last time we tried that, it really didn't work out."

"I'm sorry I made you leave. I just couldn't stand the thought of you getting hurt. I care about you, Will."

"I care about you too."

"Then you've got to listen to me. The tape was destroyed years ago, Paddy was in a car accident—end of story. You've got to give up this fantasy trip you're on."

"You're the one who started all this, I'm just trying to finish it. For once in my life, I'm not giving up on something I believe in."

"It's like the cops said, I was hysterical over Paddy's death. I was drinking too much and taking too many tranquilizers. I was wrong. Leave it alone, please."

"First you say you don't want me to get hurt, then you say nothing happened. Which one is it, Jackie—it can't be both."

"Just stop. Please."

"I know this is real and you do too. Stop pretending nothing happened."

"I just want you to be safe. I don't want to lose you, not again."

"I'm safe, Jackie. No one is going to hurt me. I know that for a fact. And I've been working on some things, making progress. There are some good people who are helping me. You have to believe me, it's going to be all right."

"What kind of things are you working on? Is it that computer thing you talked about? What have you found out?"

"I really don't have time to go into the details over the phone, I'm heading into a meeting. I'll see you soon and tell you all about it. Until then you just have to trust me."

"I love you, Will. If you love me, you will stop."

She hung up before he could reply.

Chapter Forty-five

At Least We Didn't Die

Will and Murphy held a pre-meeting in the bar below his office, where a band called Footnotes to Fame made it easy to have fun but hard to talk. The pre-meeting concluded after two drinks and they headed upstairs.

They could still hear the band loud and clear in Murphy's office, but now they could hear each other as well. Will brought Murphy up to speed on the events of the afternoon, including the explanation the studio executives gave him for the missing section of chalk line and his meeting with Cody Brown.

"So they told you that dirt from some of the earlier explosions covered the line? Do you believe them?"

"At this point it's hard for me to believe anything the studio goons tell me, but that story was confirmed by a friend of a friend whom I trust. I'm pretty sure it was an accident. But the slab that fell from the roof wasn't an accident—I know that for sure now."

"You believe what the kid told you? That there were two guys up on the roof who pushed the slab?"

"I believe him. Don't you?"

"Yes, I do. I've actually got a picture of the two of them."

"You're kidding me. I just told you about them, how could you have their picture?"

"The other night at the Old Miami I saw two guys come in and sit at the bar. They were trying to be cool about it, but they were definitely checking you out. They made me too."

"How come I didn't see them?"

"You had your back to the front door and the bar. I'm pretty sure they knew that before they came in; they must have checked us out through the window first. They definitely didn't want you to see them. That's why I took their picture—you wanna see if you recognize them?"

To Will's surprise Murphy pulled out the latest Apple iPhone. He wasn't a hacker but he seemed to be keeping up with the technology.

"I took these after you left. They hunkered down at the bar when you stood up to leave to make sure you didn't see them. Then they waited for a minute for you to take off and followed you out the door. Tried to be nonchalant about it, but they're not going to win an Oscar any time soon—they were definitely eager to get after you. Recognize them?"

Oh shit.

"The black guy, he's the one who mugged me in the Ren Cen. The white guy is the one who joined him. I thought he looked familiar, and now I know why—he looks like Eminem. Why the hell didn't you tell me about them?"

"I wanted them to follow you for awhile, see if I could learn anything, but in order to do that, I needed you to act naturally. I knew if I told you they were on your tail, it would freak you out, and they'd figure out that you knew about them."

"Two guys are following me around, maybe going to hurt me or kill me, and you don't let me know about it?"

"I've been recording and monitoring the conversations in Sam's office ever since you put the bug there. He is keeping these two on a short leash, with strict orders not to hurt you."

"I can't tell you how little comfort that gives me. Did you at least find out something useful by putting my life at risk?"

"Their handlers are too smart to meet with them in person. The only thing I know for sure is that they drive a black Dodge Magnum with tinted windows. I got an old friend in the police department checking to see if he can ID them."

"You still trust the police?"

"Most of the cops I know are honest and hard-working. They put their lives on the line to make the city safe. The fact that there are a few bad cops working for the other side pisses them off."

"They're going to be really pissed when they find out the Central Precinct commander is one of the bad guys. Have you heard anything that links him to Sam and what's happening to me?"

"Not yet. Sam keeps talking to somebody on the phone, telling him to keep the goons in line. It's like I told you before, I'm pretty sure that's Letner, but they're too smart to use names."

"Can't we check the phone records, prove that they are talking to each other?"

"We'd need a subpoena for that, and they're not real keen on giving those out to private investigators. Besides, Sam is shooting a movie in Letner's backyard. There's nothing suspicious about the head of a movie studio talking to a precinct commander about street closures, traffic control, security, all that stuff. The fact that they talked to each other on the phone proves nothing."

"So what do we do now?"

"Go downstairs and have another drink, listen to the band. They're kind of old-school punk, I like 'em."

"That's it? Go have a drink?"

"Maybe two. Then you go back to work on the movie and try to pretend that you don't see the two punks who are following you around. I'll keep listening to the conversations in Sam's office. If I hear anything useful or if your 'don't hurt him' status changes, I'll let you know. And if my buddy gets us an ID on Ebony and Ivory, I'll let you know that too."

"What about this Cody kid? He might know something that's helpful."

"I doubt it very much but give me his number. If it will make you happy, I'll talk to him."

"So that's it then? I nearly get blown up today, and our plan is stay the course?"

"Kinda scary when them bombs start going off all around you, isn't it? You should try it for real, see how much fun that is. It was pretend, Will. If they were trying to hurt you, we wouldn't be having this conversation. We have a picture of the two guys who are following you around. We know they're the ones who nearly dropped a rock on your head. I'm guessing they had something to do with your friend Paddy's accident."

"I appreciate everything you're doing, Murphy, but that still doesn't seem like much to me."

"Buddha said: 'Let's rise up and be thankful, 'cause if we didn't learn a lot, at least we learned a little, and if we didn't learn a little, at least we didn't get sick, and if we got sick, at least we didn't die; so let's be thankful.' Anything else you need to know before you buy me a drink?"

Will had dozens of questions swirling around in his head, but he knew there weren't answers to them, at least not yet. With one possible exception.

"Yeah. Why do you keep that telescope in the corner?"

"I use it in my work sometimes. I keep it in that corner between jobs because I can see the old Michigan Central Train Station out of one window and the empty field that used to be Tiger Stadium out of the other. It reminds me that life is short and glory is fleeting."

"Sounds like you should join the Principals of Entropy. Speaking as an old ruin myself, I love this city and everything in it. Isn't there something you can look at that isn't a ruin, something that would give you hope for the future?"

"Of course there is, but I don't need a telescope to see it. It's all the crazy kids downstairs. We fucked this place up, but they're bringing back the magic we used to have here. They embrace the city—the good, the bad, and the ugly—and bring a wonderful karma to it. They're fighting back against the Nain

Rouge. That's why I want to go have a drink with them. C'mon, let's go."

"Wait a minute—what's the Nain Rouge?"

"He's a little red devil, supposed to be the sign of bad things happening in the city. Been around for more than three hundred years, back to when the city was run by the French. Nowadays these kids have a parade every year to banish him. You know what, it's working. Detroit is kicking ass right now and so should we."

Murphy led the way out of the office. When they reached the top of the stairs, the noise from below got substantially louder. By the time they got to the bottom of the stairs, talking would be impossible once again. Murphy turned to Will before they descended.

"I almost forgot, there's one more thing. One of the phone conversations Sam had in his office was with a woman. It was someone he knew pretty well; he kept calling her 'sweetheart' and 'baby.' He told her she did a good job and that trying to hack into his computer would keep you distracted. Any idea who he was talking to?"

Chapter Forty-six

Roxanne

Will called Roxanne from the parking lot of O'Cac's. "Where are you?"

"I'm in my hotel room. Why?"

"Can I come to your room?"

"Are you drunk, Will?"

"I need to talk to you right away."

"Then start talking."

"Not on the phone, in person."

"I'm getting ready to go to bed, Will."

"Please. It's important."

"How soon can you get to the hotel bar downstairs?"

A half-hour later Will was going over his strategy for a final time as he walked over to where she was sitting.

Back at O'Cac's he had discussed various options for confronting Roxanne with Murphy, and the detective had nodded in approval at his final choice, which was to directly accuse her of working against him. Will did the math and it amounted to a triple cross: pretending to double-cross Sam by helping Will while really being on Sam's side the whole time.

He felt like the Burt Lancaster character in *The Killers*, a naïve nice guy who is duped and double-crossed by femme fatale Ava Gardner. *The Killers* was one of Will's favorite films, based on a story by one of his favorite writers, Ernest Hemingway. It was said to be the first film adaptation of one of his stories that Hemingway genuinely admired. Will had seen and enjoyed it a dozen times, but reenacting it in real life wasn't nearly as entertaining.

An angry confrontation with Roxanne was his first choice; it certainly would make him feel better. But on the drive over to the Book Cadillac, Will had begun to have second thoughts. For one thing, the discussion with Murphy had taken place in the bar with the band playing. He had nodded in approval at everything Will said, most likely because he couldn't hear him.

Direct confrontation also would let the other side know that he knew about the triple-cross, taking away a potential advantage going forward. It might even tip them off to the fact that there was a listening device in Sam's office.

Most importantly, it could cause Sam to have second thoughts about the restraining order he had issued to his two henchmen, putting Will in danger once again.

By the time Will sat down next to Roxanne, he was ready to deliver the alternative plan he had thought of on the drive over. He was pretty sure it would buy time and keep him safe until he really had the evidence he needed. In any case it was too late to change his mind again.

"I hope you don't mind, I ordered you coffee. I'm guessing you don't need anything more to drink right now."

"Coffee is fine, thanks."

"So what's so urgent that you had to see me right away?"

"I have some good news. I wanted to see you in person so I could share it with you and thank you for making it possible."

A waiter interrupted their discussion briefly to serve them a green tea and a coffee. When he left, Will continued.

"I've got proof that Sam stole the tape and used it with other artists. Also that Bronson Rogers is on his payroll, taking bribes in exchange for supporting tax breaks for the studio."

"You got all that from hacking Sam's computer?"

From what Murphy heard Sam say, Will was pretty sure her story about the secret computer diary was a MacGuffin designed to keep him busy looking in the wrong place.

"You sound surprised, Roxanne. You're the one who told me to do it."

"I just didn't think you'd be able to do it so quickly. What exactly do you have?"

"The things you said to look for—notes he took that show what he did."

"Are you going to take them to the police?"

"No. I want to talk to Sam about what I have and then negotiate with him."

"What is there to negotiate?"

"I'm not trying to destroy Sam or stop him from building a studio. All I want is a copy of the tape. It's my music and I want it back."

"Won't people wonder about how you got it?"

"There's only a handful of people in the world who know about the tape; nobody else has even heard about it. If anyone asks, I can just say I found a copy that had been missing all these years."

"What about your friend Paddy?"

"First of all, he wasn't my friend. I don't know what happened to him, but everyone says it was an accident. I believe that and I'm okay with it. I can let it go."

"I'm happy for you, Will. When are you going to talk to Sam?"

"Before the city council votes, so he won't have to worry about it."

"That's next week, isn't it? You'll talk to him before then?"

"Yeah."

"The sooner the better. You don't want to deal with any more falling concrete."

Will couldn't decide if that was a genuine wish or a veiled threat. They sipped on their drinks and talked about the picture. Roxanne had seen the footage of him running through the battlefield. She said it looked fantastic.

"You're doing a great job. Keep it up and you might get that three-picture deal."

"I don't have much more to do, tomorrow's my last day of filming."

"I know—why do you think I'm buying you coffee and not Manhattans? It's your grand finale. You run back across the battlefield and get shot, then send the Army Rangers off in the wrong direction. It's going to be a long day."

"I'm ready for it."

"Have you seen the call sheet yet? They're shooting your scenes in reverse order—you say your last line, then your second-to-last line, then you get to run across the field again. Do you know your lines?"

"Two of the most memorable lines in movie history? Of course: 'It's too late for me, download these coordinates into your Locater if you want to catch the rebels.' And my personal favorite, as Martha Reeves once sang: 'Can't forget the Motor City.'"

Roxanne gave Will a hug and kiss that almost convinced him she cared, then wished him good luck. He left the bar feeling confident that she would once again betray him by telling Sam all about their conversation. By pretending to have conclusive evidence and using it to call a truce, he had bought himself time to keep searching.

But on the drive home, it occurred to him that the hastily conceived Plan B he had put together on the drive to the hotel overlooked two key facts: Once he finished his scenes tomorrow, his services on the movie would no longer be needed. And instead of a truce, his bluff about having new evidence might cause Sam to declare all-out war.

Oh cac.

Chapter Forty-seven

Last Call

When Sam took the call in the den of his Grosse Pointe rental home, it was after midnight.

"Sweetheart, what's up... I told you before, when I'm busy I don't like to be disturbed. You got me now, so why don't you tell me why you've been trying to call me all night... He told you that? In those words exactly... You did the right thing, this is very helpful. I'm glad you kept trying to reach me... No, I'm not going to hurt him... I promise you... Thanks again, babe. You earned your money. I'll talk to you later."

Sam walked over to a table in the corner, loaded a glass with ice from a bucket, and poured himself a generous portion of scotch. Then he sat down in an overstuffed chair and made a call.

"It's me. The son-of-a-bitch may finally have something he can use... Remember the option we talked about before? He's shooting his final scene tomorrow, we can do it after that. Remember, I get the first shot at him. You keep those two idiots on a tight leash until I'm done... We're doing the 'fo' sho' my way."

Sam had two more generous drinks before he went to bed.

Chapter Forty-eight

The Final Shot

Considering he was a dying man, Will was pleasantly surprised by how well the day was going.

Following the inverted logic of movie production scheduling, he began the day covered in Karo syrup blood, saying his dying words, which were also his last two lines of the movie. The scene where he gets shot while running across the field would be next.

The director and assistant director were polite and professional, if a bit cold and impersonal. They set up the scene, asked him to repeat his lines a few times, and declared themselves satisfied. Will was happy with his performance, given the incredible stupidity of what he had to say. He was also delighted that he got to speak his lines to the surprisingly voluptuous Lexie Tisdale.

As promised in the script, Lexie, playing the Army Ranger platoon leader, had somehow managed to get most of her uniform torn off during the fight. After the makeup people covered Will in blood, they spritzed Lexie with a fine mist of water to simulate sweat. Will thought it looked good on her.

They filmed the scene in the middle of the rubble-strewn field he had run across the other day. He lay down on a couch missing a cushion and riddled with squib-induced bullet holes that sat in high grass next to a rusty shopping cart. Will thought the setting made his final line, which was dumb to begin with, unwittingly ironic or perhaps even insulting.

He said it anyway and the third time was the last:

"Can't forget the Motor City."

He closed his eyes until he heard the director yell "cut." When he opened his eyes and stood up, he found himself on the receiving end of a long and extremely pleasant hug from Lexie.

"That was wonderful, Will. You were so intense. It was like we were really there."

"Thank you, Lexie. I had a great time working with you."

This was no phony Hollywood kiss-up; Will was pretty sure it was the most sincere thing he had said in the last fifty years. When she finally released him from her hug, Lexie was covered in a thin layer of Karo syrup that was even more flattering than the fake sweat.

She started to say something about drinks in her trailer when one of her handlers threw a towel over her shoulders and started walking her away. Lexie called out something over her shoulder, but Will couldn't make out what she said.

When he turned to walk back to the costume trailer, Connie was waiting for him.

"C'mon, I'll walk you back."

Will didn't think Connie was in on the high-level treachery that Roxanne was dealing in. But he had been wrong about so many things lately that he decided to be careful about what he said around her, just in case.

"That's it for me, my career as an actor just ended."

"Don't forget your action scene this afternoon. You still have to run across the field screaming."

"It's easy to scream and looked scared when everything around you is blowing up. That's not really acting."

"There aren't any bombs or bullets in your scene. Those come later, we'll be filming different battle scenes all afternoon. Alan is really pushing to stay ahead of schedule."

"Thanks again for helping to get him and his flying monkeys off my back. They were actually civil to me today."

"From what I could see, Lexie was more than civil to you."

"You're not going to rat me out, are you?"

"No. I don't want to burst your bubble, but she does that to all the guys she works with."

"So I shouldn't be flattered by the things she said?"

"Actually, I think what she said about your acting was sincere, and she was right. You did a great job with some really terrible lines. You should keep at it. Have you heard anything more about the three-picture deal?"

"No."

"Well, I heard Sam is coming by the set this afternoon. He usually doesn't do that. Maybe he's got an offer for you."

Will felt a sudden sense of foreboding. Was she sending him a signal? Did that mean she was working with them? In the end it probably didn't matter, but it was nice to think that at least one person on the set was on his side.

When they reached the costume trailer, Will went inside to clean up and change. Connie said she would look for him shortly in the actors' lounge and take him to his final shot. Depending on how he viewed her involvement with Roxanne and Sam, her parting words were either comforting or disturbing.

"Are you ready for your last scene?"

"I think so, but I'm not exactly sure what they want me to do."

"It's easy. Did you ever play cops and robbers when you were a kid?"

"Yeah."

"Then you know what to do—you just run around until they shoot you, then you fall down."

Will found a seat in the lounge inside the house, sipped on his coffee, and tried to battle his irrational fears with logical thoughts.

For a while logic won.

He had, in effect, called a truce. He had sent a signal that he was willing to negotiate and received a signal in return: Sam was coming to the set. The highly skilled private detective he had hired kept assuring him he was safe. Best of all, Murphy was monitoring the conversations in Sam's office, so if his status as a not-to-be-harmed person changed, he would know about it.

On the other hand…

In sending his signal, he also confirmed that he had enough evidence to go to the police. In addition to not being true, there were no guarantees this information would motivate his enemies to call a truce—in fact it might even have the opposite effect. And although his private detective was highly skilled, he also was usually drunk. And most of the discussions Murphy was monitoring were one-way phone call conversations by a very clever business executive who was trying to conceal what he was doing.

Suddenly Will felt as if his logical thoughts had turned traitor on him and joined sides with his irrational fears. To avoid pure panic, he decided to forget about logic and fear, and instead embrace irrational optimism. He had always considered confidence to be a mild form of stupidity; now it was time to make it work for him.

He told himself everything was going to be okay.

This worked until he left the overstuffed chair he was sitting in to get another cup of coffee. On his way back he stopped by a window to see if they were getting ready to start his scene. He quickly realized that the only view this window offered was of the VIP parking lot and was about to turn away when he saw something that blew away his false bravado.

A black Dodge Magnum was parked in the lot.

There was no talking himself out of this one; it had to be the car driven by the two guys who dropped the slab. They were here, which meant it was very likely that he was in danger.

"Are you ready to go, Will? They're all set to shoot you."

Connie was standing behind him, and he flinched noticeably when she spoke.

"Nervous?"

"I'm just ready to get this over with."

"That's the spirit. Let's go."

As they walked out into the field, Will considered his options, none of which were good.

He could tell someone that two thugs were here to either hurt him or scare him, he wasn't sure which it would be. But who should he tell that to? The only people who would believe him were the ones making it happen.

He could quit and leave, get out of town and never come back. But the only good thing to come out of all his recent struggles was that quitting was no longer an option in his life. Anyway, it probably wouldn't make him any safer, and it certainly wouldn't make him any happier.

In the end he decided that the wisest thing to do in this situation was the thing that was the wisest to do in any situation. It was the philosophy that had gradually revealed itself over the past few months, one that he was trying to run his life by these days: no matter what happens, keep muddling on toward the things you value most and hope for the best.

Connie walked with him to the couch where he had died earlier in the day, and they met up with the stunt director, who walked him back to the row of houses where his first run had ended.

"The last run you made was to cross over to talk to the Army Rangers. Now you've finished talking to them and are going to run back to where you started."

"No bombs this time?"

"No bombs, no bullets, so there's no chalk line to follow. You just run back the way we came to the couch. When you get there, you'll hear a single gunshot, and when you do, you fall down."

"A gunshot?"

"It's in the script. You've talked the Rangers into a temporary truce; that's why there's no bombs or bullets. But one of your own guys, an Anarchist, shoots you by mistake. We'll have a camera by the couch, one on the crane, and one on the roof. All you have to do is run and fall down."

"Any special way you want me to fall down?"

"Just drop straight down when you hear the shot. Don't try to ham it up, it won't look natural. And don't worry, if you screw it up, we can shoot the part where you fall down over again by itself. We won't make you run all that way more than once."

"You say 'we'—where are Alan and his buddies?"

"They're getting ready for the shots after this one. Don't worry, I got your back here. You'll be fine."

A moment later Will was alone with his thoughts, waiting for the stunt director to call "action" through a bullhorn from the camera position behind the couch. His thoughts were once again divided into two camps—extremely afraid and firmly resolved. But this time the argument in his mind was escalating into a shouting match that made it hard to think.

He was relieved to hear the call for action and start running.

Will made his way out into the field, through high grass and barren dirt, running in and around the flotsam of failure—heaping towers of garbage bags, stacks of old mattresses, random items of clothing, clumps of bushes and trees. In a number of places, houses had been bulldozed into tangled mountains of wood, metal, and glass.

He had to watch his step as he was running, but it was nice to do it without explosions going off around him. His only concern now was the gunshot that would end his career in the movies.

He hoped that was all it would end.

Will came around the remains of a house and saw the couch ahead of him. On the far side of the couch, the stunt director and crew stood behind the camera. The stunt director was pointing a gun in the air with one hand and waving him on with the other. As far as Will could see, there was no one else around. He suddenly felt much better about his chances of making it through the scene unharmed.

As he got closer, he noticed someone standing off to one side, just out of the range of his peripheral vision. If he tried to get a good look at this person, it might ruin the shot, so he just kept running. He was almost to the couch now, thinking about where to fall and hoping that when he heard the shot, he wouldn't feel it.

A shot rang out and he dropped.

Will lay on the ground, breathing hard and running an emergency inventory on his body to see if anything hurt. His knee was throbbing and his shoulder was sore, but in both cases he was pretty sure it was from the fall, not a bullet. When the stunt director yelled "cut," he opened his eyes and continued the search visually.

No holes.

No blood.

He had not been shot.

A moment later he was surrounded by the crew, being helped to his feet and congratulated. The stunt director told him his run and his fall had looked great on camera—his role in the movie was done.

He made his way over to the couch where he had died to sit down and catch his breath. Now that his scene was over, it seemed preposterous to think that someone would have shot him on camera in broad daylight. He tried to tell himself that he never really believed that would happen, but the memory was fresh and, for the moment, wouldn't go away.

Will was trying to figure out what they might actually do next when the person who had been off to the side while he was running stepped up and spoke to him.

Sam Rainier said simply: "We need to talk."

Chapter Forty-nine

The Deal

Sam led Will back in the direction he had just come running from, toward the row of houses at the far end of the block. He explained there would be shooting and explosions later when they filmed more battle scenes, but his temporary on-site office on the block would be relatively quiet.

He did not say what he wanted to talk about.

They entered the white frame house from the back porch and walked through the kitchen into the living room, which had been converted into an office. Sam sat down behind a massive mahogany desk and waved Will over to a chair on the opposite wall, next to an entrance to a hallway. He did not waste time or mince words.

"Let's cut the bullshit, Will. It's time to make a deal."

"Okay."

"I'm going to lay all my cards on the table, and then I'm going to make you an offer. If you take the offer, we're all square and everything's cool."

"And if I don't take the offer?"

"That would be unpleasant for everyone but mostly for you."

It suddenly occurred to Will that he should have brought some sort of wire or bug with him to capture the conversation they were about to have. On the other hand, he had already stripped completely and changed costumes twice. It would have been nearly impossible to sneak something in.

He would just have to stick to the plan—arrange a truce, stall for time, and keep trying to find something solid he could use to expose the truth.

"So what's the deal?"

"What you asked for—a three-picture contract with Future Tense Studios. You've done a nice job on this picture; we can give you some bigger parts going forward. I said I was going to cut the bullshit, so I will—we're not going to make you into a leading man or a movie star, but you can make a damn good living as a character actor these days. What do you say?"

"What do you want in return?"

"It's simple. You've been snooping around, asking questions about things that happened years ago, things that don't matter to anyone anymore. All you have to do is forget the past and stop asking people about it."

"That's all?"

"That's it. Enjoy your new life as an actor. Go to bars, tell women you're working on a picture, I guarantee you'll get more pussy than you ever dreamed possible. When we draw up the contract, you'll see the money's not bad, either. What's not to like about this deal?"

Will was confused. It was the truce he wanted, but on the terms he had offered when he bugged Sam's office—the three-picture deal. Sam hadn't mentioned the demand Will had passed along through Roxanne, which was a copy of the long-lost master tape of the Exits' second album. He didn't know what happened but figured the best way to learn was to put it out there.

"What about the tape?"

Sam jumped up from behind the desk and started pacing back and forth.

"The tape, the tape, the fucking tape. I told you to forget about the past, so why do you keep asking about the tape?"

"I want a copy of it. I won't use it against you, I just want it for myself. I want to hear it again."

"You have a lot of fucking nerve. You ask me for a deal, I jump through hoops to make it happen, and when I give you what you asked for, you make another demand. You are messing with things you don't understand and with people you don't want to mess with. You don't know my associates, what they can do to you."

"Which associates are you talking about? Bronson Rogers? Joe Letner? Or the two thugs who are following me around?"

Sam sat back down at his desk. When he spoke again, his voice was quiet and he sounded tired.

"I know that ungrateful bitch Roxanne told you about my computer files, and I know you hacked them. I went through them again myself. There wasn't much there, and what was there is now gone. Whatever you think you have on us, it isn't much. I'll deny everything and say you wrote it yourself. It'll be the *Detroit News* stripper story all over again."

Now Will was really confused. After Murphy told him about the woman who was ratting him out, he was certain Roxanne was working for Sam and double-dealing him. Could it be the other way around? Or was Sam pretending to be mad at her to throw him off? He decided to keep pressing and try to find out.

"How do you know Roxanne told me about the files?"

"I'm a very private person, by nature and necessity. I don't share secrets with too many people. Roxanne has worked with me for years. I never had any reason not to trust her until she got the hots for you. She's the only one who knows about my notes besides me. Who else could have told you?"

"But if she's trying to help me, why would she tell you that I'd hacked the files?"

Will regretted asking the question the moment he said it. It was clear that Sam had figured out that Roxanne had betrayed him by telling Will about the computer files. But as convoluted and confusing as things were getting, it still felt like he had revealed something he shouldn't have. The uneasy feeling he had that somehow he had slipped up was confirmed when Sam started roaring with laughter.

"You dumb son-of-a-bitch, you still haven't figured it out, have you? You think Roxanne double-crossed you to help me, when it's the other way around."

"Then who told you I hacked your files?"

"Think about it, Will. Take your time. I'll give you a clue: who's the crazy bitch who has a proven track record of double-crossing you and screwing you over?"

As obvious as this clue was, it still took Will a moment to arrive at the truth. When he did, he could barely say the name out loud.

"Jacqueline."

"I always thought you were the smartest one in the band."

"But she's the one who put me on to this whole thing. She wanted justice for what happened to Paddy."

Sam's response was more laughter. When he finally stopped, he stood up again, walked over to a credenza by the far wall, and filled two glasses with scotch and ice. He handed Will a glass without asking if he wanted it and sat back down at his desk.

"I want you to listen very carefully to me, Will. I'm a ruthless bastard but I draw the line at physical violence. Unfortunately some of the people I'm dealing with don't share my feelings. I said I was going to put my cards on the table and I will. I'm going to tell you what happened, and then I want you to take the deal I've offered. 'Cause if you don't, bad things are going to happen. You got it?"

"Yeah."

"Okay. Here's the executive summary: Paddy was jealous, he wanted you out of the band, but he didn't want you taking your songs with you, he said they belonged to the Exits."

"Why did you go along with Paddy? I was the one writing the songs."

"Paddy was the lead singer, he had a lot of charisma. I thought I could make him into a rock star. He wanted to destroy the tape, but I talked him out of it. I thought some of the other bands I was producing might be able to use the material."

"You didn't think I would figure that out?"

"I was going to change the songs up a little bit and deny like hell if you said anything, but that never worked out. I put the tape aside and forgot about it."

"Was Mickey in on it?"

"Mickey was the fall guy. He was such a stoner, we knew it would be easy to put the blame on him. We even ground up some downers and put them in his drink, just to be sure he didn't remember anything. We ended up almost killing the dumb son-of-a-bitch and had to take him to the hospital. The next day we told him he had destroyed the master tape."

"So if your other bands didn't use them, how did samples from my songs end up on all those techno tracks?"

"Years later I was producing this electronic music artist named Ted Pender; you know him by his stage name: Curtis C. He went digging around in a cardboard box full of old shit in my home studio, found the tape, and really dug it. I let him use a few samples from it, they sounded great, and the word got around. Pretty soon the tape was this legendary underground thing: nobody knew where it came from but everybody wanted to sample from it. And the only way they could use it was if they signed me up as their producer."

"I'm glad everything worked out so well for you."

"It's called the music business, Will, not the music philanthropy. They don't give out medals for being a nice guy."

"That's too bad, you could have stolen one. Let's fast forward. I know Paddy figured all this out at some point."

"He was trying to shake me down for money. Not too different from what you're doing. He thought it would embarrass me and hurt my chances of building a movie studio here if people found out about what we had done."

"Did you kill him?"

"I told you, I'm not a violent person. Letner has a couple of ex-cons he uses when he wants to do something that isn't in the Detroit Police Department's policies and procedures manual. They followed Paddy around, like they've been following you around, tried to intimidate him. We weren't going to hurt him, we just wanted him to come down a little on his price. He freaked out and crashed his car, just like the police said. It was an accident, Will."

"That's not what Jacqueline thought. She wanted me to find proof that he was murdered."

"You're still a big fan of movies, aren't you? You remember *Double Indemnity?*"

"With Barbara Stanwyck and Fred McMurray? One of my favorites. I liked the remake with Kathleen Turner too—*Body Heat*. Mickey Rourke has one of the greatest lines in the history of movies in that one. Sorry, don't get me started on movies—why are we talking about this?"

"Because the woman in those pictures played the guy for a sap, which is what Jacqueline did to you. You thought she was the distraught widow, trying to find justice for her husband's murder. I bet she acted like she still had feelings for you, maybe even fooled around a little. You want to know what was really going on?"

"I'm not sure I do, but I'm sure you're going to tell me."

"She was no grieving widow. She knew what Paddy was up to; hell, she probably was egging him on all along. When he died she carried on the blackmail scheme without him. She asked me for the money herself, wanted even more because of the accident."

"What did you do?"

"I tried to give her a little bit of money, just to help her out and shut her up. But she wanted more, so I called her bluff. She went to the cops and nothing happened. That would have been the end of it if you hadn't shown up after thirty-some years. You really made a mess of things, Will."

"How did I do that?"

"Jacqueline figured you were a smart guy, an investigative reporter, maybe you could find something to give her more leverage. It didn't take long for me to find out what you were up to and who was behind it; she told me herself. After you talked to Mickey, she called and told me you were working for her. If I paid her the money, she would tell you to stop."

"So what happened?"

"I told her to go fuck herself, that you would run into the same dead end that she did. After that I offered you a role in my movie, just to sweeten the odds in my favor. I thought you wouldn't be so eager to poke around if you had some skin in the game."

"But that didn't work."

"I figured that out when you went to see Letner. That's when I said enough is enough. I was negotiating a price with Jacqueline when she sent you to the Ren Cen. That was her way of raising the stakes to get more money."

"How's that?"

"She said Paddy's copy of the tape was locked in his office and that she had sent you to get it."

"Wait a minute—Paddy had a copy of the tape?"

"I made him a copy after we stole it. He put it in a drawer and forgot about it, just like I did, until all those years later when he figured out I'd been giving out samples from it. You want to hear the best part? Jacqueline had it the whole time, locked in a safe at home. She knew it wasn't at the Ren Cen, she sent you there to try to scare us into settling. The funny thing is, it worked—just not the way she planned."

"What do you mean?"

"Letner's associates were tailing you when you went to the Ren Cen. They weren't supposed to do anything but follow you around, but when you came out of Paddy's office, they decided to pat you down and see if you had the tape. I hate it when people don't stick to the script. Once again it was an accident, but you almost ended up just as dead as Paddy. That was the final straw for me. I called Jacqueline and told her I would meet her price if she would give me her copy of the tape and call you off."

"And?"

"She agreed."

"I don't believe that."

"Think about it, Will. When was the first time she asked you to stop trying to find out what happened? Was it right after you took that fall in the Ren Cen? I'm betting it was because that's when we made the deal. Unfortunately the only thing she delivered on was the tape. She couldn't get you to stop. So here we are, I'm asking you to stop. Take the deal."

Between the good scotch and the bad news, Will's mind was beginning to get a little fuzzy. For the second time in his life, he had been played big time by Jacqueline. But right now he couldn't afford to indulge in self-pity. He had to keep muddling through.

"Just to be clear—a three-picture contract *and* a copy of the tape?"

"Holy shit, Will, you really don't understand who you're fucking with here, do you? You are not in a position to make demands. I'm going to excuse your ignorance, but you better wise up in a hurry because my associates will not do the same."

Sam took a big drink of scotch, then set down the empty glass. He sighed, then spoke again.

"All right, I'll give you the contract and the tape, but I never want to hear about any of this shit ever again, you understand?"

"I understand. I do have one more favor to ask. Can you let your two goons know we have a deal before I leave your office? I'd hate to have an accident on my walk back."

"Don't worry, they have standing orders not to come onto the grounds here."

"Well, then they must not be following the script again because I saw their car in the parking lot earlier today."

"Bullshit."

"Black Dodge Magnum. Tinted glass."

Sam stood up and hurried around his desk, motioning to Will. "C'mon, let's get out of here."

Will started to follow behind Sam but ended up almost knocking him over when he stopped in his tracks. The two men Murphy had taken a picture of in the bar were standing in the doorway to the kitchen, pointing guns at them. The Marshal Mathers look-alike said nothing, leaving it to the Renaissance Man to greet them.

"We met but I don't believe we've been formally introduced, Mr. Harkanen. We're the violent associates Mr. Rainier has been warning you about."

Chapter Fifty

The Battle of Detroit

"It's okay, fellas, I got this covered. Your services aren't needed here."

Sam waved them away with one hand, but the two gunmen didn't move.

"Shut the fuck up and sit your ass down. You're not in charge anymore. How did you say it—we're not following the script anymore."

Sam returned to his seat behind the desk; Will sat back down in the chair. Marshal Mathers sat down on a couch to Will's right, on the other side of the entrance to the hallway. The gunman who had started chasing Will around the Ren Cen remained standing in the kitchen doorway and did the talking for the two of them.

"We followed you in here, heard everything you said. You really are a dumb shit, aren't you, Rainier? You just made a full confession to the guy who's been trying to nail your ass. How stupid is that?"

"He knew everything already. I filled in a few details to help close the deal, make sure there were no more itches he needed to scratch. We're all set now, we have an agreement—it's over."

"You're half right. It's over for him."

"I've said all along I didn't want any violence. You don't have my approval for that."

"We don't need your approval, we ain't working for you. The guy we're working for wasn't too happy with your plan to begin with; he told us to keep an eye on things. When we texted him and told him you were spilling your guts and naming names, he was very unhappy. So unhappy that he made up a new plan."

"What are you going to do?"

"It's real simple. We're going to wait here for fifteen minutes while the coast gets cleared. Then the boss is going to pull into the driveway with a car for us, and my partner and I are going to take Mr. Harkanen for a ride. You and the boss are going to wait here another fifteen minutes, then go back to your movie set. When they ask, you tell them Will left before you did, and you didn't see him after that."

"What if I tell you I'm not going along with your plan?"

"Boss says if you don't like it, then you can come along on the ride with us."

"What, you're going to kill me? Are you out of your mind? Do you know—"

"Shut the fuck up!"

The Renaissance Man stepped forward and pointed his gun at Sam's head.

"We ain't having a debate here. Do you understand the plan?"

Sam slumped down in his chair, looking pale. He looked at Will, then the gunman, then nodded his head yes.

"Are you in?"

Another head nod yes.

"Any questions?"

Sam shook his head no, and the Renaissance Man stepped back and lowered his gun.

"I'm glad you like our plan. We'll be out of here in a few minutes, then you can go back to making your movie."

As they sat in silence, Will began to gradually regain control of his mind and emotions, moving from shock to terror to panic to dread. He forced himself to breathe slowly, which worked, and forbid himself from making second guesses, which didn't work.

A lifetime of playing it safe, if nothing else, had at least given him a lifetime. Whatever hippie-dippy pipedream he had pursued for the last few months—live your dreams, follow your bliss, grab for the gusto—was about to get him killed. With great effort he let these thoughts come and go, and tried to focus on what it would take to keep muddling through.

He began looking around the room to think of an escape plan. Sam's desk was in front of him; the Renaissance Man stood in the kitchen doorway to the right of it. The front door to the house was beyond Sam and to the left, at the far side of the room.

Too far to run from a man with a gun.

To Will's immediate right was the entrance to a hallway that went around a corner. He had seen a second back door when they came in; most likely the hallway would take him there. But Slim Shady was sitting on the couch on the other side of the hallway entrance. He could get there as fast as Will could—or remain seated comfortably on the couch and shoot him at close range.

Will was concentrating so hard on what to do next that the Renaissance Man startled him when he spoke.

"What you looking at, man? You thinking of running away again? This ain't a cell phone, I got a real gun this time. You need to relax, understand? Otherwise we'll have to end it right here."

Will nodded. He quit looking around but he didn't quit trying to come up with a plan. For awhile he tried to think of a movie that would help him figure out what to do, but the horrific reality he faced made it clear that distracting nonsense was no longer acceptable—it was up to Will to create this scene himself. After an eternity passed, he was startled out of his thoughts again, this time by the man on the couch.

"Hey, man, what was that line?"

"What?"

"You said something about one of the greatest lines in the history of the movies, but you didn't say the line. What was it?"

Despite his circumstances, Will had to smile. The line was eerily appropriate for the occasion. For a moment he wondered if he should say it and run the risk of pissing them off. Then he thought, what are they going to do, kill me?

"In the movie *Body Heat*, William Hurt hires Mickey Rourke to help him murder someone. They talk about it for a while, then Mickey says, 'Anytime you try a decent crime, you've got fifty ways to fuck up. If you figure out twenty-five of them, you're a genius, and you ain't no genius.'"

Slim Shady starting laughing but Renaissance Man cut him off.

"Shut up, man. That shit ain't funny. We got about five minutes left. Everybody just shut the fuck up."

It took everything Will had to ride out the wave of fear that flooded his body. He tried to concentrate on what to do next but nothing came to him. He had just about given up trying to think of something when the shots rang out.

"What the hell is that?"

Renaissance Man went to the window behind Sam's desk, pushed open a tiny crack in the curtains, and looked out. From what Will had seen of the shooting schedule, he was pretty sure the shots were coming from the far end of the block but they sounded much closer. When they continued and were joined by screams and shouts, Eminem got up off the couch to have a look. A moment later they were both peering out through the curtain with their backs to Will.

He had a few seconds to decide what to do with the rest of his life. He decided it was time to take a proactive, positive approach in pursuing his aspirations.

He ran.

In one swift movement he jumped up, pivoted to his right, and began running down the hallway. He heard someone yell "hey"—could it have been Sam?—and then heard gunshots behind him. As he turned the corner at the end of the hall, he felt a sharp sting in his right shoulder.

He kept running.

In this hallway there were doors on the left and a staircase on the right. More importantly, what he was praying for—the door to the outside—was at the far end. He made one more quick prayer, and it was answered: the door wasn't locked. He burst through it, jumped off the small wooden porch, and headed for the fallen remains of a cinderblock wall that was straight ahead.

As he ran through an opening in the wall, he heard more gunshots behind him, and a couple of spots on the wall exploded in dust. He was surprised at how calmly he noted they were not squibs.

On the other side of the wall, he took a hard left and kept running. He was headed toward the rubble-strewn field, hoping to find a place to hide. He thought about screaming for help, but decided it wouldn't be noticed while the battle scene was being filmed on the other side of the field, and it might give his position away. He crashed through a clump of bushes, climbed over a pile of bricks, and jumped down into the remains of a basement crawl space filled with random junk.

The space was an open hole about four feet deep that matched the dimensions of the house that once stood above it. It was lined with a short cinderblock wall; the floor was dirt. He made his way on his hands and knees to a corner and slid under what once, in another lifetime, had been a coffee table. He reached around with his left hand and shuddered when he felt wetness on his right shoulder. He pushed down hard to stop the bleeding and nearly screamed from the pain. The next minute was spent trying to quiet his breathing while pressing firmly on the wound.

Then he heard footsteps.

He tilted his head and peered through a small opening in the pile of garbage that was heaped in front of the table. The Renaissance Man was crouched down and walking slowly past the far side of the crawl space with his gun drawn. Will pulled his face back, waited and listened. The steps kept going, then faded away. In the distance an occasional gunshot still rang out.

If he didn't bleed to death, maybe he could wait them out.

He had just closed his eyes to settle in and wait when he heard someone whisper from a few feet away.

"Will, you okay?"

It took all he had in him not to scream or try to run. Instead he turned his head toward the sound and saw Murphy crawling toward him with a gun in his hand. Murphy stopped short when he saw the blood, then pulled off his coat and began tying it around Will's shoulder.

"I'm sorry I'm late. I didn't listen to what the bug picked up last night until this morning. It didn't sound good so I tried to call you."

"My phone is with my clothes in the costume trailer."

"I figured something like that was going on, so I rushed right over here, but the bastards wouldn't let me in. They got rent-a-cops all over the place."

"So how'd you get in?"

"I remembered you telling me how your friend the egg man had snuck in here. I called the number you gave me, and he told me where to find the steam tunnel entrance. It's pretty cool, I went through the tunnel and came up inside the perimeter not too far from here."

"So what do we do now?"

"There's two of them, right? The guys I spotted in the bar."

"Yeah, and they've got guns."

"Well, we can't wait around for someone to find us. Not to alarm you, but if we do that, you're going to bleed to death."

"Why don't you call the cops?"

"The average response time for a 911 call to the police in this city is fifty-eight minutes. Ambulances aren't much better. Same thing as just waiting—you would bleed to death before they got here."

"Then I really hope you have a better plan."

"Of course I do. My car's not far from here. I'm going to take care of them, and then I'll come get you and take you to a doctor."

"If you leave me alone here, they might find me and kill me."

"I thought of that too—take this."

Murphy handed Will a heavy gun with a long barrel and gave him instructions that weren't really necessary.

"If you see them, shoot them."

"But if I take your gun, what will you do?"

Murphy reached down and pulled up his pants leg, revealing a large knife in a sheath strapped to his calf. He took it out and held it up.

"This is all I need. Maybe not even this. See you in a few minutes."

Of all the dumb plans they had tried, this one seemed like the dumbest by far to Will. One old fat guy with a knife against two young men with guns in a field of broken dreams being used to make movie magic. But as Murphy crawled away, Will was too weak to protest or to think of anything else they could do. The intense pain was beginning to fade, and in its place came an overwhelming sleepiness. The coat tourniquet Murphy had tied around his shoulder was helping to slow the bleeding, but he couldn't have a whole lot of time left.

He hoped Murphy knew what he was doing.

Will drifted in and out of consciousness, holding up the gun when he was awake, dropping it back down when he wasn't.

Finally he drifted out and didn't drift back.

Minutes or hours later—he wasn't sure which—he heard voices that snapped him awake. It was two men, talking in heated whispers, but close enough for Will to identify them.

Sam Rainier and Joe Letner.

Chapter Fifty-one

The Good, the Bad, and the Baddest

The two men couldn't be very far away from Will; even in his semi-conscious state, he could hear everything they said. Letner was doing most of the talking, berating Sam for trying to make a deal with Will, then not stopping him when he ran.

"I told you, Joe, I tried to warn them he was taking off."

"You think I give a shit about what you *tried* to do? 'Cause here's what you *did*: you gave him a full confession, then you let him get away."

"Look, you can blame me all you want for what's happened. The question is what are we going to do now? I don't want any more shooting or killing. I never wanted any of that."

"What are *we* going to do now? You think you still have any say in this?"

"Okay, what are *you* going to do now?"

"We're going to mop up your mistakes and finish this thing up for good."

"Are they going to kill him?"

"What do you think?"

As if on cue, several gunshots rang out in the distance.

"Was that them?" Sam asked.

Joe Letner laughed.

"Mr. Big Shot Producer, you don't recognize the sounds of a movie being made? That's your actor friends playing army on the other side of the block. Lucky break for me, not so lucky for you."

"What do you mean?"

"Hearing those gunshots gives me an idea. I want to go help find that son-of-a-bitch Harkanen, but there's a loose end I need to tie up before I do."

"What are you talking about, Joe?"

"You've already confessed once. I'm not going to give you a chance to do it again."

"What, you're going to shoot me? Are you crazy?"

With great effort and considerable pain, Will scooted forward and peered around the corner of the coffee table he was lying under. He looked up and saw the two men standing twenty feet away at the edge of the basement crawl space he was hiding in. Joe Letner had his back to where Will was hiding.

He was holding a gun on Sam.

"I was going to wait until after the guys took care of Harkanen and we all drove off together. But now that I think about it, you're kind of the nervous type, aren't you? You might not be that eager to go for a ride with a dead body in the car. Maybe you'd do something stupid, try to get away or yell for help or something. Plenty of room for two bodies in the trunk, gunshots going off all over the place, so why not do it now?"

With a growing sense of horror, Will realized that he was going to have to make a life-and-death decision, and make it quickly. Actually there were two decisions to make: whether or not to try to stop Letner, and if he did want to stop him, whether or not he had the strength left to do it.

Sam was unwittingly buying Will time to decide by doing what he did best: arguing and negotiating.

"You're going to shoot me in broad daylight with all these people around? You'll never get away with it."

"You'd be surprised what you can get away with if you know what you're doing. They're still looking for Jimmy Hoffa, aren't they? Nobody ever did any time for that one."

"What about all the money I've given you? There's more where that came from, you can name your price."

"All the money in the world isn't going to help a cop who goes to prison. You talk too much, Sam, I can't take that chance."

It was now or never for Will.

He rolled out from under the table, stood up, and with great effort, lifted Murphy's gun and pointed it at Letner.

"If you move I will shoot you. Lower your gun."

Letner lowered his gun and turned his head slowly.

"Is that you, Harkanen? It is you, and you've got a gun. You think you can shoot me before I turn around and shoot you?"

"Let's find out, Letner."

"Ordinarily that's a chance I would love to take, but it looks like I won't have to. That's not fake movie blood all over your shirt. So now we know that you got shot when you ran away, and you've lost a lot of blood. Which makes me wonder: how long can you stand there pointing that gun at me?"

"Either way's fine with me. I've got all day."

Will hoped his voice projected confidence, because his body was sending a very different message. Stars were swirling in front of his eyes, and a thousand red-hot needles were tearing into his right shoulder. His left arm, which was pointing the gun at Letner, was trembling.

He didn't have long and Letner knew it.

"Why don't you just shoot me, Harkanen? Don't want to shoot a man in the back in cold blood? That's very noble of you. I was counting on your moral code to screw you over again. Before you pass out, I want to thank you for helping me."

Will didn't have much strength left, but he knew he had to stay engaged in the conversation or Letner would decide he was too weak to be a threat, turn around, and shoot.

"Are you going to tell me how I'm helping you, Letner, or do I have to guess?"

"When you pass out, I'm going to shoot you with my gun, and then I'll shoot Sam with your gun. Wipe 'em clean, stick 'em in the appropriate dead man's hands, and presto—you've got yourself a fatal shootout. Explains everything nice and neatly and saves me the trouble of hauling bodies around."

Will wanted to point out that he had another wound from a different gun in his shoulder, but he was sure Letner would have a ready reply—and he wasn't sure he had the strength to keep talking.

The stars were getting brighter, and his vision was starting to blur.

"What's the matter, Harkanen, you running out of things to say? Or maybe you're running out of blood. Is it time for us to have that shooting competition we were talking about? I think we should wait a little longer."

As he finished the sentence, Letner ducked and began to spin around, raising his gun as he turned. Will followed Letner's movements with his gun and fired one shot as he turned. Then something knocked him on his back, and he wasn't sure whether or not he had been shot again.

Will lay on the ground trying to assess his wounds, but the only thing he could determine with certainty was that everything hurt. He finally decided that the best way to sort things out would be to see if he could stand. He rolled over, braced himself against the wall, and slowly rose to his feet.

Sam stood alone opposite him, staring in disbelief.

Will staggered but recovered, leaning against the wall for support. His ears were ringing and his eyesight was failing, a circle of black slowly closing like the end of a silent movie. He put the gun down carefully on the coffee table and took a seat beside it.

A moment later he collapsed to the ground.

Chapter Fifty-two

What's Going On?

"I guess you can cross getting shot off your bucket list."

Will opened his eyes and saw Murphy and Baxter standing next to his bed. Murphy was smiling, Baxter was not.

"Getting shot was never on my bucket list. Is this Henry Ford?"

Will quickly found out why Baxter wasn't smiling.

"Damn right this is Henry Ford. You're here because you almost got killed. Why the hell didn't you tell me what was going on?"

The front of Will's bed was tilted at an angle. When he tried to push himself up the slope to a more upright position, he felt a sharp stab of pain in his right shoulder.

He was now fully awake.

"I was pretty sure we were going to be doing some stuff that was illegal or dangerous, and I didn't want to put you in a bad place."

"Haven't you ever heard of attorney-client privilege?"

"I must have skipped that class. Seriously, I don't think these guys would have been too concerned about the fine points of the law."

"You think I don't know how to deal with low-life hoodlums? I'm not the one who was raised in the suburbs."

"Sorry, Baxter. The next time I get involved with violent criminals, I'll make sure to include you in the fun."

Baxter shook his head but Will was pretty sure his anger had passed. What he said next made him certain.

"I didn't come here to bust your chops, I came to give you some good news. I figured you could use it. For starters, Jane has signed the divorce papers. You're a free man."

Will wasn't sure if the ultimate failure of his marriage counted as good news, although he was grateful that Baxter was now trying to cheer him up instead of yelling at him. But there was a lot more news he needed to know.

"What happened to Letner? I remember shooting at him, but I don't think I hit him. He must have ducked or something, because he just disappeared."

This time Murphy spoke.

"You hit him."

Will wasn't happy to hear this news but he wasn't sad.

"Is he dead?"

"No. You just wounded him. I brought him with us when I took you here. He's down the hall. Some of his former employees are keeping watch over him."

"What's the deal with the gun you gave me? It recoiled so hard it knocked me on my ass. I thought I got shot again."

"It was .44 Magnum."

"You mean like *Dirty Harry*? Why didn't you tell me?"

"I didn't think we had enough time for a lecture on gun safety. Besides, I really didn't think you would use it."

"I didn't think so either. I'm glad I did. So I shot Letner—what happened to the two guys who were chasing me?"

"Murphy took care of them. He disarmed and immobilized them."

"With a knife?"

"I didn't use my knife. There are ways to kick a guy in the leg that will keep them from running away."

"But they had guns."

"Not when I finished with them. I took their guns and broke a few bones so they couldn't get away, then I came back to get you and take you here. I told Sam what I had done and said if he didn't want to end up the same way, he needed to go back to his office, call the police, and show them where his friends were. That's what he did."

"You left those two goons out in the field?"

"They weren't going anywhere. The police found them where I left them."

"I told you he was very good at what he does, Will."

"So what's next? What's going on with Sam Rainier and Bronson Rogers? Is anybody onto their scam besides us? Have they figured out these guys are crooks?"

Baxter and Murphy looked at each other and Baxter spoke.

"It didn't look too good at first. Sam Rainier and Bronson Rogers must have talked before the police came. They were going to stonewall, find a way to blame it on you."

"Me?"

"They hadn't laid out their entire story yet; they were going to talk to their attorneys first. But from what they did say, I'm pretty sure they would have said you wanted revenge for what happened years ago with Letner and the police department, and with Rainier for getting you kicked out of the band."

"That's crazy, no one would have believed them."

"It would have been your word against theirs, and you're the guy whose credibility was badly damaged years ago. But don't worry, that's not going to happen. There's been a new development overnight that changed everything. That's the other good news I have for you."

"What happened?"

"Sam Rainier changed his story. He made a full confession and told the police everything."

"Did they believe him?"

"Yes. They're being very cautious; there are some very powerful people involved. But I'm certain there'll be indictments and warrants soon. As Murphy's teacher Buddha once said, 'Three things cannot be long hidden: the sun, the moon, and the truth.'"

"Why did Sam change his mind?"

"I'm not sure, but before he confessed, he came by my office to tell me what he was going to do, and he asked me to give you something."

Baxter handed him a thin, white cardboard box with faded writing on it that read *The Exits—Master Tape*. Inside was a reel-to-reel tape that looked as fresh and new as it had more than thirty years ago. A feeling that he hadn't experienced in years came over Will, a kind of calmness and contentment suffused with optimism and anticipation.

Whatever it was, it felt good, and he wanted to share it.

"Hey, Murphy, what did the Buddhist monk say to the hot dog vendor?"

"I don't know, Will, what did he say?"

"Make me one with everything."

They continued sharing the details of what had happened for the next half hour, until a nurse came in to give Will more pain medication. The two men left and Will drifted off to sleep. When he woke up again, Jacqueline was sitting in a chair next to him.

Chapter Fifty-three

My Girl

"Hey, Will. How are you feeling?"

"Are you pretending to be my wife again? Because if you are, you should know that we just got divorced."

"I didn't have to pretend to be your wife this time. They let anybody in."

"You got that right."

"Will, I know I wasn't very supportive of what you were doing. But I was trying to get you to stop because I was worried you might get hurt. This is exactly what I was afraid would happen."

"I'm going to stop you right there, Jacqueline, before you dig yourself in any deeper. I know exactly what happened. Sam told me. You got me involved in all this to try to keep your extortion scheme going. You didn't try to stop me until Sam said he would pay you to do it. You played me for a fool again, Jackie."

She stood up and walked to the window.

"Can you see Motown headquarters from this room?"

"I wouldn't know. I've been flat on my back and wacked out on drugs since I got here."

"You said you would take me there someday. When you're feeling better, can we do that?"

"No, Jacqueline. I'm not taking you anywhere. I would like you to leave, and I don't want to see you again."

She walked back to the chair and sat down, her eyes filling with tears.

"I went after the money, Will, that part's true. There's nothing sadder than a Bloomfield Hills widow with no money, especially an old one. You said you were going for a second chance in life. This was my second chance."

"They killed Paddy."

"Paddy was a terrible driver. I don't doubt that the crash was an accident like they say. But those idiots were chasing him, trying to scare him. They owed me something for that."

"And when they wouldn't give you what you wanted, you got me into it."

"I did. But when I asked you to stop, it wasn't just for the money. I was genuinely concerned for your safety. I didn't want you to end up like Paddy or back here in this hospital again. You said you had feelings for me, Will. I have them for you too. When this was all over, I wanted us to get back together."

"I have no way of knowing whether that's the truth or not. But that doesn't matter, because either way we are through. I'm going to ask you to leave one more time. If that doesn't work, I'm going to hit the call button and get someone to escort you out. Good-bye, Jacqueline."

She stood to leave, then bent down and kissed him fiercely on the lips. It was painful to Will in every way possible, but it was a damn fine kiss. When she finally stopped, her tears covered his cheeks. She walked away but turned in the doorway to speak.

"Maybe we can try again sometime? I swear I won't screw it up this time."

"Call me in thirty years."

"I'm not waiting that long, Will."

She turned to leave and Will called out to her one more time.

"You need to get yourself a lawyer, Jacqueline. I'm sure the police are going to want to talk to you."

After Jacqueline left, Will fell back into a restless, drug-induced sleep. He dreamed he was Sam Spade, only he was sitting in Baxter's office, and instead of the Maltese Falcon, he had the Exits' tape. He had gotten rid of the bad guys and was waiting to turn the villainess over to the police when he heard someone knocking, which woke him up.

Roxanne was standing in the doorway.

"I'm sorry, did I wake you up? Is it okay if I come in?"

"Of course it is, come on in."

She came in and sat in the chair by his bed.

"I've been calling the hospital every hour to get an update on how you were. They told me you were doing okay. Are you?"

"All things considered, I'm fine."

"I would have been here sooner, but I had to talk to the police, and after that all of the studio's financial backers. They're pretty nervous. It's not looking good for Sam right now."

"Roxanne, before you say anything else, I have to say something. For a while there, before I talked to Sam again, I thought you had double-crossed me."

"Why did you think that?"

"Because someone told Sam I was trying to hack his computer files. I thought it was you."

"It wasn't me."

"I know. It was Jacqueline. I told her about it and she told Sam. She was the one who double-crossed me."

"So why are you telling me this now?"

"Because I felt horrible when I thought it was you. And when I found out it wasn't, I was so relieved and happy. Do you know why?"

"I have an idea but why don't you tell me."

"Because I realized how much I cared about you. I didn't want you to be my enemy."

"What did you want me to be?"

"I don't know. Maybe we can figure it out together."

"Another mystery to solve? Like *Chinatown* or *North by Northwest*?"

"I was thinking more like *The Thin Man*. Lots of drinking and clever banter. What do you think?"

Roxanne stood up, bent over, and kissed him.

It was the best kiss he'd had all day—maybe the best kiss of his entire life.

Chapter Fifty-four

Turn the Page

"So what's the deal with your girlfriend, man? How's that working out?"

"The studio's financial backers freaked out when Sam got into all this trouble, and they put Roxanne in charge. Depending on how things come out with his trial, it might be permanent."

Mickey laughed and took a hard pull on the neatly rolled Detroit Killer in his hand. He and Will were sitting in folding chairs on the bandstand in the Lower Bar. Will had his guitar in his lap; Mickey was behind an electric piano. Will's right shoulder was still heavily bandaged, but he could pick and strum without moving it too much, and his prescription medication eased the pain considerably, especially when he combined it with this homegrown medicine.

It was after hours. They were the only ones in the restaurant. The jam session had gone well, and now they were taking a smoking break.

"No, man, that's not what I meant."

"You mean like what she's doing with the studio? Since they're not going to get any tax breaks from the city, Roxanne decided to scale things back. They're going to build a green-screen sound stage on the block they've already demolished and leave the other blocks alone. They're not going to blow up Detroit."

At this point in the conversation, Mickey began laughing hysterically. He handed the Detroit Killer to Will, shook his head, and tried to speak. He could only manage to get out two words before he started laughing again.

"No, man…"

"You mean the movie? She was cool about the movie. She even made that asshole director reshoot the scene where I said the dumb line about smacking some peace into them. I thought of the new line myself. It was a Buddhist saying I got from Murphy: 'Better than a thousand hollow words is one word that brings peace.'"

Mickey fell on the ground and shook with laughter. It was several minutes before he recovered and sat back down in his chair. By then the Detroit Killer had been smoked down to a stub and was smoldering in an ashtray on the piano. Mickey picked it up and finished it off before he spoke again.

"This shit is making you goofy, man. We sound like a Cheech and Chong routine. It's me, Dave, open up. Dave's not here, man."

"I liked *Up In Smoke*, that was a great movie."

"Wait. You still haven't answered my question."

"I forget what the question was."

"What's the deal with your girlfriend?"

"What do you mean?"

"I mean, are you guys having some awesome sex? Does she have any crazy Hollywood moves she puts on you? Is she as good-looking with her clothes off as she is with them on?"

It was Will's turn to laugh.

"You asshole, it's none of your damn business."

"You must really like her if you won't tell an old friend all about it in graphic detail."

"What, are we still in high school? Let's play some more before the drugs wear off and my shoulder starts hurting."

They sat in silence for several minutes before Mickey asked another question. This one was rhetorical, although at the moment neither of them could have spelled or defined rhetorical.

"The tape sounds pretty good, huh?"

"The tape sounds awesome. Let's play some more before my shoulder tightens up."

This time Mickey made his way over to a couple of small Fender amplifiers and turned them up. When he sat back down, he had another question for Will.

"Are they really going to let us play at the Movement festival next summer?"

"I talked to Curtis C. He wants the Exits on stage with him, playing the parts he sampled from our album live. I wasn't really that into techno music, but I'm starting to like it a lot more. It might be fun to play with him. I think Tommy will do it if we do it."

"There's only three of us left now, that's a bummer. But it would be cool to play in Hart Plaza in front of thousands of people. It would be like the old days."

"It wouldn't be the old days, it would be the new days."

"With the old guys."

"The new days with the old guys."

"I like that, Will."

"I like it too, Mick. Maybe it will turn into a Rodriguez thing."

"*Searching for Sugarman*? Late-life success? Cool."

"We could even come back here to the Lower Bar and play a set after the Movement show. It would be like a reunion concert."

Without saying another word to each other, they both looked across the room to the doorway that led upstairs. What they were looking at was illuminated in a glowing red light; it was easy to see in the dimly lit bar.

It was a sign.